Dead City Omnibus

Dead Devil's Night

Dead Devil's Playground

Maree Rose

Dead City (Dead Devil's Night and Dead Devil's Playground)

by Maree Rose

Cover Art and Formatting by Maree Rose

Foreword

Hello readers!

Thank you so much for choosing up my book!

Please be aware that this book is a Why Choose romance, meaning our leading lady Rylan will not have to choose between her men, because #whychoose.

Warning, this book is a dark contemporary romance. It contains very explicit 18+ dark, sexual content, and straight-up smut.

There are no heroes here, only characters with psycho tendencies and therefore there is unaliving people, and lots of dark and twisted content.

All the characters are 18+

Please proceed at your own risk.

Thank you and I hope you enjoy the Dead City.

THE CONTENT NOTES....

I know we all love a shopping list of warnings and I usually love giving them to you. However, there aren't too many warnings to be had.

In saying that there is a big blaring warning right from the get go.

There is r@pe/SA and v!olence in the prologue. It is not detailed but it is there and does set the scene for the whole story.

From then on it is a very dark revenge story with a LOT of v!olence and detailed unaliving. Like really, the main character is unhinged... and she remains unhinged throughout both books (maybe to a lesser degree in book 2... maybe...).

Dead Devil's Night

Maree Rose

*For everyone who has dreamt of a
blood soaked revenge, I got you!*

Prologue

Traumatic experiences are always unique to the individual experiencing them. There is no gauge for how something will affect a person.

Watching my best friends slowly bleed out from multiple stab wounds as they are forced to watch a group of men rape me and then stab me can absolutely cause lasting trauma.

I had grown up with the twins, Rev and Kai. From the moment the authorities threw me into the foster home, they took me under their wing. We had been inseparable since that day twelve years ago.

They had been there to cheer on my successes, wrap me up in their arms when I was sad, and beat the shit out of the guys that turned into assholes and cheated on me in high school. And then they were also there to watch me die.

When the twins aged out of the system, they found an abandoned apartment building and created a home out of the ruined remains on one of the upper floors. For the two years after that, while I was still at the foster home, I spent all available free time there. What I could steal from the foster home without it being noticed, I did.

And when the time came, there was a room waiting for me.

For four years after the day I turned eighteen, we had each done what we could to provide for our family. We took jobs wherever we could to put food on the table and buy whatever we needed to survive.

They were my everything.

We respected the space we had created and kept all of our sexual encounters far away from our home. Or, at least, the few attempts I had made to find someone I did. But every one night stand always felt wrong, so it wasn't long before I stopped looking. Because in the end those men weren't the two men I lived with.

If the twins still looked, they never flaunted any of their encounters and never spoke of their conquests.

They were even at the bar with me the last few times I tried to meet someone. After my dates abandoned me when my back was turned, they would walk me home.

We were like any normal family, coming and going depending on our work or whatever else we were doing. But we always made sure to have at least one night dedicated to being together, cooking, eating and watching a movie until we fell asleep.

And every year on Dead Devil's night, without fail, we locked ourselves within the safety of our home together. We played board games by candlelight and ate the worst food we could get our hands on. It was our own Dead Devil's tradition.

We had an entire night planned, as we did every year on that night. The night everyone called Dead Devil's night. It was the one night of the year where there was no law. The crazies come out of the woodwork and terrorize the streets, killing and causing utter chaos to anyone stupid enough to not stay behind locked doors.

I had the day off my bike courier job, so I had spent the morning cleaning the apartment and dyeing my hair a pretty violet color. While the twins chose to decorate their bodies with tattoos, I chose to change my hair color. I had chosen some pretty extreme colors in the past, but the violet became my favorite and seemed to make my dark blue eyes pop.

We had spent the afternoon cooking a light meal and then gathering our junk food and supplies for our tradition. As usual, Kai teased me about my hair color, but I could tell he secretly liked it with the amount of times he played with it. Rev, on the other hand, just kissed my forehead and then smacked my ass in his effort to get me out of the kitchen.

It wasn't long after the sun had set that the noises started.

My heart sped up. They seemed louder than normal, closer.

Rev and Kai were sitting on either side of me as our laughter and happiness sputtered out at the sounds of screams and howling. The sound of shattered glass came from the street below, and Rev quickly got up to look out the window at the street below.

I could see the moment his jaw clenched, his tattooed hands gripping the longer parts of his black hair before he turned back towards us. He came over and started blowing out the candles, Kai quickly hopping up to help.

The building we were in wasn't in the heart of the city where all the chaos normally happened. They didn't normally come out this far. Rev and Kai said they had chosen it to keep me safe and away from the potential darkness people had to embrace to live in the cesspit at the center.

What happened next was the stuff of nightmares. A person could wonder whether the light in our window was what drew their attention, or if it was when the candles were blown out that caught their eyes.

The boys had gone to retrieve the bats they kept in their bedrooms as protection, but it was already too late.

Their bats did not stand a chance against the five men who broke down our door wielding spiked bats, knives and other weapons. The small amount of self defense training that the boys had taught me was useless.

The men took their time taunting the twins, tying them up and stabbing them before positioning them on their stomachs with their faces held in a position to see me.

They had to watch while each of the men forced themselves on me, stabbing me with both dicks and knives until I could no longer scream. Until I could no longer feel anything.

My head was turned toward them, watching the tears and blood flow from them in utter devastation and pain.

The blackness had started to eat away at my vision as the last man forced himself between my legs.

I couldn't fight anymore. I couldn't scream. I couldn't make any sounds.

I was screaming on the inside. I was trapped in a nightmare that I wasn't going to escape from.

It was even a struggle to keep focusing on the twins' faces.

I just wanted to sleep. I was so cold, the chill of the night was sinking into my bones.

Rev's eyes started to lose focus, his blinks becoming longer and more drawn out. Kai's face twitched as he tried again to fight against the ropes, but he slumped again after only a second, the effort doing more harm than good.

Blinking my eyes became harder, and between one blink and the next, I watched as Kai's eyes shut, not opening again.

When my eyes closed the next time, they wouldn't open again. The blackness was all-encompassing.

I couldn't see. I couldn't feel. I couldn't survive.

Chapter 1

Rylan

12 Months Later

The dreams always came every night without fail. They were never about the attack itself. In some ways, it would have been easier if they were. Instead, other memories haunted me, happy memories of times I had spent with Rev and Kai before the attack. And that made it far worse.

I was walking back toward the bar after needing to use the ladies room when I noticed that my date was no longer where I left him. Instead there was someone else far more familiar. Sliding back onto the barstool, I quirked an eyebrow. "Where is Matt?"

Kai flashed me a grin. "I saw him as he went out the exit. Seemed like he was in a rush."

I huffed in response. "Did you scare away my date?"

He chuckled, picking up the glass of bourbon in front of him and then tapping it against the matching drink in front of me. "I didn't do anything, gorgeous. Drink up, and I'll walk you home."

It wasn't the first time this exact scenario occurred, which was why I asked the question. I knew they felt protective of me, but lately it was like their protective nature was in overdrive.

Picking up the glass, I knocked it back in one swallow, expecting to cringe at the harshness but finding myself pleasantly surprised. He had somehow scored a decent quality from the bartender. Grinning at the look on my face, he swallowed his own drink and gestured for me to walk ahead of him.

"Luckily there aren't that many people here or I may have had to make a scene poking out a few eyes for seeing you in this outfit."

I rolled my eyes, but when I looked over my shoulder at him, he was just scowling in the direction of the two other patrons in the bar. When his eyes returned to mine, he just grinned as though he wasn't doing anything wrong and then took bigger steps to catch up again as we exited the bar.

He tugged on a strand of my hair when he's beside me. "Have I told you red is my new favorite color?"

I laughed at his absurdity and shoved a hand into his side, pushing him away as he continued to grin at me. I dyed my hair a cherry apple red only that morning for my date. Matched with the one simple black dress that I owned and red lipstick, I thought I looked pretty hot. And I had gotten the impression that Matt thought so too, but I guess I was wrong.

Suddenly an arm landed across my shoulders, and I tensed up momentarily until the familiar spicy scent of Rev washed over me. He dragged my head closer to him as we continued walking and smacked a kiss to my forehead. "Hey, little bit. How was your evening?"

"Well, it didn't have the happy ending I was hoping for, but the bourbon Kai got me made up for it."

Kai barked out a laugh from my other side. "If a mid level bourbon is better than a fuck then you aren't being fucked right."

I swear Rev actually growled at Kai, but I was throwing a frown Kai's way, so I couldn't be sure. I was about to say something when something else caught my attention, my hand gripping the fingers of Rev's hand where it's hanging over my shoulder. "What did you do to your hand? Are you okay?"

Rev just chuckled and turned his fingers to give mine a squeeze before letting go again. "I'm fine, little bit. Just accidently hit something hard. I'm all good."

Kai starts cackling beside me, and I frowned in his direction before looking back at Rev's grinning face. Focusing back on the walk to our apartment, I dismissed it; if they aren't concerned then I won't be either.

The memory fades away, instantly replaced by another. It's the way it was every night, like my mind wasn't satisfied with tormenting me with only one memory alone.

I heard stories that in hell, the thing that tortures the souls isn't the fires of hell themselves, it's the memories of our loved ones and our happy moments played on repeat. A reminder of the life we could no longer have and the people we could no longer touch.

If that were the case, then I lived in hell every single night.

The red was fading from my hair so I knew it was time to dye it again. I was toying with the idea of some shade of purple; Kai had just gotten a new tattoo on his neck with a swirl of purple at the heart of it. The color had been on my mind ever since.

I knew that Dead Devil's night was coming up soon so whatever color I chose, that seemed like my best day to do it.

We were all in the kitchen cleaning up after our weekly dinner and even though Rev wanted me to just sit on the couch and wait for them, I preferred helping and spending as much time with them as I could. "What do you think of the color purple?"

Kai looked at me in confusion, though he still had a grin on his face. "Why?"

I flicked a section of my hair that had fallen out of the loose bun I put it in earlier. "Time for a new color."

He laughed before putting on a fake pout. "Awww, but we liked the red, it helped advertise the too hot to handle attitude."

I gaped at him in indignation.

Rev flashed a grin. "Why not just go with a rainbow and then you wouldn't have to choose."

"Too much work," I responded with a scowl, still wanting to growl at Kai.

"Hell no, we don't want any of those dipshits deciding they want to chase the rainbow'."

This time, I do growl at Kai, flicking the cloth in my hand at the bare patch of skin above his sweatpants. He just grabbed the cloth and pulled me toward him to start tickling me. I wriggled in his soapy arms as he cackled hysterically at me.

Rev grabbed my chin, causing us to stop playing. "No matter what color you choose, you will always be beautiful to us." Stealing the cloth from my hands, he pulled me away from Kai and pushed me in the direction of the couch. "Now go pick a movie out, this is almost done."

Grumbling under my breath, I stomped across the room, and I swear I heard him call me a good girl under his breath. I just flipped him the bird and got laughter in response.

I can feel the tears leaving paths of sadness down my face as I start to wake. I wipe at my eyes desperately, as though simply dismissing the tears will push the memories back into their box in my mind. But my heart aches too much.

Rolling onto my side, I allow myself to sob into my pillow. It has been a year since that fateful night, and the pain in my heart is still a fresh and open wound. My body may have healed, but my heart and mind would always remind me that sometimes the worst part wasn't the physical pain at all.

Chapter 2

Rylan

Closing the bathroom cabinet in front of me, I take in my reflection.

I just finished dyeing my hair in honor of their memory, but seeing the fresh violet color makes my heart speed up and a wave of sadness wash over me.

Controlling my breathing and steeling my spine, I force myself to look at every part of my reflection in the mirror.

I have plans for the night. It is Dead Devil's night after all.

The plans I have, though, are vastly different from all the other years.

After I woke up in the care of an older police officer, David, who hid me away and nursed me back to health, I started making my plans.

When David told me that the twins were dead, it just fueled the burning rage that consumed me. He told me about coming across the scene at our home the following morning. He at first assumed that we were all dead, but then I made a noise.

He then quickly picked me up and got me to a doctor he knew to try to save my life.

He succeeded.

I then spent many weeks recovering in David's spare room while plotting my revenge. And then when I was back on my feet, I started to expand on those plans.

After what happened, I did consider myself lucky to have not had any lasting issues. The doctor that David had taken me to managed to get a massive amount of antibiotics into me as well as the morning after pill. I had scarring all over my chest and stomach, but it was easily covered with clothes.

David knew about my plans for the night, and had even gotten me as much information as he could to assist me. Including the identities of the men who attacked me.

But a few months ago, he was killed in a shootout at a local liquor store near his house.

From that moment, I was truly alone.

And I had nothing left to lose.

I stayed in David's house after he died. It was even further out of the city than the apartment I lived in with the twins. It was small, only a two bedroom little home, but it was all I needed.

Criminals and crime lords ruled the city. Power was in the hands of those who killed to take it and rule over everyone else below them. It was a cesspit of evil and corruption. An almost dystopian landscape of abandoned and ruined buildings. Most places in and around the city were not monitored or maintained. Law was minimal at most times, but there was none at all tonight. And I was going to use that to my advantage. Just like the men who attacked me and killed the twins did.

But I was going to give new meaning to the name Dead Devil's night. Because technically I was dead. Those men were going to meet the devil tonight, and I would be the one to introduce them.

I had spent the last two months following each of the men closely from the shadows. I now had their routines completely memorized. I knew their likes, their dislikes, every little detail about them.

At this point, I could probably predict when they needed to take a piss.

I lived and breathed them for months, perfecting my plans.

Taking another deep breath, I put a final touch on my light mascara and added a touch of gloss to my lilac painted lips. My reflection looked like a picture of innocence. My dark blue eyes are large and framed with black lashes, my skin pale and my cheeks rosy.

Paired with my newly refreshed violet hair, I appear sugary sweet.

But it was just that, an appearance. It was skin deep.

There was no innocence left in me. The plans I have are the opposite of innocent, but I need to look sweet as pie to get into some of the places I need to go. And to get the attention of who I need to.

Finishing in the bathroom, I make my way back to my bedroom. One of the walls is covered in photographs, plans and maps. But five images take center stage on that wall. The five men whose images are burned into my memories.

As I pull on my long black boots, I look at that wall. Refreshing myself again of all the details, even if I don't really need to.

The images are pinned to the wall, one above the other, and looking at each image, I let the memories play in my mind. I worked hard to move past the trauma of that night so that I could remember without breaking down. The last thing I need tonight is to have a trauma response while I get my revenge.

At the end of the column of images on the wall is Karver Walkin.

He was the first one in the door that night. He had instantly swung the bat in his hand at the closest target: Rev. I remember screaming as I watched the wood hit Rev's body, the spikes wrapped around the end tearing at his clothes and flesh as he tried to fight against Karver. But he was distracted by the next person through the door.

Damien Kane. The second image on the wall.

He went straight after Kai, who was on his way to help Rev. Damien also had a spike-wrapped bat. The bats that Rev and Kai had never stood a chance. The arm that Kai used to grip his weapon was shredded. Damien landed the spikes in Kai's upper arm and dragged them down to his elbow.

Next in the door and on the wall is Kasen Jekle.

By then Karver already had Rev on the ground, landing blow after blow. But Kasen took pleasure in tying up Rev's hands and feet.

Then came Ash Dean.

He also had rope in his hands that he used on Kai.

And while I screamed, they just laughed. Cheering each other on as they took turns using their weapons on the twins.

I was so busy concentrating on the twins that I missed the last person to enter the apartment.

Silas Holt.

But he didn't miss me.

The pain that exploded across my face and the impact of the strike sent me crashing to the floor. Silas was the one that dragged me across the floor of our home by my hair until I was in the center of what was our living room.

He was the one who ordered the other men to move the furniture out of the way and position Rev and Kai so they could see everything they did to me. He was the one in charge of them, moving everyone around like pawns in his own twisted game.

He was the one that gave the orders for them to stab the twins.

He was the one that gave the order to assault and stab me.

He was the last one to force himself inside me.

There were no reasons given for the attack.

They didn't care about our lives or who we were. From what I could tell, we were just entertainment for them.

They probably don't even remember me.

But they would soon know my name. And they would leave my life in the same order that they entered it.

And they would go to hell regretting ever meeting Rylan Coal.

Chapter 3

Rylan

The sun is just creeping low in the sky as I pull on my purple leather jacket.

I paired it with a flared black leather skirt and a low cut cream blouse that was just sheer enough to hint at the black bra I was wearing underneath.

Yes, I need to look innocent, but I also need to look sexy as well. And after doing some research, the leather would be easy to clean any blood off of. Practicality for the win.

But just in case, I had multiple changes of clothes in a bag that I threw into the trunk of David's car. It had taken me a little bit to start using it after David died, but in the end, I was thankful the twins had given me at least a few lessons so I could get around. Because tonight, I needed it.

I check the supplies in the trunk along with the bag for the final time. I would need to be careful that the vehicle didn't fall victim to the chaos of the night.

It isn't a flashy car; it was an older nondescript sedan in navy blue. It had no special accessories that called attention to it and the windows were clear so everyone could see that there was nothing inside to steal.

In other words, it was a 'nothing to see here' sort of car. The whole point of it is to blend in and last the night.

I already knew where Karver would be, they were all creatures of habit. And Karver's habit at this time of day was a fuck at his local whore house. Well I hoped they all stuck to their normal habits and routines tonight, otherwise shit was going to get real.

Sliding into the driver's seat, I check the time and realize that I need to hurry my ass up or I would be cutting it a little too close.

I make the quick drive to Ninth Street and pull up down the street from Karver's favorite spot. It's run down and seedy, but there is nothing surprising about that. The fact that it's still open for business on Dead Devil's night speaks volumes.

Stepping out of the car, I can already hear some of the screaming and chaos starting closer to the heart of the city. I couldn't see anything through the buildings yet, but the sound of glass shattering and laughter was faintly reaching me. I knew the closer I got to the center of the city, the more difficult it was going to get, and the harder it would be to hide.

Opening the trunk of the car, I slide two knives into my long boots, tucking them in sheaths so only enough of the handle shows that I can pull them out easily. I had already tested it and knew that when I pulled them out the sheaths would stay in the boots for convenience.

I had already done a lot of groundwork leading up to tonight. There were supplies positioned where I needed them, hidden from thieving hands. Or in some cases, even placed in plain sight weeks ago, so they didn't raise questions tonight.

But I still had plenty in the trunk of the car if something did happen outside of my control. I had spent too long planning this night that I was not going to let anything ruin it.

Reaching further in, I pull out a small case. Opening it, I grab the pretty steel ring I kept hidden there, sliding it onto my finger. It didn't look like anything much. But then again, neither did I.

Adding another couple of knives into the inside pockets of my jacket, I close the trunk of the car again, shoving the keys into one of the zippered parts of my jacket for safekeeping. I make my way across the street and towards my destination. The gravel and broken glass crunches under the soles of my boots.

If I have timed it right and he sticks to his schedule, Karver should be here shortly, and I need to be in the right place.

The closer I get to the whore house, the more I can hear what was going on inside the building. The exaggerated moans and porn worthy sounds from inside almost make me roll my eyes. I doubted any of the men inside even knew how to use their cocks properly enough to make it even slightly pleasurable for any of the girls.

Knowing Karver will be approaching from close to the back, I move around the side of the building and lean against the wall. Pulling out a packet of cigarettes and a lighter from another of my jacket pockets, I quickly light one up and tuck them back away. Nothing to see here, just a whore taking a smoke break from sucking cock.

Or at least that's the look I was aiming for.

I had done enough research to know that he had a type. If pretty, innocent looking slut was a type.

The cigarette was at least doing a good job of dulling the smell of piss and garbage that was coming from the alley behind the whorehouse. I knew from experience it was stronger back there.

I close my eyes briefly, taking in all the sounds for a moment. It was a symphony of disgust and depravity. But suddenly under that was the crunch of footsteps on gravel and glass.

Perfect. Show time.

Opening my eyes again, I flick the ash from the end of the cigarette in my hand and glance in the direction of the approaching figure. But not for long. I can't look too eager.

Even after looking at his photo every day and stalking him for months, just seeing him still makes me burn with hatred. His hair is buzzed close to his head and the blond color makes him look almost bald. He is covered in tattoos, there are even some on his face, and he is dressed in loose jeans and a wife beater.

Taking another drag, I cross an arm across my chest under my breasts, loosely holding my other elbow. It pushes my decent sized breasts further up in my blouse, making them more noticeable.

I tilt my head down as though I am looking at the ground in front of me before flicking another look in his direction from under my lashes. He's now a lot closer, and I can tell I have his complete attention. It was predictably easy.

His pace slows as he gets closer, coming to a stop only a few feet away. "Hey pretty little thing, you on a break?"

Bingo.

Time to see just how good my acting skills are.

I tilt my head back again, giving him a better view of my face as I watched him, but not a full view. This would be over before it begins if he remembers me.

"Can't work all the time, right?" I respond, taking another drag on the cigarette.

He chuckles in response. "You new? I haven't seen you before."

Good.

Looking up, I give him a little playful smile. "I'm new, just started. Not sure if I'm going to stay here, though. The cut they give us is pathetic."

Internally, I hope he isn't super loyal to whoever owns the fine establishment behind me.

A slow grin slides across his face as his eyes give me another once over. I feel like scrubbing myself clean just from having him look at me.

"How long is your break, pretty? I could give you all the cut I would have paid inside."

I let a flirty smile play across my lips as I flutter my eyes a little and pretend to think about it, tugging my lip between my teeth. His eyes focus straight on the movement, and I let go of my lip to give him a full look at them as I part them. I know he's fantasizing about my lips now, and I have to hold back a shudder at the thought.

"I'm sure I could stretch it depending on what you want. Like I said, not sure I'm staying here anyway, so it won't matter to me what they think."

His grin gets wider and more shark-like as he takes a few steps back in line with the alleyway and indicates to it with a jerk of his head. "Well then, pretty, let's negotiate for a little fun away from prying eyes." *Hook, Line and Sinker.*

I smile slyly and flick my cigarette away, following him as he walks backwards into the alley, as though he doesn't want to let me out of his sight. Oh, don't worry Karver, I'm going to be the last thing you ever see.

He keeps walking backward through the clear path that I previously made until his back is against a protruding brick wall toward the end of the alley. It's darker here, harder to see. Perfect.

I use a hand to push against his chest, flattening him more against the brickwork. I see a small flinch cross his face, and I let a look of concern cross my own. "Are you okay? Did I hurt you?"

He grins again, disregarding the moment in an effort to look like a macho man. "Of course not, sweetheart, pretty little thing like you couldn't hurt me."

I let the smile cross my lips again as I take a few steps away again, letting one of my hands slowly slide down the center of my blouse. "Do you like what you see? I do try to look extra pretty for my clients." I look down at my fingers as they play with the fabric a little, peeking up at him again through my lashes. "And you are a very giving client, right?"

His body is starting to relax into the moment as he watches my movements with a twisted grin. "Of course, I'll be extra giving for you, pretty girl."

I let my fingers walk further down my body until they reach the edge of my skirt, hooking one of the fingers on the material and ever so slightly dragging it up an inch. His eyes are following the movement with an eagerness that almost makes me nauseous. I stop and pretend to pout a little. "How giving though? I still don't see any money. Maybe I should just go back inside..."

Letting the material drop again, he frowns for a second in disappointment; the grin returning to his face quickly as he digs his wallet from his baggy pants. He opens it and drags out a wad of cash as he looks at me, probably hoping I will be impressed by it.

"I want to bury my dick inside you, but I also want to see those pretty lips wrapped around it too."

I give a fake giggle, but don't move. I just keep watching him. "Both is extra."

He chuckles and just folds up the wad of cash and holds it out to me. "I'm sure this will cover it and more. Something tells me you're worth it."

That does actually make me laugh, but I'm sure not for the reasons he thinks. "Oh, I absolutely am."

He frowns slightly, his eyes flicking down to the money in his hand. The frown deepens as his eyes come back up to mine and he takes a long blink.

I wait for another moment and when he doesn't move anymore; I let a real smile spread across my lips. I step closer to him again and put on a fake concerned look. "Are you okay? Are you sure this pretty little thing didn't hurt you?" I grin again. "Oh, that's right, you can't respond, right? Can't speak, can't move."

Moving forward, I pluck the money from his fingers and slip it into my pocket. I hate the man, but money wasn't something I would ever throw away. I don't bother counting it, not like I really care. Money isn't really the goal. I push his arms back down to his sides and tilt my head as I look into his eyes. "But you can feel." Holding my hand up in front of his eyes so he can see the tiny needle on the underside of the ring. "Tetrodotoxin. It's amazing what you can find on the black market when you're determined enough."

I remove the ring and throw it to the side. I have another one of them in the trunk of the car, and this one is useless now.

Reaching down, I pull out the knives from my boots. They are long and wicked sharp.

"Look, I'm sure whatever you thought was going to happen here would have been a ton of fun for you. But from what I remember, your dick was pretty pathetic." I grin as I hold up the knives for him to get a good look and for it to sink in, what is about to happen to him. "You may not remember me, but I remember you. We met a year ago. A year ago tonight, to be exact."

I see his eyes widen, and a garbled noise comes from him.

"Oh, you remember me now? I'm sure you are sorry, but it's just a little too late for that. You killed my best friends. Now let me see if I have the order correct. It was their arms you attacked first, right?"

With that, I stab the knives into the fleshy parts of both arms and drag downward. Blood starts gushing from the wounds as

Karver makes a louder, garbled cry. His attempt at screaming, I'm sure. Either way, it's too much noise.

I pull the knives back out of his flesh and hold the bloody tips against his lips. "Hey now, none of that. I know I need to be quick, but please allow me to at least enjoy this for a moment without having to listen to you whine like a baby."

Stepping back, I look at him and the blood running down his arms. Some of it has already started to stain his white tank red.

"Now what next? Oh yes, there were stab wounds to the stomach." I plunge the blades into the flesh there, burying them deep and turning them as I pull them back out. He didn't listen to me and that awful noise is still coming from him, so I point the knives at his face again. "Stop it, you're annoying me. I'm trying to enjoy this, remember? Hush."

There are tears streaming from his eyes. And fuck, that feels good to see.

Taking a moment, I swing a couple of chains down from where I stored them a week ago. I wrap a chain tightly around one arm and bolt it in place on the wall, repeating the process with the other arm.

"You know what came next, right?" I slide the blades between the skin of his hips and the fabric of his jeans, jerking outwards in both directions. The knives cut through the fabric like butter. I'm not sure if I consider it lucky or unlucky that he wasn't wearing any underwear underneath when his jeans fell to his ankles. What little there is of his flaccid dick hangs between his legs. "You remember now, don't you? Raping me with that pathetic little dick. I suppose I should be glad you're a two pump chump."

I cross my arms over and slide the blades to either side of his shriveled flesh, pausing to look at his eyes again. "Did you even take the time to find out who it was you raped? Did you ever learn my name? Or the names of the men with me that you killed?"

His face is a mess of tears and snot and flecks of blood. I'm actually surprised he hasn't passed out yet, but I'm happy not to have had to waste an ammonia capsule on him.

"Their names were Rev and Kai Draven. My name is Rylan Coal. Remember that when you reach hell. And when they ask your name, make sure to tell them; it's Dead Devil Number One."

I move my arms in a quick motion; the blades acting like scissors in his flesh. After giving him a moment to scream to himself at the loss of his dick, I then slide the blades across his throat, silencing him for good. The noise was too annoying to wait any longer.

I was right, though. I was going to need that change of blouse.

It was surprising that there was still so much blood able to come from his neck, the warm liquid hitting me and dripping down my skin. I frown. I was going to need to account for that with the others.

Pulling a towel that I stored behind some garbage in the alley, I wipe down my jacket and skirt. I remove the jacket to pull off the blouse, and wipe my skin before putting the jacket back on over my black leather bra.

I really hope there is no blood on my face. I don't have time to reapply my makeup now.

Making sure I wiped off all visible blood from my body and blades, I throw the towel and blouse into a tin can positioned next to the body. Pulling out another cigarette and lighting it, I breathe a sigh, taking a long drag before throwing the lit cigarette into the can. The instant whoosh of it igniting the fuel soaked material in the bottom is satisfying, as was the little wave of heat that hit me.

Turning away and walking out of the alley, I make my way back toward the car. I have plans. I have a timeline to stick to.

One down, four more to go.

Chapter 4

Rev

I NARROW MY EYES at the sight in front of me. We had plans for Dead Devil's night. And someone is already ruining them.

We tried to time it right, knowing that the asshole Karver would be leaving the whorehouse at a certain time. Like he does every day.

He would be relaxed enough not to see us coming or put up as much of a fight.

But when he didn't appear I almost thought that, like last year, his routine was different. Then we noticed the fire behind the building.

I guess I can't be too upset, he looked like he died a bloody and painful death. We can only assume that he pissed off one too many people in the whorehouse and they took out the trash.

I cross my arms across my chest as I take in the carnage.

From the moment we woke up in that derelict hospital, we made plans to hunt down the men who invaded our home. The men who murdered the love of our lives.

Starting with Karver.

It seemed fitting that we did it on the anniversary of the day they took everything from us.

We both loved Ry since the moment she came into our lives, we just hadn't realized it until we were forced to move out of the foster home. Before then, we tried our best to fuck her out of our systems. But nothing worked, we always came back to the same thing, she was ours, she was meant for us.

She was the missing piece that connected our souls and made us one. One family, one love.

And they killed her.

Not just killed her, they utterly destroyed her. And for that, they had signed their own death warrants.

We weren't even sure what they did with her body. Taken for their own depravity, we assumed.

When those men entered the home we had created for her, our safe haven, all of our thoughts had been focused on protecting her. But we never predicted how many would storm our home, or the weapons and violence they used.

Even as the pain ripped through me and the spikes tore into my flesh, all I could focus on were her screams.

And then came the living nightmare they forced us to watch as we lay there dying from the knife wounds, our blood spreading across the floor of what had been our home. Our safe place.

The feeling of utter devastation I felt when I woke up alive and without her still haunted the back of my mind. And after lengthy discussions with Kai, I knew he felt the same.

Kai huffs out a breath beside me and allows the spike covered bat in his hand to smack against the ground. "Well, that was anticlimactic."

He steps forward and lifts the end of the bat to push Karver's head back and look at his face. Looking back at me, he grins. "Somehow I don't think he enjoyed Dead Devil's night as much this year."

My own grin pulls at my lips in response.

I narrow my eyes again as I look a little closer at the blood covered body from head to feet, noticing something I didn't the first time. "Is that what I think it is?"

Kai looks at where I'm indicating and then jumps back with a grimace, his hands automatically going toward his own junk. "Jesus, fuck. I wonder if he was still alive when that happened."

Even I flinch at that thought.

We missed the chance to take our revenge on Karver, but at least we knew he suffered anyway. "We should get out of here before anyone else comes along that might not be so happy about this prick's death."

Nodding in agreement, Kai gives the body one last look before turning with me and heading back out of the alley. Our motorcycles were parked further down the road closer to the city.

Once we reach them, we return our bats to the holders we created for them. The ones that matched the four others of the same kind around the front of our motorcycles.

The next one should be easier.

Damien Kane.

At this time of day he was usually at the pool hall only a few blocks closer to the city. Buying and doing drugs before he dragged his ugly ass further into the city to follow orders like a good little soldier.

Swinging a leg over my bike, I give Kai a renewed look of determination. "Let's keep moving, we have places to be."

Kai grins and swings his leg over his own bike. "And people to kill."

Chapter 5

Rylan

PARKING THE CAR A block away from the pool hall where my next target routinely frequented, I can hear the chaos even louder the moment I open the car door. I know a part of that is the noise of the pool hall itself, the laughter and screams echoing through the streets.

I put on a skin tight black tank underneath my jacket. It molds to my curves and after accessorizing with a few thin steel chains to my neck and rings to my hands, it gives the outfit a more grungy look. Perfect for the pool hall. Adding a couple more items to the outfit from the little case, I call it good enough.

Quickly checking my face in a small mirror, I make sure there is no obvious blood on my skin before locking it all up and starting toward my destination. It wouldn't really matter if there was blood there. I already checked the inside of the building a few times and the lighting was murky at best.

Damien only liked to play pool long enough to find his next fuck and score his next high. If I timed it correctly, then he should have a slight alcohol buzz already and be one game of pool in.

Pushing my way through the door and into the building, I'm met with a cloud of smoke and a blast of music and noise. There are barely clothed women everywhere, draped over guys that look like they have spent too much time high and drinking to be good at anything. Even now, in some corners of the large room filled with pool tables and people, I can see women bent over as creeps pump pathetically away at them.

It only takes moments for me to spot my target at one of the pool tables at the side of the room, still playing, but with a few girls in skimpy outfits trying to grab his attention. I've been here enough in the shadows to not instantly draw attention.

He has medium length brown hair. Just long enough to pull back into the knot behind his head and show off the undercut and the tattoos that cover the skin showing above his black shirt. The tattoos stretch across his skin, from his shirt across the back of his neck and even on the sides of his head. He may have been attractive at some point, but too many drugs and too much power had gotten to him. He was a piece of shit that would have been more fitting in the sewers below the rotting city, but even now the girls still tried to get his attention for the potential of being on his arm at the next city event in the hopes of catching a bigger fish.

Good luck girls, but I'm setting this river on fire.

After my initial scan of the room, I walk up to the bar, not paying close attention to anything in the room, but still aware of everything. I know the moment I have his attention. It's akin to the feeling of skeletal fingers sliding along my skin. Cold and creepy as fuck.

Ordering a bourbon that I'm not going to actually drink, I see Damien indicate to the bartender from the corner of my eye. Right on schedule.

I knew he wouldn't be able to resist something new and shiny.

When the bartender returns with my drink and I go to give him the money for it, he waves me off. I raise an eyebrow at him, and he just indicates where Damien is standing.

Finally turning my attention in his direction, I see he's already focused on me, leaning against an empty pool table, cue in hand. A small smirk appears on his lips when he sees he has my attention.

If only he knew he has had my attention for a year now, he wouldn't look so cocky.

Pretending to take a sip of the brown liquid, I can smell that it's higher quality than what I ordered, but that still won't make me actually drink it. I knew that the bartender was on Damien's dime and regularly slipped things into the drinks of unsuspecting girls. But he was a problem for another day.

Slowly making my way over to where Damien is standing, I allow him to look his fill, seeing his eyes heat in appreciation. But not in recognition.

Trailing a finger along the edge of the table, I step closer and give him a coy smile. "Hi there."

He grins in response. I can almost see the thoughts running through his mind, thinking that it's his lucky day. He's about to have the unluckiest day of his life.

"Hey, sweet thing."

Even his voice sounds oily, dripping in fake honey tones.

I raise an eyebrow at him with another smile. "Sweet thing?"

He chuckles in response, and I force down a shudder, the memory of that sound from a year ago tugging at my mind. Stepping closer, he brushes a finger across my collarbone.

If I didn't need to play a part, I would have snapped that finger the moment it got close to me, but patience is a virtue. And I have a shit load of patience.

"Yeah, you look good enough to eat. What's a sweet thing like you doing here?"

I struggle not to roll my eyes at the pickup line.

Instead, I let my smile get wider as I keep thinking about the end goal and flutter my lashes at him. He continues to trail a finger along the edge of my tank and when his finger scrapes along the plastic bag tucked into my bra, I almost grin at just how easy this was turning out to be.

Because with Damien, I may be the hook, but what is tucked into my bra was definitely the line to drag him in. He rubs his finger across the plastic a little harder and the edge of it peeks out from where it's hidden.

"I don't like partying alone." I respond to him finally, giving him a sly smirk so now he will know exactly what I'm talking about.

He chuckles, and I feel his fingers pinch the edges of the bag, but I grab his hand before he can pull it out.

"I don't like crowds, though. Maybe we can have a private party." Sliding my other hand up his black shirt, I purposely let my nails scrape against his chest and hear his breath hitch.

And he takes the bait.

Grabbing my hand, he throws the cue in his hand onto the table and turns away to lead me behind him, toward the back of the building. I ignore all the hostile looks thrown my way by the other girls in the room while I silently follow behind him. I already knew where he was leading me. I had watched him take this path several times over the weeks of watching him from the shadows.

I let a true smile flit across my lips as I walk behind him. He is a dead man walking, he just doesn't know it yet. But he would very soon.

He pulls me into a dimly lit staff room at the back; I already know it has a small couch and a table but not much else. But I still don't move my eyes away from the man in front of me.

I reach back and close the door behind me, flicking the lock as he watches and gives me what I'm assuming is his version of fuck me eyes.

All it does is make me want to dig his eyes out with a rusty spoon.

Reaching into my left bra cup, I bring out the little bag of white powder and hold it out to him with a grin. When his eyes flick to it, I see the moment his eyes squint and the flair of temper that flashes onto his face.

"Not too much there for a good party, sweet thing," he says. "Maybe I should have seen if there was a better party out there."

I laugh in response before pulling another plastic bag from my right bra cup with a grin. I pull a straw from both bra cups and offer him the one in my left hand. He waves it off before starting to cut the powder.

Knowing he is watching me carefully, I wipe a shelf close by and start doing the same with the contents of the bag in my hand. Putting the straw in my hand to the first line, I inhale, turning back toward him when I'm done to watch him lean over and inhale his first line.

He grins at me when he's done and puts his straw down to lean back on the couch with his arms spread, allowing the hit to take effect.

"Come here, sweet thing. I want to watch those tits move as you bounce on my dick."

I laugh, and even to my own ears, it has an edge to it. I don't move toward him, and he tilts his head with a slight frown.

"Get that ass over here," he demands.

I only grin at him in response and watch as a drop of blood starts making a slow path from his nose.

"I had a different party in mind," I respond as my grin gets wider.

His frown deepens, and he gives a slight cough as he sits up straighter. He looks at the other line of drugs he cut and then looks at where I left my other line. Then he looks back at me in confusion.

Stupid, pathetic man.

"Oh, don't worry about me, it was just yours that was bad. Hell, mine wasn't even drugs." I reach a hand out and dip it into the powder from my line and bring it to my mouth, flicking my tongue out to lick it from my finger. "Mmm, powdered lactose. It's what they use in the movies."

He coughs again and this time blood sprays from his mouth across the table in front of him, the droplets stark red where they land on the white powder.

I can see the panic entering his eyes as he tries to speak, only to cough up more blood.

"Oh, don't worry, yours was definitely cocaine. Along with a few extra ingredients just to make it that extra spicy for you." I flutter my fingers at him with a grin.

I hear the rattling in his chest as he struggles to draw breath into lungs that are already being eaten away by chemicals.

His hands start to claw at his own chest as his pain-filled eyes plead with me for help.

I hum a tune as I move closer to him. It was one of the twin's favorites, totally fitting for the occasion. "You don't remember me. Your friend Karver didn't remember me until just before I slit his throat, either. We met a year ago. My name is Rylan Coal. And the men you killed that same night were Rev and Kai Draven, my best friends."

Moving even closer, I watch as the veins expand under his skin, hardening and turning black. He is still aware. I see the fear and realization in his eyes. I knew he was feeling every last second of his life slipping away, feeling as the chemicals ate away at his insides.

And I watched every last second of it with satisfaction.

Once his hands fell limply to the couch and his eyes remained open, vacant and unseeing, I knew I needed to move on. Looking down at myself, I see a few specks of blood on my skin but otherwise this method had no mess.

It was cleaner than the last time, but not as good as cutting off his dick.

Frowning slightly to myself as I grab a cloth from a shelf and wipe off the blood, I consider the differences. I preferred the personal touch. This one felt too impersonal.

I'll have to account for that with the rest.

Throwing the cloth aside, I exit the room and turn toward the back exit instead of going through the main room. I don't want to draw attention, and leaving so quickly will draw attention.

Two down, three more to go.

Chapter 6

Kai

WE DON'T SPOT OUR target anywhere in the room. We had circled the pool hall now for a few minutes and he wasn't there.

But he should have been.

I walk up to the bar. Bartenders always know where the big players are. And in his mind, Damien is a big player.

After a moment of watching the guy behind the bar actively avoid looking toward us, I hold up a twenty. It only takes him seconds to come in front of us after that, asking what he can get for us.

"Where is Damien Kane?" I ask him as he goes to take the money from my fingers. But I don't let the note go until he sneers at me.

"Why should I tell you that?"

I raise an eyebrow at him and give him a look as though he isn't worth the money or time. "Boss wants him and he isn't answering his phone."

The reaction is almost instant, the color leaching slightly from his face, and a tremor running through his hand, still gripping the money as though he has forgotten what he was doing. He has never seen us before, never seen Damien's boss either, only knew him by reputation, just enough to be scared of someone who could be here on his behalf.

With a loud gulp, he points toward the back of the room to a darkened hallway. "He went into the back room with a piece of ass."

I let the money go and watch as he scrambles away from us, as though the demons of hell are on his heels. The thought almost makes me laugh out loud. We are so much worse.

Motioning to Rev, I make my way toward where the bartender indicated, inwardly hoping we aren't about to walk in on him balls deep in some skank.

As we turn the corner into the hallway, a flash of violet catches my eye seconds before the back door closes behind the girl that stepped out of it. I stop in my tracks as memories of the last time I saw that color hit me. Memories of Ry are never far from my mind. In that moment it was almost like a slap in the face to see someone with the same color hair she died with.

Rev puts a hand on my shoulder and squeezes. "What is it?"

I frown as I keep staring at the now closed door. "Just something I thought I saw." I shake my head. It won't do us any good to be dragged down by the memories when the night was still so young, and we had a lot more to get done.

Rev grumbles and moves around me to the back room. My head jerks toward him when I hear him swear viciously, taking the step to look into the room also.

Damien Kane was already dead.

It didn't look nearly as violent as Karver, however it did look like it had been painful. But, dead was still dead. And frustratingly not by our hands.

A growl leaves Rev as he takes in the room. But I only need to see one thing for my brain to take a leap that has me running. There had been someone else in that room. Another line of drugs was on a shelf away from the one in front of Damien.

I throw the back door open and look around as I run toward the street. I can hear Rev behind me, hissing at me to stop while trying not to draw attention to us. I make it to the street, but still don't see anyone else around. It was like the person I saw walking out the door disappeared like a ghost.

Rev catches up to me and grabs my arm on a growl. "What the fuck?"

After giving the street another look, I turn to him. "I saw someone leave out the back door as we were getting there."

He tilts his head with a frown. "You think some other guy is hunting these guys too?"

I give him an intense look as my mind races. "It wasn't a guy. It was a girl."

He scoffs at me and looks at me as though I'm delusional. And frankly, I'm starting to feel he may be right with the thoughts going through my head. "She had violet hair."

The color drains from his face and he blinks at me in disbelief. I watch as he tries to process what I just said. He looks around the street in a rapid movement before looking back at me.

"Are you sure you weren't imagining it? Could it have been the lights?"

Maybe I am going crazy. There was a good chance after everything.

"No. But there is only one way to find out," I respond and start jogging toward where we left our motorcycles. Rev swings his leg over his own bike moments after I get onto mine. "Who would they be going after next?"

I gave him a look. "The same person we were going after next, Kasen Jekle."

Chapter 7

Rylan

Everything was going exactly to plan. These men were so predictable it was pathetic.

But then, at the same time, I wonder why last year was different. Why are these same men not causing the same chaos they did only twelve months ago? Why are they not out raping and killing again?

Not that I was sad that they weren't. It made my night that much easier that they were following their normal routines.

I don't exactly remember when they attacked us that night, and it is slightly disturbing to think that even last year they may have gone through the same routines and habits they did every night. Before they chose death as a hobby.

Shrugging it off though, I continue to watch Kasen walking in my direction. He doesn't know he's walking in my direction, he's just following the same path he does every night at this time.

It took me several weeks to pick this exact spot. I knew that I could get him when he reached his run down apartment just above me. But when I saw the path that Kasen walked to his apartment, I knew exactly how I wanted to do this. The memory of this man laughing as he kicked and stomped at Rev and Kai still haunts me.

So what I planned seemed fitting. Almost poetic.

Kasen let his dirty blond hair grow over the last year, past the point of being tidy, becoming more shaggy. He was lean and only slightly muscular. He looked like a surfer boy lost in a dark city while wearing black pants and a simple blue shirt. His hand was currently wrapped around an unopened bottle of bourbon. He picked one up every night on his way to his apartment.

He reaches the steps leading down from the street to the back entrance of his building. It is a stroke of luck that the back entrance is lower than street level. I watch with keen interest as his foot goes straight through the fake step that I created. The loud mechanical snap echoes through the small area.

Then comes Kasen's scream, like music to my ears.

If there is one thing I am truly thankful for tonight, it is that everyone ignores the sounds of screaming to stay safe in their own beds. I wasn't so thankful for that last year though.

I move from the shadows towards Kasen who doesn't even notice me. His entire focus is on his mangled leg and the bear trap that snapped shut on it.

It hadn't been an easy find, but fuck, it had been worth it.

For someone who was in what I imagined was some extreme pain, he still hadn't let go of the bottle of alcohol in his hand.

Forcing the smile off my lips, I look at the man in front of me clutching at the metal claws embedded in his leg. "Oh my god, are you okay?"

He looks up at me from where he is bent over his own leg, tears coating his face. It's such a pretty, pretty sight, it's hard not to smile at that alone.

"Please help me."

I tilt my head and start walking backward. "Please help me? Now why does that sound so familiar?" I stop walking at the end of the little alleyway and pick up the ends of two ropes that are on the ground. Exactly where I put them. "Oh, that's right, I remember screaming that same thing this time last year. And you just laughed."

I heave on the ropes in my hands as his eyes widen. The ropes were tied to two anchors sitting high on ledges. Those anchors had chains that wrapped around security bars that residents of the apartments on either side used to keep themselves safe from men like Kasen. And the ends of those chains were bolted to the sides of the bear trap embedded in Kasen's leg.

The anchors weren't as hard to come by as the bear trap was. In a derelict city, there were a lot of dilapidated boats in the little harbor.

As soon as the anchors slid off their ledges, it was like magic. And once again, the scream that leaves Kasen's mouth as the chains pull him into the air by his mangled leg was like music to my ears.

This time, he lets go of the bottle. I am happy that he did so while he was still mostly on the ground, so it just rolled along the concrete but stayed intact. Because when he finished being pulled by the anchors, he was dangling in the air by the bear trap, so far above the ground that I didn't even need to bend far to look into his face. The chains spun him so that he is now facing the mouth of the alley, on display for anyone walking.

I let him swing on the chains for a moment while I walk past him and pick up the bottle, taking a look at the quality of bourbon he buys. "Nice!" Setting it aside, I move back over to the crying and whimpering man.

Leaning down slightly, I look into his face. "Do you remember me now, Kasen?" I ask him.

He reaches out, trying to use his now free hands to grab onto me, but I'm just out of reach. "You can't be here. We killed you."

I do laugh at that, a grin stretching across my face. "Then I must be the ghost of Dead Devil's nights past, right?" He whimpers again. I reach down to pull the knives from my boots. "I know Karver and Damien didn't find out my name, but did you?"

The look on his face tells me everything I need to know. I was insignificant to him. Just another person to torture and kill among the many that he has probably killed.

"It's Rylan Coal. And those men with me were Rev and Kai Draven. They were the best people in this shitty world, and you killed them. Something tells me you won't forget those names now for the rest of your life."

I step forward and stab my knives into the flesh of his stomach before stepping back and out of his reach again. "Well, the few minutes you have left of your life, anyway."

There he goes, singing that sweet music for me again.

He's trying to put his hands against the stab wounds, but he is already so weak he can't raise his arms more than a few inches before they drop back down. Stepping back up to him I swing the knives high and then down, and his screams become more high pitched as the blades embed into his pathetic dick.

Then the music stops.

I pull the knives out and step back. I see he has lost consciousness.

I'm just contemplating using an ammonia capsule to wake him up when a strangled noise comes from behind me. Disappointment floods me, knowing that not only is my fun about to be cut short, but that I may need to take care of witnesses.

Turning slowly, I look into green eyes I never thought I would ever see again. I wonder if I am somehow a ghost after all. Because the two men in front of me surely are.

They can't be real. Maybe I have truly gone over the edge of insanity. All I can do is stare slack-jawed at them as they stumble closer to me with looks of shock that I'm sure mirror my own.

"Ry?"

I'm not sure which of them asks, but then we are all moving, colliding in a tangle of limbs.

"I thought you were dead."

"How are you here?"

"Where have you been?"

We are talking over each other. I can't stop my hands from moving across their skin, not believing that they are really here, in front of me. Their touch is familiar but foreign. Their hands are also touching me all over, their eyes searching over my whole body and taking in everything.

The swinging man behind me is now completely forgotten as I try to understand what I am seeing.

Rev wraps his big hands around the sides of my neck, resting his forehead against mine and looking deep into my eyes. "Little bit." His old nickname for me makes my heart clench and tears finally come to my eyes. "They told us we were the only survivors pulled from that building. How are you alive? Where were you?"

Bringing trembling fingers to his cheeks, I still can't believe my eyes as I touch the smooth skin there. "A cop pulled me out and hid me away to recover. He said you were dead. I thought you were dead, Rev. I've spent the last year planning to avenge your murders."

He lets a sardonic laugh slip out as he gives a slight shake to his head. "And we have been doing the same."

And then his lips are on mine and nothing else matters.

Chapter 8

Rylan

I STILL THINK THERE is a fair chance I've finally cracked or this is a dream, but fuck if it isn't the best dream ever.

Rev's lips move over mine before his tongue flicks at the seam of my mouth, and I open for him instantly. His tongue plunges into my mouth to tangle with mine as he takes what he wants. His fingers press hard into the skin of my neck, pulling me closer to him like he wants to crawl inside of me completely.

My hands are clutching at him in response, trying to drag him closer to me and merge our bodies into one. He tastes like the grape gum he always used to chew, and to me that tastes like home and happy memories.

I feel his heart racing through the shirt he wears under his black leather jacket.

He moves back from my mouth, his breath panting softly across my lips as he looks deep into my eyes. But then I am turned in Rev's arms and Kai's mouth is devouring mine.

Kai pushes my back more solidly against Rev's chest as he presses himself to me, his lips and tongue moving against mine. The taste of caramel and coffee hits my senses and brings back moments of fighting with him over the caramel coffee syrup that Rev bought us.

I can't stop the moan when Rev's lips softly touch the back of my neck, leaving soft kisses in a path up to my ear as Kai continues to kiss me.

"The thing we regretted the most when we thought you were dead was not showing you how we really felt about you." Rev's voice is soft and full of emotion.

Kai finally allows me to breathe, resting his forehead against mine in a mirror of what Rev had done. "We love you, Ry. The only thing that kept us from following you in death was the thought of vengeance."

I don't even realize I'm crying until Kai pulls back and wipes the tears from my cheeks. "Vengeance has been all I have thought about for the last year. I couldn't let myself stop, or I would have broken. You were both my whole world. I'm sorry I didn't tell you," I whisper, closing my eyes as I try to pull myself back together.

Rev brushes my hair to the side and kisses my temple. "No one will ever take you away from us again. We will slaughter anyone that even tries."

A whimper and cry reminds me of the slaughtering I was in the middle of before they appeared.

Kai looks behind him at Kasen hanging from the chains, then he laughs. "Speaking of..." He grins as he looks back at me, the humor still dancing in his green eyes. "Can we join in on the fun?"

I chuckle in response, picking up my knives from where I dropped them in order to touch them. Just looking at them has the biggest smile on my lips. "Not sure there is much fun left in this one, but sure."

He steps back up to me, grabbing my neck and smashing his lips against mine in a quick, brutal kiss. "Fuck, you're beautiful."

Releasing me, he holds a hand out toward Rev, who passes a bat to him. A spike-wrapped bat like these men attacked us with. A giggle bubbles up and out of my lips as I raise an eyebrow at Rev with a pointed look at the bat in his hands.

Rev grins and swings the bat in a circle. "Fucking karma."

I cackle as he moves around me to stand next to Kai, who stands pushing the end of his bat against one of Kasen's stomach wounds. "You awake asshole?"

Kasen whimpers again in response.

"Good." I hear the humor in Rev's voice as he growls out the word. And then he takes the first swing.

It was like watching them play a gruesome game of pinata, taking turns to swing their bats at Kasen until they were covered in a red haze.

And fuck me, it was the first time in over a year that something has turned me on. Watching as they destroy one of the men who tried to destroy us has me all sorts of fucked up. I feel the beating pulse of my pussy as I watch their muscles bunch and move and the blood fly from their bats.

Maybe I cracked after all, because that shit is the hottest thing I have ever watched.

They stop after a few minutes and it's easy to see that Kasen is no longer with us. But I couldn't care less.

Both of them turn back towards me, panting. I'm not sure what is showing on my face, but after a moment I can see the heat burning like fire in their own eyes.

Kai is the first to reach me like a blood covered freight train. He picks me up and takes me along with him until my back is against the closest brick wall and his mouth is on mine again.

I moan loudly into the kiss as I wrap my legs around his hips, my hands fisting in his short hair. I don't care that I'm being covered in blood as Kai's body rubs against mine.

"Fuck," Rev curses from next to us as Kai's mouth moves from my lips to my jaw. Rev's bloody hand wraps around the front of my throat and he uses his fingers to turn my head toward him, forcing Kai's lips to the side of my jaw, his tongue licking up to my ear.

"Eyes on me, Ry." Rev says and I force myself to look into his green eyes. "If you don't want this, say so. If you need us to stop, we will."

I moan again as Kai's teeth gently tug on my earlobe. "Fuck me, please, I need to feel you."

Rev's fingers dig in harder in response, as though his restraint is being tested, but a pained look enters his eyes. "I don't want to make you remember them."

Reaching out, I take a handful of Rev's hair, dragging him closer to me. "Then give me new memories."

He doesn't hesitate again, his lips crashing into mine and his tongue plunging into my mouth to tangle with mine as Kai slowly lowers my feet back to the ground. I almost protest, not knowing what he is doing until his hands slide under my skirt, gripping the underwear I have on and tearing them from my body.

Then he has one of my legs over his shoulder and his mouth on my pussy, and I must officially be in heaven.

There is no other explanation, because the feel of his mouth on me is divine. Rev's mouth continues to devour mine as Kai licks from my opening to my clit, swirling his tongue around it before sucking it into his mouth.

The sound I make is obscene, but Rev swallows it, one of his hands moving to fist my violet hair. His other hand travels down into my bra and rolls my hard nipple between his fingers.

Kai's mouth continues to move, his tongue flicking, his teeth nipping at the sensitive flesh. I feel an orgasm slowly building. I haven't touched myself in over a year, too afraid of triggering my memories, but nothing about the way they touch me reminds me of that night.

Kai sucks my clit into his mouth again, at the same time he slowly pushes a finger into my pussy, and I tighten around him as he pushes me closer to the edge of oblivion. His tongue flicks as he adds another finger, thrusting them inside of me before curling them and scraping his teeth against me.

I lose it, screaming into Rev's mouth as I cum hard. My pussy pulses around Kai's fingers as he continues to suck and lick at me.

Rev moves his face back from mine and holds my head so that all I can see is him. "Give me another, Ry. I want to watch you cum on my brother's tongue."

Fuck, why is that so hot?

Kai pushes a third finger inside of me, and I know that Rev won't have long to wait. My body is already starting to tighten around Kai's fingers again. I'm already panting and moaning in response, my eyes staring into Rev's as I hurtle toward the edge again.

Rev leans closer and flicks his tongue against my panting lips before he nips at my chin. Kai's fingers are moving harder, thrusting into my pussy and curling to rub against that spot inside of me that I know is about to have me seeing stars.

"Cum for us, Ry," Rev breathes and I shatter, my scream echoing around the alleyway.

I'm coming back down from my orgasm when Kai moves my leg from his shoulder and slowly stands back up. Then he watches me with burning eyes as he sucks his wet fingers into his mouth, licking them clean like he is licking his favorite ice cream. And I have seen him lick an ice cream. The sound he makes is not something he makes when he eats ice cream, but it has my body throbbing.

Rev nips at me again. "Do you still want our cocks, baby girl?"

I moan, "Yes, fuck yes."

He doesn't ask again, moving in front of me and then lifting me up against the wall again. Kissing me deeply, he wraps my legs around him, and then I feel him undoing his pants. The first touch of the head of his cock against me has me moaning and dropping my head back against the bricks, my eyes fluttering closed as he bites and licks along my jaw.

And then he starts slowly pushing inside of me.

He is bigger than anyone that I've ever been with before. I can feel him everywhere, as he starts stretching me inch by inch.

The men who raped me have nothing on this man. There is no comparison, and yet panic starts to claw at my chest.

A whimper rips from me as a flash of memories from the previous year hits me.

Chapter 9

Rylan

Rev stills, his hand coming up to grip my jaw. "Eyes on me," he growls, and I automatically obey. His green eyes lock with mine as he watches me focus back on him.

The panic eases, and my breathing slows down again.

Once he sees that I have calmed down, his fingers dig harder into my jaw. "Keep your eyes on me, baby girl. Don't look away, don't close your eyes, just watch me as I fuck you and make you ours."

Fuck if that doesn't have me dripping for him again.

He pulls his cock back until I almost lose him, but then he pushes back inside of me. My eyes don't leave his. I watch every emotion that crosses his face as he pulls back and then presses into me again.

When he's buried inside of me completely, he grinds his pelvis against my clit and my pussy tightens around him as I moan at the sensation. Pleasure crosses his face as he groans, then sets a steady pace, thrusting inside of me as he keeps his eyes locked with mine.

Then a stream of filth starts pouring from his hot mouth. "Your pussy was made for me, Ry. Such a perfect fucking pussy. That's it, baby girl, squeeze my cock with that perfect pussy."

I'm on the edge of cumming when he pauses and I growl. A grin flashes across his face and then he adjusts his arms. I catch sight of Kai behind Rev, his cock in his hand as he strokes and squeezes it, his eyes burning as he watches his brother fuck me.

Rev lets go of my jaw to hook my knees over his arms and grip my hips tightly. When he moves again, he is no longer gentle, and he doesn't hold back.

His hips snap forward, his skin slapping against mine as he thrusts his cock deep inside me.

I don't even recognise the sound that escapes me. "Fuck, yesss."

He chuckles, but starts moving faster and harder, setting a rhythm that has me moaning like one of those bitches in the whorehouse. And all the time his eyes don't leave mine and his mouth doesn't stop with the dirty filth. "You like my cock buried in this pussy, Ry? I wish I had done this years ago. You're ours, baby girl. Who does this pussy belong to?"

I moan in response, but he somehow wants me to think and respond to him. He slaps the skin of my hip hard and I clench around him. I'm so fucking close.

"Say it," he growls, his pace still not slowing.

"Yours," I moan in response.

"Good, now cum on my cock."

My body obeys him, like it too knows exactly who it belongs to. My orgasm hits me and nothing else matters but the rush of absolute pleasure sweeping me up like a wave.

My vision blacks out for the briefest moment but no memories come to me, it's just ecstasy and him. But when I blink again, he's all I can see.

His own pace stutters as my pussy tightens hard around him and with a low groan he follows me over the edge. It's the sexiest fucking noise I have ever heard and it's now become my new favorite soundtrack.

And the look on his face when I focus on it is what I assume mine looked like. Like he found heaven.

It's a look I want to see on his face every chance I can get. And if Kai gets that same look then even fucking better.

Rev leans in to me to brush his lips against mine before gently lowering my legs to the ground again. I chuckle because there is a good chance I'm not going to be able to stand for a little while. He just grins at me like he can read my thoughts and holds me against the wall while shooting a look over his shoulder at Kai.

Rev slides away from me only to have his body replaced by Kai, with a hand on my hip and one brushing some sweaty strands of hair from my face. His grin is big as he looks at my flushed face. "You all weak in the knees for us, gorgeous girl?"

I laugh as I drag his lips to mine. For twins, they kiss so differently. Rev is pure possession while Kai has a playful edge as his tongue flicks into my mouth, playing with mine until he deepens the kiss to scorching.

While he kisses me, my legs become steadier, so I take charge of the moment. Using my body pressed to his blood covered chest, I reverse our positions until his back is against the brick wall. Wiping my hand and reaching down, I wrap my hand around his hard cock and savor the groans that come from him as I move my hand along his length.

When our lips part, his head falls back against the bricks and he looks at me with hooded eyes. "What are you doing, gorgeous?"

I grin at him and then lower myself to my knees. The ground is rough and hard against my skin, but I don't care. There is blood everywhere, all over us, all over the ground. It's dark and dirty, and I love it.

"Fuck," he groans as my tongue comes out to flick against the head of his cock.

"You got to taste me. Now I want to taste you," I reply, giving him another lick.

He growls softly and threads a hand into my hair, gripping it hard as he tilts my head back to look at him. "Don't tease, Ry. I've dreamed about watching those big blue eyes as you swallow my cock a hundred times."

My grin spreads even wider before I wrap my lips around the head of his cock and move slowly down his length. His hand tightens almost painfully, and he moans long and low. Looking back up at him from under my lashes, I see his focus is completely on me. His mouth is open slightly as he breathes heavily.

He is just as big as his brother, so I only make it halfway down his length, wrapping my hand tightly around the base of him that doesn't fit in my mouth.

"Fuck, you look so fucking good with those pretty lips wrapped around my cock."

I set a slow pace, moving my head up and down his hard length. I swirl my tongue around the head before taking as much of him as I can, my tongue continuing to flick and my teeth gently scraping against him. It's his turn to moan obscenely.

When I hum around him with my mouth as far as it will go, his hips jerk away from the wall, thrusting into my mouth and hitting the back of my throat. It makes me moan and hum around him harder.

His hand tightens even further and his other hand comes up to take another handful of my hair as I move back to just the tip. "I'm not sure how much longer I can control myself, Ry."

I lick the end again and grin. "Then don't."

He pulls my head away from him to lean down and brush his lips against mine. "You want me to fuck that pretty throat, gorgeous?"

"Yesss," I moan, loving the hold he has on my hair.

He growls again. "Relax your throat, and tap my hip if you need me to stop."

The first thrust of his cock back into my mouth has me gagging, but then he gives me a moment to do what he said and I force my throat to relax. His next thrust has him sliding a little into my throat. The next thrust he goes even further, his hands clenching in my hair and tilting it just the way he wants.

Then he is sliding in until my nose brushes the skin of his pelvis.

I moan and swallow around him and his control snaps. Holding my head, he sets a hard and vicious rhythm, fucking my throat the way he wants. And fuck if I'm not dripping and throbbing again from it.

Reaching down, I slide my fingers over myself, but Rev has already seen my intentions. He crouches down beside us, knocking my hand away and replacing it with his own. "From now on, you only cum on our fingers or cocks, baby girl."

He thrusts three fingers deep inside me, pressing the heel of his palm against my clit.

I'm moaning loudly around Kai's cock, my hands grabbing his blood soaked pants in some attempt to drag him closer to me.

"Yes, fuck, that's it. Swallow my cock. You're such a good fucking girl."

Rev's other hand comes up and wraps around my throat, squeezing gently as he thrusts his fingers inside me and grinds against my clit. It takes only seconds before I'm screaming my release around Kai's cock.

Two more thrusts and Kai is cumming deep in my throat as I struggle to swallow around him while coming down from my own climax. I give him one last lick as he pulls himself from my mouth, and he gives me a heated look in response.

Grinning, I stand back up and look around the alleyway again before walking over and picking up the bottle of bourbon. Unscrewing the lid, I take a deep swallow of the harsh liquor and then hand the bottle over to Rev.

I wander over and retrieve a towel I had stored behind some trash cans, using it to wipe as much of the blood from my body and clothes as I can. The tank is ruined, so I pull it off and throw it into the trash can closest to me.

Turning back to the guys as I shrug the leather jacket back on, I see their eyes heat at all the skin I have on display until they see the scars. The fury that crosses both of their faces heats my blood as I walk back toward them with two more towels.

They clean their own skin, loosing their shirts to the trash and putting their jackets back over tattooed and scarred chests. I could melt into a puddle at the sight of them. But the same anger burns in me when I see their own scars.

Setting the trash on fire I start walking backward out of the alley, grinning at them.

"Come on boys, we still have people to kill."

Chapter 10

Rev

I CAN'T BELIEVE SHE is alive.

Our girl is right in front of us with a grin lighting up her beautiful face. There is evil in her eyes and fuck, it's a good look for her.

When Kai mentioned that the girl he saw leave the pool hall had violet hair, I almost stopped breathing. But then I pushed away my hope that she was somehow alive. It had been a year, not only did she not come back to us, but why would she still have that hair color when she had only just dyed it that day last year?

But finding out she too thought we were dead, and that she was avenging us, just made it all that more clear. She owned us, body and soul, just the same way she is ours.

I would watch the whole city burn before I lost her again.

Looking across to where Kai is watching her, I see that slight crazy edge to his eyes that he's had for the last year. I know he feels the same way as me.

I don't think that there would even be anyone left alive when he pours gasoline on the flames if something happened to her again. He would pile the bodies high and light those fuckers on fire.

But I would be right there beside him.

They signed their own death warrants the moment they touched the Draven family.

Chapter 11

Rylan

Ash Dean wasn't where he was meant to be.

I knew the risks of my plans when we had our fun after killing Kasen. But I knew Ash's schedule and routines back to front, so I wasn't too concerned at the time.

But that fucker wasn't where he normally was right now, and I didn't know where the little cockroach crawled to.

After we left the alleyway, the twins followed me on their hot ass motorcycles to Ash's apartment building on Third Street. But when we got there, it was empty.

I had changed into a new black mesh top over my bra and the twins keep sending me heated looks as though they both hadn't cum inside me not long ago. Admittedly, the moment I saw them on their motorcycles, I wanted to ride them on their bikes. But I had plans and this current situation was what happened when I allowed distractions.

Picking up one of the empty beer bottles on Ash's coffee table amongst the other trash, I throw it at the wall in frustration. Kai just grins at me and raises an eyebrow in response.

Huffing, I fist my hands on my hips. "Where the fuck is he?"

I see Rev tilt his head out of the corner of my eye and when I look in his direction, I notice he is looking at something in the other direction. He wanders across the room in the direction he is looking and moves some trash off the kitchen counter. Then he presses a button on the machine that's revealed.

"Ahhh man, are you there? Karver's dead man. Slaughtered. Ash, are you there?"

"Yeah, I'm here, what the fuck do you mean he's dead?"

"He didn't show up to the dropoff, so I went to the whorehouse, thinking he got distracted like last time. Man it was fucked up. He was strung up behind it, hacked up. They even cut his dick off."

Rev sends a vicious grin in my direction, and I can't stop my own grin in response.

"Fuck. Get Damien over there, he's closer."

"He's not answering either, man."

Kai chuckles, and I swear I hear him mumble under his breath something that sounded like 'Try a ouija board.'.

"For fuck sake, you're all a bunch of incompetent fuckers. I can't call Si with this shit, he's at the club. I'll be there shortly."

The recording cuts off with a bang as though Ash slammed the phone down. Rev laughs as he moves some more papers aside to unearth the old phone on the bench. "Not that we aren't grateful for making shit easy for us, but who the fuck still uses landline phones anymore?"

Kai shrugs. "Emergency line maybe?"

Rev picks up a beer bottle on the bench beside the phone. It's only half filled. "He didn't leave that long ago, this is still cold."

I frown, my thoughts moving rapidly through my mind. "We can't let him have the opportunity to warn Silas. We need to go back to the whorehouse and cut him off."

The look on Kai's face is far too eager, like a psychotic puppy. "Cut him off or cut him up? Does this mean we get to watch you play with knives again? Cause that shit made me hard as fuck."

I'm laughing as I walk out of Ash's apartment. I hear them following me as I make my way back down to the street, not bothering to sneak out the same way we snuck in. It's not like we were trying to creep up on anyone now.

Seconds from stepping out the front door of the building, I freeze, Rev almost running into my back with how suddenly I stop walking. What I see outside has a smile stretching across my lips. "Change of plans, boys."

Rev frowns before following my eyeline. "It can't be that easy."

Across the road and down a few buildings, crouched down beside his car changing the tire, is Ash Dean.

A hand takes hold of mine, spinning me back and into Kai's arms who then spins me around before bowing me backward like we are dancing. It was something we used to do all the time and laughter bubbles up and out of me. For the first time I see the real emotion in his eyes as he looks down at me.

"So how are we doing this, gorgeous? Somehow I think he might be on the defensive if he sees us coming," he asks as he returns me to an upright position.

"Then let's make sure he doesn't see you coming," I reply, putting my hand against the door.

Rev grabs my arm, stopping me and I almost growl in frustration.

"Just give me a few minutes and trust me."

He uses a finger on my chin to tilt my face back toward him before brushing his lips against mine. "We do, just be careful."

With that he lets me go, and I push through the door, letting it swing closed behind me as I start moving along the sidewalk. Reaching inside my jacket, I retrieve what is stored there and put it on. I'm now in line with where Ash is finishing with putting the new tire on his car.

I look him over as I cross the street, pushing the rage back down. It wouldn't work to have that emotion on my face.

His brunette hair is short at the sides and long on top like the twins'. He doesn't have any visible tattoos, but likes to show off his status with gaudy chains. The type you look at and just want to choke him out with. He spends too long at the gym, and I know if it came down to a fair fight he would overpower me in moments.

Reaching out, I grab his shoulder and he jerks away from me sharply. "Oh, I'm so sorry, I was just trying to see if you needed any help." I flutter my lashes at him and try to look as innocent as I can.

Ash scoffs, brushing off his initial surprise as I knew he would the moment he saw I was a woman. "I got it, sugar, don't you worry your pretty head about it."

I stand to the side and clasp my hands behind my back, the picture of sweet and naive as he finishes with his tire and then stands up. He pulls a rag from his trunk after throwing his tools back in there and cleans the dirt from his hands.

"Are you sure I can't help with anything?"

He leans against the car and gives my body a slow look over. When his eyes reach my face he frowns slightly. For a moment I think he recognizes me, but he then dismisses it and gives me a condescending smile.

"Nah I have somewhere I need to be. But a sweet, innocent little thing like you shouldn't be out on a night like tonight."

I can't stop the laughter that escapes me. "I stopped being those things a year ago."

He frowns at me again, his eyes flicking over my face as he lets his hands drop to his sides. He scoffs at me again, but I can see the mental struggle starting to take place behind his eyes. "And what could you even do?"

The smile stretching across my lips gets even bigger; I just loved how men underestimate women. It made moments like this all the sweeter. "Maybe you should ask Karver what I can do. Or Damien. Or Kasen." He blinks at me owlishly. "I mean, you can't right this moment, but maybe when you get to hell you might want to broach that subject. Just out of curiosity."

I step closer to him again, he doesn't move away, and only the slightest flinch crosses his face. Because that's all the toxin will allow at this point.

Grinning, I look past him and back to the building I just came from and wave an arm. It only takes a moment before the twins are jogging across the street to meet me. Rev's hand fists a handful of my hair and drags my lips to his while Kai pokes a finger at Ash's cheek.

"That's fucking creepy." Kai shudders and turns to me, dragging me from his brother's arms. "Hey, gorgeous."

Kai gives me a hard smacking kiss as Rev circles Ash's still body until he returns to stand beside me again, flicking a hand at Ash. "So how did you do that?"

I pull the ring off my finger and show them the sharp needle in the underside. "Tetrodotoxin, it's what I used for Karver too. He can see and feel everything, but he can't talk or move."

Kai cackles beside me. "Savage. I fucking love it. So Karver actually felt it when you sliced and diced his dick?"

Nodding, I grin at them. I don't care that my crazy is showing.

Rev once again fists my hair and pulls my mouth to his, kissing me deeply before pulling back and mumbling against my sensitive lips. "So fucking perfect for us." He lets go again and smiles at whatever he sees on my face. "So what is your evil mastermind plan for this asshole?"

Looking back at Ash, I watch his eyes as I say what's in my mind. "Did you know that a burning car can get as hot as fifteen hundred degrees Fahrenheit?"

The look of panic and fear that fills Ash's eyes is priceless, and the shocked laughter from the twins is even better.

"Besides, it's Dead Devil's Night. Burning cars are common tonight, and no one gets near them until the cleanup in the morning."

"Fucking perfect," Kai gasps out between his laughter.

Once the twins control their laughter, we move Ash until he is sitting in the driver's seat of his car. When I start opening the windows a fraction, they look at me in confusion.

"The fire won't spread without oxygen, boys. We want a furnace, not an oven."

Rev chuckles but starts doing the same on the other side of the car. I open the cap on the car's gas tank and then once the twins have stepped away, I reach under the car and yank the fuel line away from the tank and move back. The street thankfully has a small slope to it so that when the fuel starts spreading from under the car, it creates a small stream in our direction.

Reaching into the pocket of my jacket, I pull out the packet of cigarettes and offer them to the twins. They were the ones that got me into the habit in the first place. They each take one with a chuckle while I light two in my mouth at once.

Taking one from my mouth I flick it at the spreading gas and watch with glee as it ignites, then I take a drag from the other as we watch the flames race back toward the car.

I do strangely wish that Ash wasn't paralyzed because the sound of his screams would have been so beautiful, but instead all we got was the muffled cries that to me just sounded annoying.

Taking drags of our cigarettes, we stay there and watch the fire eat away at the car and then at Ash. Before long, the annoying sounds he was making stop and the car is completely engulfed.

We all turn away and they both wrap an arm around me as we head back toward my car and the bikes.

"Four down, only one more to go."

Chapter 12

Rylan

We just reached my car when I found my back pressed hard against it and Kai's lips were moving hungrily against mine. He presses himself against me while gripping my hips, grinding against me and turning me on even more than I already am.

He slows the kiss to a stop, almost reluctantly pulling back from me a fraction, his lips still brushing mine as he speaks. "That was so hot, I really want to fuck you over the hood of this car until you're screaming my name for the whole goddamn city to hear who you belong to."

I hum because fuck yes. "Then why don't you?"

"Because we don't have time on our murder schedule to add more bodies if they see your gorgeous ass."

I grin wickedly at him before pushing him away. He looks confused for the two seconds it takes for me to unlock the car and jerk open the back door. When I sit down on the back seat and scoot further into the car, his eyes are almost as hot as the car fire we just left behind.

He licks across his lower lip as he steps up to the open car door. "Hands and knees, beautiful. We only want your mind on us when we fuck you."

Understanding and appreciation hit me briefly, but the moment I turn over and he runs a hand up my bare skin under my skirt, they are washed away by pure need.

Flipping my skirt up and baring me to his eyes brings a flush to my body. It seems ridiculous since he has already had his mouth on me there, but presenting myself seems even more intimate.

He makes a noise as his hands rub over the bared skin, trailing along my legs and over my ass cheeks and teasingly at the edge of my pussy. "So what you're showing me is that this whole time, including when we burned that asshole alive, you were walking around with no underwear and Rev's cum dripping from this pretty pussy?"

I'm about to respond when his hand cracks against my bare ass cheek. I'm not quick enough to stop the moan that escapes and his laugh is low and his voice is raspy. "You're so fucking perfect."

The door opening on the other side of the car in front of me is enough of a distraction that I don't pay attention to what Kai is doing until he is thrusting his cock inside of me to the hilt in one sharp movement. The force propels me forward, almost into Rev's lap as he slides in to sit on the back seat of the car in front of me, closing the car door behind him.

Obviously Kai doesn't care about anyone seeing his own ass with the limited street light and firelight close by because he leaves the door behind him wide open. Leaning over me he moves one of his feet to the footwell and lodges his knee between mine and the worn leather of the back seat.

This time when he thrusts into me harder he must be happier with the position because he digs his fingers into my hips and doesn't stop again. I'm gasping and moaning, my arms trembling as I try to keep myself upright even with the movement.

"Fuck, when I do die, I want it to be when I'm buried in this pussy."

I can feel him everywhere, his cock stretching me so good, just like his brother's did. I can feel every bump and ridge on his cock as it moves inside of me, his hip bones slapping so hard against my ass I wouldn't be surprised if I get bruises from that alone.

Rev fists a hand tightly in my hair, pulling my attention back to where he is sitting in front of me, his own cock now gripped in his tattooed hand.

"Wrap that hot mouth around me, baby girl."

He doesn't really need to tell me what to do. Leaning forward I use the momentum of one of Kai's thrusts to lick against the head of his cock above where his hand is. Then I swirl my tongue around him briefly on the next thrust. I make a frustrated sound when Kai pulls me back again and stops moving.

They both chuckle at me before Rev moves, changing his position so that he is turned toward me and leaning his upper back against the door. Now his cock is a lot closer. He uses the grip he has on my hair to tilt my head back until I'm where he wants me and then he is feeding me his hard cock.

I look up at Rev's face as I slowly swirl my tongue around the head of him again before closing my lips around him and taking as much of him in my mouth as I can. He is at the back of my throat when I choke around him briefly. I force myself to relax and take him even further, pushing past my limits. The groan that comes from him is the best fucking reward.

"I don't know what's better, your pussy or this fucking mouth. That's it, baby girl, fuck."

I breathe through my nose as I move my mouth up and down his length. Kai still doesn't move behind me yet, allowing me to take a moment. I grab Rev's other hand and move it to my hair beside the one already there.

He groans again when I swallow around him and squeeze his hand before putting my hand back on the seat for balance. "You want it hard, baby girl? You want me to take control?" His voice is husky, and I am so fucking on edge.

Kai grunts behind me, shifting his hips, his cock moving inside of me with the movement making me tighten around him more as he pulls back. "Fuck, yes she does. She likes that a lot. Don't you, gorgeous?"

I can only moan in response and the moment I do, Rev's hands twist in my hair as his hips jerk forward in response. Bites of pain pull at my scalp as he then pulls almost fully from my mouth.

He thrusts all the way back in, the head of his cock pushing down into my throat as I force it to stay relaxed and continue to breathe through my nose.

The next time he withdraws Kai slams his cock inside of me.

They set a primal, savage rhythm, one thrusting as the other withdraws. And I'm held between them with hard hands and tight fingers as they take complete control of my body.

I feel like I am exactly where I was always meant to be. I have never felt as much pleasure as I do at their hands.

It's not long before I'm riding the edge of release, my pussy tightening around Kai and the pressure building inside of me.

And then Kai stops.

I growl around Rev's cock, rocking my body back in an effort to chase him. But the vibration makes Rev twist his fists in my hair and push me down onto his cock, groaning deep and long as he jerks in my mouth. I swallow his cum greedily, momentarily forgetting my frustration.

Rev finally slumps back onto his heels, panting and mumbling under his breath about Kai being an asshole. Kai just laughs in response, knocking Rev's hands away from my hair to take a handful himself and pull me up and backward as far as the car would allow.

He lifts my leg and hooks it over the one he has bent and planted in the footwell, spreading me open wider.

My hands hit the roof and I cry out as Kai thrusts into me again. The angle is different, deeper and rubbing against different parts inside my pussy.

I'm not frustrated anymore. I'm in fucking ecstasy.

Kai reaches his free hand and starts circling my clit. "Tell me you have always wanted this, gorgeous. Tell me you have always secretly wanted our cocks like we wanted this pussy."

My moan is obscene. "Fuck, yesssss."

I'm not sure when my eyes fall closed but Rev's hand wraps around my throat moments before he breathes against my lips.

"Keep those eyes open, baby girl. I love watching them shatter for us."

He doesn't kiss me, just holds me there as his brother keeps thrusting his cock hard and deep inside of me.

I moan again, my body tightening as the pressure keeps building. It's different and almost painful. "Godddddd."

Rev huffs a laugh against my lips. "I doubt he will help us after tonight, baby girl."

The pressure is too much, my body too tight. I can feel Kai struggling to keep thrusting. When he presses and rubs more firmly against my clit, my body shatters, my pussy pushing him out completely as liquid gushes from my pussy. His fingers keep rubbing hard across my clit back and forth as more liquid sprays across his cock and the leather car seat.

I can't catch my breath to scream. My mouth is wide open but no sound is coming out as waves of pleasure roll over me.

"Fuck yes," Kai moans before thrusting back into my pussy hard. I'm still coming down from that earth shattering moment when he grabs my hips again and starts pounding inside of me. It throws me straight into another smaller orgasm, my body clamping down on him once again, but this time taking him with me. His pace stutters as he groans deep in his chest.

The moment they groan out their release is now my new favorite sound. I want it on repeat.

I almost collapse onto the seat again, but Kai holds me up with a chuckle. Rev pulls off his jacket and then his shirt, using it to clean my dripping pussy before mopping up the mess we made on the seat. Once he's done, he throws the shirt into the footwell on his side and slides his jacket back on.

Kai releases me to take his own shirt off to clean himself and then puts his own jacket back on over his bare chest.

I think I'm drooling. They are dangerous to a woman's brain.

"You need to stop distracting me. I had a schedule and you keep blowing that and me out of the water."

Their laughter surrounds me and it's a light sound. Almost at odds with the purpose of the night. Even now, since our own sounds have died down there is no mistaking the sounds of chaos happening in other parts of the city streets. We were lucky to have avoided the chaos for as long as we have.

Rev runs a tattooed hand through his hair, clenching it in a fist, a habit he has when he is thinking. "Right, Silas."

I reach over and tug his hand from his hair, giving it a squeeze. "Ash said on that voice message that Silas is at the club tonight. He bought a nightclub about a month ago in the heart of the city and my guess is it will be one of the only places open all night tonight to celebrate Dead Devil's Night."

He frowns down at our joined hands as Kai leans over to kiss the back of my neck.

"So what was your plan?" Kai asks when Rev doesn't say anything.

"You need to trust me," I reply.

Both of their eyes narrow at me as almost identical frowns cross their faces.

"I'm going to get his attention. He prowls the club for what he wants... and he then takes it, willing or not. It shouldn't be too hard to catch his eye and then when we are alone, I will make my move. He has not counted on someone truly fighting back one day. And he will underestimate me."

Rev's frown deepens. "I'm not sure I will be able to stand by if he touches you."

As I go to say something, he looks at me with a savage look, his hand tightening on mine.

"You don't understand, I'm broken. I want to bathe in his blood for ever touching you. But I will try to control myself for you."

My heart thuds in my chest and I smile softly at him. "I think what happened last year broke something in all of us."

He is deep in thought for a moment before he gently lifts my hand and kisses the tops of my fingers. "We will be broken together, little bit. We will build a mosaic out of our broken and shattered pieces. We will make the world stare in awe at the masterpiece we create together."

Kai takes a hold of my other hand and also kisses it. "A masterpiece of death."

Chapter 13

Rylan

The nightclub was appropriately named Devil's Lair. But on the streets it was called Hell.

And Hell is fucking pumping.

The seductive deep beats are playing loudly, I can feel the pulse of the music through my whole body. There is more people than I had planned for, especially given it is Dead Devil's Night, but I still had hope that my plan would work.

When we arrived and hid the car and bikes a street away, the twins almost had a fit when they remembered I still had nothing under my skirt. Luckily I came prepared. I pulled out some black leather booty shorts, which made them happy.

Until they also realized I still only have the mesh top on, which I wasn't going to change.

They had also devised their own plan to take out Silas, which involved them making their way to the rooftop access to get to the upper floor where Silas lived. It is the first time since we reunited where we aren't in eyesight of each other. And I hate it.

The security at the door meant that I couldn't bring my knives. All I could wear is my clothing and accessories as I walk into Hell. But I manage a few rings and necklaces that compliment my outfit.

There is people everywhere. The area had a large bar to the left and right side of the room with lounges and tables spread out surrounding a lowered dance floor called The Pit. There are stairs leading up to a mezzanine floor that hold another bar and all of the VIPs.

Moving through the bodies toward The Pit, I try to take it all in, taking peeks in all directions but never lingering. It only takes me a few moments to spot my target.

Silas Holt is surrounded by clingers and whores. But instead of paying attention to them, he is leaning against the railing watching The Pit and the writhing mass of bodies.

He has a black suit on, but the white shirt underneath is open halfway down his chest. It shows off the tattoos covering most of his skin and the thick gold chains that he is wearing to flaunt his wealth in a dead city. He is older than all the others, around his mid forties. His short black hair is slicked back on top and shaved at the sides and he has kept a thin layer of stubble on his face.

He might be attractive if he wasn't the epitome of Satan.

Focusing most of my attention back in front of me, I keep moving towards The Pit. If that's where he is looking, then that's where I need to be.

Pushing my way through the bodies, I find a spot toward the center, then I start moving to the beat. It doesn't take long to get into the rhythm, the thump of the base winding through my body as I dip and sway.

My hands snake up and into my hair, gripping it and giving it a shake before I raise them high. Moving them back down my body, I touch every part of me on the way back down, pulling my jacket just off my shoulders to give anyone above me a teasing view through the mesh of my top.

Throwing my head back, I close my eyes and part my lips like I'm in ecstasy just from the act of moving to the beat. My hands continue to move over my body, touching everywhere. If I didn't have a date with the devil, then the music and movement might have actually turned me on.

I feel hands on my hips and when I open my eyes a fraction, I can see that I have the devil's attention. Turning toward the hands that are touching me, I silently hope that the twins do not have a view of me from wherever they are, otherwise this poor unfortunate sap may not survive the night either. Dismissing any potential concern, I step into the body, draping my arms over the broad shoulders and allowing him to wedge a knee between my legs as we start grinding on each other.

The guy is relatively attractive in a boy next door sort of way. Wavy light brown hair, lightly tanned skin and a bright smile. I'm sure he thinks he is lucky at this moment, the poor misguided fool.

It doesn't take long. We are only dancing together for a few short minutes before someone appears beside us out of the mass of bodies, his fingers tapping my shoulder lightly.

I start to dismiss him as though I have no interest in him, but he leans closer to my ear to shout over the music. "Mr. Holt would like you to join him."

Looking back toward the man, I raise a brow and he points to where Silas is leaning against the railing still. He has a smirk on his face, so I play along and smile sweetly back.

Turning back to my dance partner, I lean in briefly, my lips almost brushing his ear. "Thank you for the dance. Me leaving is you getting lucky. Find a sweet girl to take home instead."

Letting him go, I move to follow the hired muscle and don't give the boy another thought. He is a means to an end.

I'm led to a private elevator at the back of the club and directed in through the open doors. Instead of getting on with me, the man just turns to stand guard in front of it as the doors slide closed, trapping me inside of it alone. It's slow to start moving, but then starts ascending toward the mezzanine floor. When the doors finally open, the Devil is waiting.

Silas is standing directly in front of the open elevator doors and instead of allowing me to step off, he steps on and presses the button to take us to the top of the building. The smirk is still on his face, and all I want to do is wipe it off.

Taking a few steps to close the distance, he braces his hands on the elevator wall on either side of my body. "Hey there, sweetheart."

I give a coy smile and look up at him through my lashes. "Hi. Where are we going?"

He snickers, moving a hand to drag a finger down the side of my face and I suppress a shudder. "A private party. Just you and me."

I hum and force myself to lean my face toward the hand touching me, playing along.

"You'd like that, wouldn't you, sweetheart? To party just with me."

I nod in response and I don't even need to fake that enthusiasm, because really, I do want to party just with him. And his blood as I slice him wide open.

His smirk gets even wider as the elevator slows to a stop, the doors opening slowly behind him. He turns and slides a hand behind my back, pressing against it and not so subtly pushing me out of the elevator and into his apartment.

The place is luxe, and I admit it is beautiful. The main feature is the wall of glass that gives the perfect view of the chaos outside. The fires can be seen all over the city and I wonder if this would have given a good view of the fire we made when we burned Ash alive.

Everything in the apartment is darkness and shadows, the only light coming from above the elevator. When I look back toward the only light source, it illuminates Silas standing there behind me.

With a gun aimed in my direction. Still wearing that insufferable smirk.

"You didn't truly think I wouldn't recognize you the moment you stepped into my club, right?"

Chapter 14

Rylan

Well, it is official, the twins are going to hunt me in hell and kill my ass again for telling them to trust me.

Trying not to show anything apart from humor, I smirk back at the asshole. "It was the hair, wasn't it?" I laugh and use a hand to flick some of it over my shoulder. "What can I say, I was feeling nostalgic."

His eyes narrow slightly and I can see the smirk become a little strained around the edges at me not cowering before him. I am pushing my luck, really, but I am never going to cower and cry in front of this man ever again.

Tilting his head, he looks me over, probably trying to see if I have any weapons on me. I wish I had another one of my handy rings, but even if I did and was able to sneak it past security, judging from the gun, he never would have let me lay a hand on him.

"So what exactly was your plan, sweetheart? Sneak in and kill me in revenge?" There is humor in his voice and it grates on my nerves.

I laugh, because seriously, did he really want me to just come out and say yes, I came with the intent of killing him? Fuck that. "Do I look like I'm sneaking anywhere? I was simply dancing. It was you who dragged me up here."

Turning around, I look around the apartment again. It was a proverbial 'fuck you' to dismiss him like that, but I know he wasn't about to shoot me in the back. Simply by being there last year, he proved he liked a more personal touch with his maiming and killing.

The furniture is black and dark wood. The apartment is large, with an open plan living and dining area and a buffet style kitchen along one section of wall. I could just make out door-ways in the darkness leading off both sides of the room, which I assumed led to bedrooms.

Stepping off the elevator landing, I walk toward the glass, watching in the reflection as Silas follows the movement. He slowly steps down after me, but doesn't follow me too closely. He keeps his distance, staying close to the landing while still keeping within shooting range. The frown on his face tells me I'm not acting the way he wants me to act, like I care what he wants.

"How the fuck are you still alive? I thought I had done a pretty good job of killing you."

I grin at him over my shoulder. "Dead Devil's Night seems to be my lucky night."

I can see amusement cross his face again and his eyes run over me again condescendingly. "So you thought you could get lucky again this year and get revenge? Sounds like the stupid idea of a crazy girl."

Humming, I turn around to face him again with a genuine grin of my own. He is still steadily aiming the gun at me. "Maybe crazy, but my luck seems to be holding out so far."

The amusement becomes strained on his face again, and I can almost see the cogs turning inside his mind as he tries to understand what I'm getting at. He keeps the gun steady as he reaches into the pocket of his jacket and extracts his phone.

I watch with my amusement growing as he tries number after number with no answer. After the last one, he growls in frustration and throws the phone across the room to be lost in the darkness.

Narrowing his eyes at me again, his face loses all the humor and amusement that he once wore. His eyes almost glitter with malice. "No great loss, I can easily replace them. I suppose you think you're something special for killing them."

"I don't know about me being special, but their deaths definitely were. Would you like to hear about them? I know you love chaos, so I'm sure you will enjoy hearing all about it."

He doesn't respond, so I continue as though he has agreed with me. I wanted him to hear all about it, to understand the joy I felt with every one of them. And I want him to imagine me doing the same to him.

I start slowly pacing in front of the window. "Let's see, Karver was first. You know he likes his whores right? He likes them on the sweet and innocent looking side." I pause and bring my hands under my chin and give him a fluttering of my lashes. "It wasn't hard to get his attention. Then it wasn't hard to paralyze him and start cutting him up. He didn't last long after I cut his dick off and slit his throat."

There is a microscopic flinch to his eyes. A purely male response.

I grin savagely but keep pacing. "Then there was Damien. He likes the girls too, but he prefers the ones that are going to supply his habit." I tap a finger to my nose so he doesn't mistake what habit I'm talking about. "Flash a little skin and a little plastic bag and he was practically drooling for me. It's a shame that it was a dirty batch with more chemicals than cocaine. His veins turned a pretty shade of black before he choked on his own blood."

If I didn't know better, I would have thought Silas looked a little green with that one. It made me wonder if he liked the white stuff too.

"Kasen was next. But I'm sure you can guess the order by now right? Kasen took a little more planning. He didn't like whores or drugs, but he did like to pick up a bottle of bourbon each day and took the same path back to his apartment. You really should have taught them not to be so predictable. He didn't even see the bear trap before he stepped in it. And then when the chains pulled him up into the air, all I needed to do was cut him up. I did get to stab him in the dick also before he was beaten to death with a bat."

I don't mention that I wasn't the one to beat him to death. He still needs to think the boys are dead.

"I almost didn't catch Ash, though. By the time I got to his apartment, someone had already called him about Karver. I thought I was going to have to trudge all the way back to the whorehouse to get him. But as I said, luck seems to be in my favor tonight and he had to change his tire first. I don't imagine he enjoyed being burnt alive when I set his car on fire with him inside."

Turning back toward Silas I stop pacing, resting my hands on my hips. I can see that he thinks I'm utterly crazy, and yeah, I probably am, but in the end he did contribute to my madness.

"Which brings me to you."

He tilts his head again with a frown. "Maybe I should have recruited you instead."

I raise an eyebrow at that. "Was that before or after you raped me and tried to murder me?"

He scoffs, and a grin returns to his face. "You think I went into that night blind? I had already done my research. I knew who you were before I even entered that apartment. Poor little orphan girl, no one was going to miss you."

The confession doesn't surprise me. I had already worked that part out. I knew more than he thought I did. "And you think I've come into tonight blind? I've done my research too. Tell me, how did it feel killing your own sons that night?"

Chapter 15

Rylan

His grin doesn't even falter. If anything, it gets bigger, the sadistic fuck.

And still the gun doesn't waver.

"Pretty and smart. I definitely should have recruited you. Maybe then you might be on the end of my dick instead of my gun."

I can't stop the disgusted cringe that crosses my face as I look at him. "Eww, no. And for the record, your sons fucked me better."

The grin finally disappears from his face as fury takes over. Men are so predictable, insult their manhood and they take it so personally. He takes a step closer to me and adjusts his grip, I can see that he is itching to pull the trigger now.

"Such a shame I took your boy toys away from you then," he sneered at me.

I let the slow smile spread across my lips. "I wouldn't be so sure about that."

The sound of the bat hitting the side of his head was almost better than the sound of my guys groaning their climaxes. Almost.

Silas is far too arrogant and self assured, so he never once checked his surroundings when he exited the elevator. He thought he had the upper hand, but he never did. I felt them the moment I stepped into the apartment. They were so ingrained in my soul that just their proximity was calming.

The sound of the gun going off is loud in the room, but thankfully, it doesn't hit anything important. The gun ends up sliding across the smooth floor and out of Silas' reach.

He isn't down though, and even with the spikes of the bat tearing into the flesh at the side of his head, he still stays standing. He turns toward his attacker with a snarl, only to get a heavy boot to the chest that finally sends him crashing to the floor.

Kai swings the bat again with a grin, landing the shot in the middle of Silas' back and drawing a shout from the sadistic fuck's mouth. And just for good measure, Kai then drags the barbs downward before pulling the bat away and letting Rev press a heavy boot where the spikes were only moments before.

It doesn't take long for Kai to drag over a chair and for them to secure Silas into it, tying his arms and legs so tightly it wouldn't surprise me if he no longer had blood flow to them.

Ignoring the snarling and cursing coming from Silas, Rev closes the distance with me, cradling my face and kissing me deeply. "I'm totally spanking that ass for that whole 'trust me' shit."

Chuckling, I brush my lips across his again. "Don't threaten me with a good time."

Turning back toward Silas, I take in the grinning Kai standing guard next to him. I can't help running my eyes over him. He shoots me a wink and reaches for something behind his back. "We brought you presents."

He's holding out my two knives, and I practically skip across the floor to take them from his hands. Once his hands are empty, he drags my lips to his in a savage kiss that tells me that the momentary distance aggravated him as much as it did me.

I grin at him when he finally releases me. "Remind me to thank you properly later."

He laughs and just picks up his bat again from where he dropped it to secure Silas.

The twins take up positions beside me as I look at Silas. Blood is dripping down the side of his face where Kai first hit him, and I can see the edge of pain that he is trying to hide behind a sneer. His eyes are looking back and forth between Rev and Kai.

"I should have hunted you down harder when that junkie cunt told me she hid you away."

Rev doesn't even need to move forward much before swinging his bat down and landing a hit to Silas' knee. This time Silas just grunts and grits his teeth, trying to portray the tough man he really isn't.

But he can't hide the flash of pain in his eyes, and I revel in it.

I chuckle again. "Well, I'm glad she did. The home she hid them in was how I met them. The biggest mistake you made was attacking me."

This time he laughs. "It was never about you. You were just a pathetic little cunt that they were obsessed with. A means to an end, a way to make them suffer. When I finally found them, I was going to let them go, but then they thought they could try to take over my territory."

Still, none of this comes as a surprise to me. This time it's Kai's bat that lands on Silas' other knee and Silas screws his face up and closes his eyes against the pain.

Stepping forward, I lean into his space. "So, how did that work out for you, hmm?" Slowly I push the knives in my hands into the flesh of his thighs and he gives a long and pained groan.

His eyes flash to mine as I drag the knives back out of his legs. "You won't get away with this, you little bitch. I'm not the top of the food chain here. You won't get away with killing me."

I give him a surprised and worried look, holding a blood flecked hand in front of my face. "Really?" My voice trembles for a second before I laugh at him again. "And when was the last time you spoke to your boss, like actually spoke on the phone with him?"

He frowns; mixed with the pain, it's an almost comical look. I could almost see the cogs turning slowly.

"I'd say it was about a month ago, right?" I ask. "Just before he was shot in a liquor store holdup close to our house."

All emotion vanishes from Silas' face.

"He told you to leave the twins alone, and then you didn't follow his orders. That was why he was even there that night and rescued me. I asked him why he left you alive, and he said that your death was no longer his to take."

The fear is finally in Silas' eyes, and the sight is better than anything else I have seen so far that night.

"So, for the past year, he helped me plot and plan my revenge. And while you licked his boots like a good little boy hoping for scraps to work your way into his legacy, he taught me how to rule."

I smile fondly at the memories. "He taught me everything, including patience. Like that old saying, the one about revenge being a dish best served cold. Is this cold enough for you?"

Pushing the knives into his groin, I finally get the scream I am waiting for. Pulling the knives back out, I can see the blood spreading faster now.

"You never knew who he really was, you just followed orders like a good soldier. I mean, David's disguise was genius, who would ever suspect an old beat cop of running a criminal empire? But I like our new disguise better. Thanks to you, the world thinks we are dead."

Stepping back to the twins, I hold a knife out to each of them with a grin. "I believe these have your names on them. This death belongs to you, too."

Kai flashes me a savage grin, taking the knife on his side and moving past me. Rev takes the knife but lays a kiss against my head and murmurs into my ear before following Kai. "So fucking perfect."

I don't bother watching. Silas' final moments no longer interest me. He doesn't deserve the extra attention.

It doesn't take long for Silas to take his last breath, and I know the twins probably made it quick in order to be sure there was no chance of Silas surviving like we had. They learned the lesson that Silas thankfully hadn't.

Turning my back on the view of the city once again, I wave my hands out the windows as though I'm a sales girl. "Welcome to our empire, boys."

Kai gives an exaggerated bow. "My beautiful Empress."

I'm suddenly in his arms as he swings me around in the air, making me giggle like I did growing up with them.

Rev reaches out once I'm back on my feet and tucks my hair behind my ear. "So what does this mean?"

I laugh joyously. I know he wants to know about who I became over the last year, but I just couldn't bring myself to discuss it that night. It had been a long night. Well, a long year, really. "Well, I believe it means you just inherited a nightclub. It's so good too! Wanna go dance?"

Not taking no for an answer, I move past them and over to the elevator. Throwing a smirk over my shoulder at them, I pull off my leather jacket and throw it to the side, fully intent on distracting them and having some fun to celebrate. "Someone was getting handsy earlier, so you may have competition."

I squeal and give a hysterical laugh when Rev picks me up and throws me over his shoulder before stepping into the open elevator. His hand cracks loudly across my ass cheek.

Kai cackles and steps onto the elevator beside me. "No such thing, gorgeous girl."

I grin. Best night ever.

Dead Devil's Playground

Maree Rose

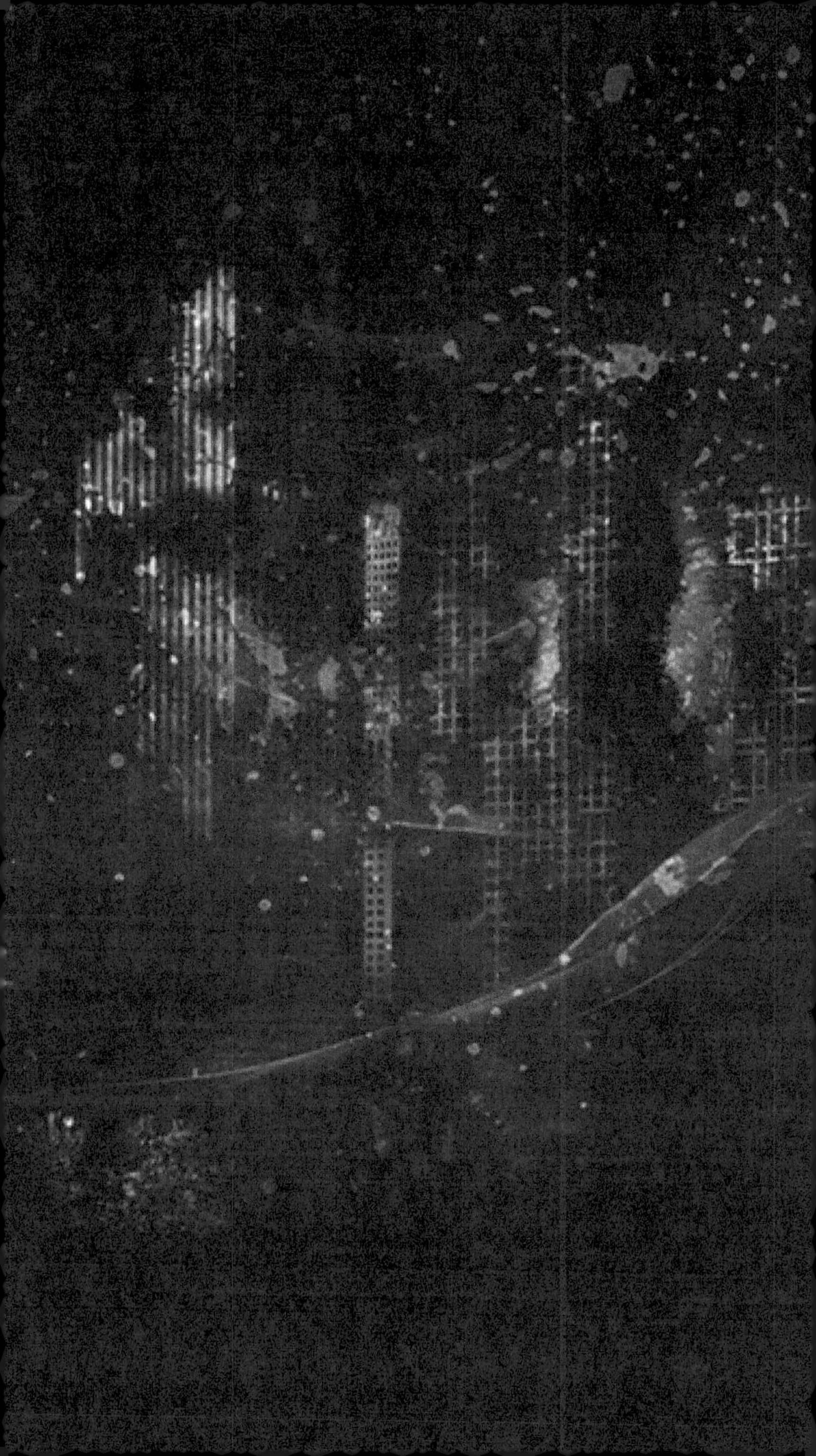

For every devil who was
told to stay quiet—
and chose violence instead...

Prologue

Two fucking years.

Two long, blood-soaked years I've ruled this hellhole from the shadows with Rev and Kai by my side. Or under me. Or behind me. Or on top... you get the picture.

Two years of anonymous enemies—faceless cowards—scrambling in the dark, trying to take down the phantom who dared step into their dirty playground, who had the audacity to end their reign of terror. No more killing, no more raping innocent lives. We made this city ours. Not with shiny crowns or sly handshakes but with guns, knives and violence.

Every year, I still let chaos off its leash for one night, allowing them a taste of the madness they crave. But even in the depths of carnage, my rules reign. Cross that line? They don't get a warning. I don't send polite little memos or hallmark cards. The stories? They whisper them in dark corners: Break my law, and I appear. Out of nowhere, like smoke. One second, nothing. The next? They're dead—they don't live long enough to describe what happens after.

I am the sweet nightmare in combat boots they can't escape.

I am the rumor that haunts their last breaths, the predator they'll never see coming, the executioner in the shadows. Better they never see my face, better they tremble in ignorance. For their safety? No. For mine.

But honestly, I don't give a shit either way.

You can't kill what's already dead.

Chapter 1

Rylan

"Don't make a sound, little bit—I'm not fucking sharing you tonight."

Well fuck, I'm not sure how he expects me to keep silent when he's balls-deep in my pussy. My eyes flick to Kai's sleeping form in front of me on the bed. I clamp my teeth together, determined to swallow every moan.

Rev angles me higher, my leg hooked over his, and I gasp when he thrusts deeper. His hand slides up my body until his fingers curl around my throat—just how I like it—claiming every breath I take. His grip tightens, and I feel the heat pool low in my belly.

The room is cloaked in darkness, the silence broken only by the ragged sounds of our breaths, each gasp of mine stifled by the possessive weight of his hand. Kai sleeping just inches away makes my pulse quicken, a wicked thrill that turns every thrust of Rev's hips into an electric current. I'm not sure how we haven't woken Kai yet, but his face is still relaxed in sleep, his breaths deep and even.

Rev knows exactly how to drive me crazy—how to push me over the edge with each deliberate movement of his cock. His fingers tighten around my throat and I can't think, the pressure sending a rush of heat through my body, intensifying the pleasure radiating from where he's buried deep inside me. My breath hitches, the struggle for air mixing with the overwhelming sensations of him filling me, claiming me.

All I feel is him inside me, and his grip tightening in that silent command for my complete surrender to him. My thoughts are consumed by the raw need he's igniting within me. My body arches up, seeking more of him, chasing that exquisite pain-pleasure, even as my voice is reduced to nothing more than desperate whimpers.

With one final, powerful thrust he brings me to the brink and I fall apart around him, my body trembling with the force of my release. My body pulses around him as my release crashes over us in waves of ecstasy. I can barely hold back the cry that wants to tear from my throat, my fingers gripping the sheets as I ride out the pleasure that he so expertly commanded.

Rev slows his movements, leaning in closer, his lips brushing against my ear. His voice is a low groan, filled with satisfaction. "I'll never get fucking tired of feeling you come on my cock."

His words send another shiver down my spine, his deep voice vibrating against my ear as he remains buried inside me, my body clenching around his hard cock. My breath is still ragged, chest heaving as I struggle to regain some semblance of control.

But the way his body presses against mine, the possessiveness in his touch, makes it clear that control is the last thing he's willing to give back to me right now.

He loosens his grip on my throat, allowing me to draw a full shuddering breath, but he doesn't pull away. Instead he moves slowly, deliberately, his hips rolling in a way that makes me acutely aware of just how deep he still is. It's almost too much—almost.

"Kai's out cold, baby girl," Rev murmurs against my skin, his lips grazing my jawline as he speaks. "But if you keep making those sweet noises, he won't stay that way for long."

I bite down on my bottom lip, desperately trying to hold in the sounds building in my throat, but it's futile. Another gasp escapes me, louder this time, and Rev's response is immediate. He pulls me tighter against him, his teeth grazing my earlobe as he drives into me harder, faster.

"Nothing will ever take you away from us again," he growls, each word punctuated by the snap of his hips.

He drags me back to the brink again, my body trembling as I feel another wave building. I know I won't be able to hold it back, not with the way Rev is fucking me like he owns me, like he's determined to imprint himself on every part of me.

"Rev…" I manage to whimper. Even after two years of being back together, we can't help but slip into the memories that haunt us. But the concern is fleeting, drowned out by the overwhelming need to let go, to give in to the pleasure that's consuming me.

Rev's hand slides down my body, his fingers finding my clit. The moment he touches me, it's over. I shatter around him, broken moans tearing out despite my best efforts. He doesn't stop, doesn't slow down, riding out my climax until I'm nothing more than a trembling, gasping mess before he follows me over the edge.

Finally he stills, chest heaving, and buries his face in my neck. We sit in the hush of our ragged breathing, the sheets rustling softly as Kai shifts once.

When Rev finally pulls free, he levers himself up beside me until his eyes lock with mine, dark and intense as if he's daring me to say something, to deny the claim he stakes on me every chance he gets. But I can't. I never could, even before we all admitted our feelings, and especially not with the way my body still feels like it's on fire from his touch.

Instead I reach up, fingers brushing against his jaw as I pull him down for a kiss, soft but lingering. Rev's lips leave mine as he slowly slips out of the bed with a predator's grace, stalking toward the bathroom. I know exactly what he's doing—fetching a cloth to clean me up, a ritual that's become familiar between us.

I turn my head to the side, my gaze falling on Kai. His chest rises and falls steadily, the picture of a man deep in sleep but as I look closer, I notice the telltale curve of his lips. He's not asleep at all, and I doubt he ever was. Kai's eyes suddenly open as though he feels me staring, glinting with mischief and desire as he locks his gaze with mine.

A slow, lazy smirk spreads across his face, one that has my heart beating faster and my pussy about to beg for more. But he doesn't say a word, just gives me a knowing wink before closing his eyes again, his expression smoothing back into one of feigned sleep. Allowing his brother to have his moment. No one could ever say they aren't good at sharing.

Before I can dwell on it too long, Rev reappears with a warm, damp cloth in his hand. His eyes meet mine as he kneels beside me, his expression softening as he carefully cleans me up, his touch tender.

When Rev's done, he tosses the cloth into the hamper and slides back into bed beside me. I turn my head to look at him, catching the faintest hint of a smile playing on his lips.

"Will that help you sleep now, baby girl?" he asks, his voice husky.

I hum in response, my body relaxing against his. It takes me a moment to recall that this late-night fuck was his attempt to help me clear my mind and ease my restless thoughts. I sink into his embrace, feeling his warmth surround me as he draws me close.

As I'm about to settle against him, I feel Kai's arm slide around me, pulling me back toward him. Rev grunts in annoyance at the intrusion, but there's an underlying amusement in his voice as he mutters, "Seriously, Kai?" I can't help but giggle softly, my heart fluttering at the warm press of both their bodies.

Closing my eyes, I allow myself to be lulled by their presence. The rhythmic rise and fall of their breathing soon syncing with my own.

But it doesn't take long for my chaotic thoughts to take root once more, gnawing at the edges of my mind. Both Rev and Kai have already drifted off again, their breathing steady and deep, but sleep remains elusive. With a sigh, I gently extract myself from their embrace, careful not to wake either of them.

I slip out of bed, grabbing the thin, soft gown from a chair nearby. I don't bother tying it; our penthouse above the Devil's Lair is at the top of the tallest building in the city, and I'm not about to turn on any lights. Instead, I make my way to the bar, pouring myself a glass of bourbon. The rich amber liquid shimmers in the low light as I walk toward the wall of glass, staring down at the city—my city.

Dawn is creeping closer; I can tell by the soft edge of blue to the sky. Dead Devil's Night is approaching, and despite my efforts to clean up the cesspit that sprawls out beneath me, I know there will always be someone trying to resurrect the ghosts of the past. Recently, there have been more reports of forces working to bring back true chaos, like what nearly killed me and the twins all those years ago.

I take a sip of bourbon, letting the burn of it ignite something inside me. It seeps through me like a slow, soothing fire. Quelling the storm of thoughts rushing in, but it doesn't quite settle the chaos in my chest. I may not rule this goddamn city with an iron fist, but I've ruled it with a blade so sharp it'll make anyone think twice before stepping out of line. If anyone dares to try and do to others what was done to me? I'll make sure their blood stains my hands.

Down below, the city lies still, a quiet so thick it feels suffocating. But I know it's not real. It's all just a damn facade, broken only by the distant hum of a world that's waking up. I stand there for a moment, lost in the taste of bourbon and the quiet hum of the chaos I'm preparing for. I'm pretending it's peaceful, but we both know that's bullshit. I'll have to confront this new threat head-on, just as I always have.

Dead Devil's Night isn't about peace. It's about blood. About destruction.

Another sip. The burn is a comfort, but it doesn't last.

Something's coming, I can feel it. A storm waiting on the edge of the horizon. Something's brewing, ready to drag me back into the mess I've spent years trying to clean up.

I take another sip, close my eyes briefly, and let the fire lick at my insides. The rush of it, the warmth, the bite. It keeps me steady for a second, but I know I won't stay steady forever.

If they think they can threaten anyone I love? They have no idea who they're fucking with.

I'll tear them apart. Piece by piece. And then I'll put their bodies on display like the trophies they are, for all the assholes in this city who think they can take what's mine.

This is my city. My playground.

And if they want to play?

I'll fucking play.

Chapter 2

Rylan

By the time the sun has crawled its way into the sky I'm already hunched at the dining table, drowning in a sprawl of contracts and permits like they're crime scene photos. The new club is supposed to open in days, but every scrap of paper feels like a live grenade waiting to blow in my face. My brain should be on numbers, deadlines, signatures. Instead, it keeps circling back to the city—how the whole rotten thing feels like it's vibrating on a fault line. Waiting to crack. Waiting for someone to bleed.

I don't hear Kai until his fingers slip through my hair, tilting my head back so he can steal a kiss. A lazy brush of lips—infuriatingly soft. It should annoy me, but instead it knives right into my chest, easing the tension I've been chewing on since last night. Still, it also reminds me I need to redo my hair. Blonde's fine, but for the grand opening? I need to look sharp. I need a statement. Something that says *look at me and know I'll carve you open if you blink wrong.*

"Did you even sleep, gorgeous?" Kai's voice is thick with sleep, still dripping from whatever dream he crawled out of, but the concern underneath makes my teeth itch.

I hum, unwilling to give him the satisfaction of an answer. Like it matters. He's already wearing that worried expression like a badge. I sigh, because ignoring him is useless. "Not really."

He's winding up for a lecture, so I cut him off with a raised hand. "Don't start, Kai." My voice comes out sharper than intended—teeth snapping. He doesn't deserve it, but I'm not in the mood to be handled like some fragile thing.

His mouth quirks, half-pissed, half-amused. "You're lucky I'm not Rev, but even I've got limits. That attitude's only cute until it's not."

Before I can bite back, Rev strolls out of the bedroom, his movements precise and purposeful as always. He heads straight for the open kitchen, starting the coffee machine without a word. Then he leans back against the counter, arms crossed as he locks eyes with me. He doesn't need to say anything, I can tell from the look on his face that he already knows I didn't sleep.

Rev just waits for the coffee machine to work its magic, but the tension in the room is palpable. He's already running calculations behind those eyes, working out the best way to approach me without lighting the fuse.

They learned very quickly when we were reunited that I am no longer the sweet and innocent girl they once knew. What happened carved me up–literally and metaphorically–it left jagged edges and shadows. It left me broken, and probably on the edge of unhinged. Or maybe it simply set me free. It would depend on the day. But they stayed by my side, accepting the darker parts of me without hesitation. Perhaps because they're just as fractured, just as wild. Just as fucked.

Kai and Rev are the perfect matches for my broken soul—unhinged in their own ways, their chaos complementing mine. They've seen the worst of me, they understand that darkness all too well, having accepted their own demons over the years. We're all a little twisted, but somehow, we make it work.

Rev finally pushes off the counter, the smell of freshly brewed coffee filling the room as he pours us each a cup. He adds the caramel creamer that Kai and I like before he hands one to Kai, then offers me mine, our fingers brushing together briefly as I take it. He doesn't push. Instead, he shifts gears. "Kai," he says, his voice deceptively casual, "you hear anything more about the building on Fifth?"

Kai straightens, rubbing the back of his neck. "Yeah. Arson. No doubt."

The knot in my stomach tightens. I knew it, but hearing it out loud? That's a different beast. Kai's eyes flick between us, warning that there's more.

"And there was a message," he adds, voice dropping. "'The reign of the current devils is coming to an end. Careful, or you might end up a dead devil too.'"

The words coil in my bones, cold and jagged. My grip tightens on the cup, ceramic biting into my palm. The message is a clear threat aimed at me and everything I've built.

Rev watches me, his expression unreadable. He's waiting to see how I'll react, ready to step in if necessary. But there's no fear in his gaze, only grim understanding. This is the kind of battle we've all been preparing for.

"Let them fucking try." My voice is steady, but anger hums beneath like a live wire. "They have no idea who they're dealing with."

Rev's nod is small, approving. Exactly what he expected. "You don't go anywhere without Hudson from now on."

The words slam into me. "Rev—" I nearly growl, "I don't need a fucking babysitter."

"This isn't up for debate," he replies, voice flat steel. "Hudson's the best. We're not taking chances."

I want to argue, to claw at the edges of the order like a caged animal, but it's pointless. The first time my life was threatened after we took control of the city, I'd been more accepting of the twins' decision to bring in extra protection. But then they'd introduced me to Hudson—the walking complication. Six foot five inches of lethal precision and inconvenient attraction. The man's been a shadow at my side ever since. Competent. Relentless. And those fucking green eyes that see too much. I hate how my body betrays me around him. I hate how much the twins love to throw him in my path like a game.

"I can handle myself," I mutter, more petulant than I'd like. Rev raises an eyebrow, trading a look with Kai.

"No one doubts it," Rev says. "But this isn't about what you can handle. It's about not giving them easy chances, baby girl."

Kai leans in, smirking. "So, what's your plan for today?"

I glance at the mess of papers, already plotting. "I need to make a trip to the club to make sure everything's ready for the opening, and maybe put a new color through my hair."

Kai twirls a strand of blonde between his fingers. "I'm going to miss the blonde," he says with a sigh. "Are you going back to purple again?"

It's tradition–I've dyed my hair purple for Dead Devil's Night every year for the last three, but I feel the itch for change. I smirk. "Maybe. Or maybe I'll surprise you."

His grin sharpens, tugging on the strand of hair he's holding. "Looking forward to seeing it wrapped around my fist, whatever color it is."

I laugh—breathy, involuntary. Rev clears his throat, dragging us back to the present. "We have business to attend to down in the Lair and at one of the pool halls toward the edge of the city," he says, his tone shifting to a more businesslike edge. "You know the one?"

I nod. The pool hall in question was once owned by the men who attacked us years ago. Taking over the places once owned by the bastards who hurt us had been... delicious.

"Well then," I say, draining the last of my coffee and shoving to my feet. "Guess I should get ready."

The elevator dings, and I force down a growl of annoyance. Hudson is punctual to a fault, arriving at the apartment every morning like clockwork. As expected, his muscular frame steps off the lift, filling the space. His eyes flare when they land on me, then smooth into professional detachment. I catch the twitch of amusement at the corner of his mouth before it vanishes.

And that's when I realize; I'm standing there in nothing but an open gown, bare skin on full display.

My cheeks burn, but I yank the gown closed and refuse to give any of them the satisfaction of watching me squirm. Kai's snicker cuts through the room sharp as glass, and when I whip him a glare he just grins wider, smug as sin. Rev stands back, unreadable as stone—except for that twitch at the corner of his mouth that tells me he's enjoying this more than he should.

Hudson clears his throat. "Ready for the day?" His tone is professional, but the teasing glint in his eyes is anything but.

I take a deep breath, forcing my irritation down. "Give me a minute," I snap as I turn on my heel to head toward the bedroom. "I'll be ready shortly."

Kai's cackle follows me, wicked and delighted. I resist the urge to flip him off, though it takes more self-control than I'd like to admit. Instead I focus on getting dressed, pulling on fitted black jeans that hug my hips with a blue satin shirt that Rev had found for me, the fabric cool and smooth against my skin. This sort of material is a luxury now, and tells everyone I'm not someone to fuck with.

Pulling my boots on, I slide my knives into place. I run a brush through my hair but leave it out, a swipe of the dark eyeliner and blue eyeshadow making my eyes pop the way I like. Good enough.

When I step back out, the conversation they were having in hushed tones cuts off. Three sets of eyes turn to look at me, all of them assessing.

"Nice," Kai drawls, winking as he saunters over. He wraps one of his tattooed arms around my waist, pulling me close. His touch is warm and familiar, and I feel the usual thrill at his proximity. When he goes in for a kiss, I bring a hand up between us.

"I'm not reapplying this lipstick," I warn, smirking, my voice sweet but firm.

His grin only sharpens. He peels my hand away like it's nothing, lips ghosting across mine before sliding to the soft spot under my ear. His tongue flicks, deliberate, making my knees weak.

"That's fine, gorgeous," he murmurs, voice hot against my skin. "I'll save my kisses for your other lips later."

The promise coils through me, dark and dirty, leaving me flushed and aching. He steps back, smug as the devil.

Rev replaces him, his intense gaze locking onto mine as he gently takes my hand. The humor fades from his eyes, replaced by a seriousness that makes my heart skip a beat. "Be careful out there, little bit. I hate when we're apart."

The weight of his words presses into my chest. His hand slides up to cup my cheek, his thumb brushing lightly against my skin. Then, without breaking eye contact he leans in, his lips touching mine—soft, feather-light, deliberate. Careful. Tender. It burns hotter than Kai's teasing.

Hudson waits by the elevator, patient, his stance relaxed but his eyes sharp. Keys on the counter catch my eye, and I scoop them up as I stalk over. His brow arches when I flash them at him.

"Like fuck are you driving," he says flatly, snatching them from my grip and tossing them back to Kai without effort.

I roll my eyes, stepping into the elevator. "All right, old man."

Ignoring the choking laugh coming from one of the twins, Hudson follows me into the elevator, pressing the button for the ground floor. The confined space amplifies his presence, the subtle scent of his cologne wrapping around me.

I lean back against the elevator wall, crossing my arms over my chest as I eye him critically. I know in reality there is only nine years between us. Ever since he started working for us almost two years ago I have put up a clear wall between us, but today, I can't resist trying to poke at his rigid control.

"You know, for someone your age, you move pretty fast," I remark, my tone dripping with faux concern. "Should I be worried about you throwing your back out?"

His eyes flick to me, amusement dancing in their depths. "Considering I can still outrun and outfight you on your best day, my back is just fine," he retorts smoothly, not missing a beat.

I sigh dramatically. "Denial is the first sign of aging, you know. Next thing, you'll be bitching about 'kids these days' and going to bed at eight."

A low, dark chuckle escapes his lips, a sound that thrums in my chest. "Keep it up, and I'll start enforcing a curfew for you. Eight o'clock was it?"

I arch a brow. "Please. Like you could control me."

He leans closer, voice dropping to a dangerous murmur. "Don't make me prove you wrong."

The air thickens, heat and irritation tangling. I hold his stare, unflinching. "In your dreams, old man."

His smirk widens, sharp as a blade. "You have no idea what I dream about."

The elevator dings, breaking the moment, but the tension clings like smoke. He slides his mask of professionalism back on, gesturing forward. "After you."

I lift my chin, refusing to acknowledge the flutter in my stomach as I stride out of the elevator.

As we walk through the dark and empty nightclub Hudson falls into step beside me, his gaze scanning the surroundings for any sign of threat.

Outside, the black SUV is already waiting at the curb, engine purring. One of Hudson's men stands by the car door, opening it as we approach. I pause, casting a look at Hudson.

"I still don't see why I can't drive. I know these streets better than you," I argue, not ready to let the issue drop.

Hudson doesn't even blink. "And I know how to keep you alive. Let me do my job."

I roll my eyes but climb into the SUV without further protest. As he settles into the driver's seat, I can't resist one last jab.

"Just try not to fall asleep at the wheel. I know it's hard at your age."

He glances at me in the rearview mirror, his lips twitching, but there is something harder in his eyes now. "Careful, sweetheart."

I huff, turning to look out the window as we pull away from the curb. The city rushes past, a mixture of dilapidated buildings and thriving establishments that we've painstakingly built up over the years.

As we pass a drug store I turn to Hudson, breaking the silence. "At some point today, can we make a stop? I need to change my hair again."

Hudson glances at me, his eyebrow raising slightly, but he doesn't question it.

As we navigate through the streets, my mind drifts to the message left at the burned building on Fifth Street. The threat was clear, and while I refuse to be intimidated, I can't ignore the nagging worry gnawing at the back of my mind.

"Any updates on Fifth Street?" My voice cuts through the quiet. I don't sugarcoat the question.

Hudson's jaw ticks, eyes fixed on the road. "Nothing concrete. A few leads. Nothing I'd bet your life on."

I nod, tapping my fingers against my thigh impatiently. "We can't afford to let this slide. Whoever did this needs to be made an example of."

He glances at me briefly before returning his focus to the road. "Agreed. But we need to be smart about it. Rushing in without all the information could make things worse."

I bristle at his cautionary tone. "Sometimes force is exactly what's needed to keep people in line."

Hudson sighs, his grip on the steering wheel tightening. "And sometimes it leads to unnecessary casualties."

I bite back a retort because he's not wrong, and I hate that he's not wrong. "Fine. But when we get a name, I want blood. No hesitation."

His gaze flickers back to me, hard, promising. "You'll have it."

The rest of the drive passes in relative silence, both of us lost in our thoughts. When we finally arrive at the new club, I take a moment to appreciate the transformation. The exterior, though still a work in progress, has a certain allure with its sleek lines and vibrant colors. It's hard not to feel a swell of pride mixed with anticipation for the grand opening.

Hudson ignores the no-parking sign, pulling right up to the curb like he owns the city. Which, to be fair, we basically do. Near the entryway of the club, a banner announces the grand opening, and workers are putting the finishing touches on the new signage. One spots me and nearly trips over himself to get closer. "Perfect timing," he blurts, excitement shining through grime. "We're about to light it up. You can let the bosses know we did a good job, right?"

I chuckle softly, always amused by everyone's assumption that the twins are the ones in charge. I nod in agreement, and the worker gives the go-ahead to one of the others. The sign blazes to life, the brightness striking even in broad daylight—though not as striking as it will be on Dead Devil's Night. I hum in appreciation.

My lips curve into a slow, dangerous smile.

The worker stares, wide-eyed, desperate. "Did we do good?"

"You did perfect," I tell him.

Lit up across the front of the building in a beautiful teal color are the words 'Devil's Playground'.

Chapter 3

Rylan

As we push through the front entryway, the hum of activity behind the closed door swells. Workers scatter like ants, setting up bars and tables, putting the finishing touches on the walls and stages. The energy is electric, frantic, and I can almost taste it on my tongue—sharp, metallic, like blood.

The club is alive. The walls are adorned in teal and blue, fabrics spilling from the ceiling like rivers of silk, twinkling lights woven through like stars caught in a spider's web. The walls are dressed in textures that beg to be touched, every detail calculated to seduce and distract. The effect is both mesmerizing and enchanting, a far cry from the warehouse it once was.

The mezzanine level pulls my attention. It resembles a scene from Arabian Nights; private lounges curtained in semi-sheer veils, shadows flickering behind them like sin on display. Even closed, the lights throw shadows of whoever's inside onto the fabric—bodies twisting, moving, putting on a show for anyone who dares to watch. Erotic as hell. Subversive. A place built for both spectacle and scandal.

Hudson's men already stalk the level, mapping the space like predators scenting new territory, preparing for their role as security.

On the main level round tables with seating are scattered throughout, providing space for patrons to relax and socialize. The dance floors are situated on each side of the main stage, strategically placed to ensure that every corner of the club can experience the energy of the dance scene. The main stage itself is flanked by two minor stages, all adorned with hanging curtains. Cages are suspended above the stages that can be lowered or retracted to suit the performance.

On the main stage, movement catches my eye. A performer—long hair tied back, muscles catching the dim light–drops from the ceiling on a sheet of fabric, catching it with one lean, muscled arm. He moves like smoke, like sin, the strength in every flex making my pulse trip. He spins with a predator's grace, his body bending, twisting, teasing the crowd that isn't here yet. He's dressed in nothing more than shorts and a muscle tank, showcasing his toned body.

I know that on the night of the opening, both male and female performers will be in more intricate costumes, which they will gradually shed throughout their performances. It will be an elegant strip show, but a strip show nonetheless.

The performer uses the curtain material to spin gracefully around the stage, his movements fluid and confident. As he lands back on the cage, he lets go of the fabric, gripping the cage behind him. His muscles ripple beneath his skin with every motion.

Even from a distance, it's clear that he's aware of his audience. His mouth parts, subtle but enough, and his hips roll like a dare as his eyes lock onto mine. My stomach twists with heat, irritation sparking because I hate how easily I'm distracted by pretty muscles.

Then he lets go, freefalling for a heartbeat that drags me to the edge of panic—until he catches another curtain, smooth as silk. Show-off. My lips twitch.

Hudson's nudge snaps me back, and I almost growl at the interruption. Stella, the manager we hired for Devil's Playground barrels toward us, flushed with stress and adrenaline, eyes wild. Hudson's voice stays dry, calm. "Looks like she's got something to discuss." Humor coils under his words, and I have to grit my teeth not to snap.

The woman starts rattling off last-minute updates, efficient and jittery. "Everything's coming together," she says, her eyes darting around the room. "We're just about ready. If there's anything specific you need, now's the time to let me know."

I smile. "It looks amazing so far. How about you give us a progress tour so we can see it all for ourselves? I'd love to get a closer look at the final setup and make sure everything aligns with our vision for the opening."

The manager's face brightens, clearly eager to please. "Absolutely, I'd be happy to. Follow me, and I'll show you around."

She leads us through the bustling space, pointing out cages, safety measures, bars, lounges, all the little things that keep chaos from spiraling too far.

Gesturing towards the cages suspended above the stage, she starts to go over the safety checks. "The cages have been thoroughly checked and tested for safety. We've ensured that all the rigging is secure, and that the cages can be safely lowered or retracted as needed. They'll be inspected every week to ensure they remain in top condition."

Her professionalism and attention to detail are reassuring. "We've also conducted extensive safety checks on the performance materials," she adds. "The curtains, the rigging, and the equipment have all passed thorough safety inspections. I know the goal is to provide an exciting experience while ensuring the performers' and guests' safety."

We move towards one of the minor stages, where she continues. "These smaller stages have similar safety measures in place. All the materials used are flame-retardant as I know we have the fire dancing performances also. The dance floors have added non-slip materials, but we have cleaners scheduled for the entire establishment morning after closing to clean and double check for safety."

At the bar area, she adds, "The bars are ready, with secure shelving and staff trained for any emergencies. The privacy lounges upstairs are also well-prepared, with secure curtains and safe lighting. Each lounge area will be monitored and cleaned as needed. The girls we have set up for those duties will just blend in seamlessly with the other staff and performers."

Finally, she looks at Hudson as she points out the security stations. "As you know, your team is already familiar with the layout. We've got surveillance and patrols set up to ensure everything runs smoothly and no one gets out of hand."

When she's done, she scurries off, leaving the club's thrum around us. I take it all in. It's perfect. Dangerous. Erotic. Ours.

Hudson leans close, voice low. "I need to brief my team. Don't go far."

"I'm stepping out for a smoke," I shoot back, rolling my eyes before he can give me that lecture look. "Back alley. Close enough I can still feel you breathing down my neck."

The growl in his chest is low, warning, and it makes me grin as I slip away.

Outside, daylight slams into me. I blink, digging out a cigarette, but freeze when I notice him—the performer. Leaning against the brick wall, smoke curling from his lips, hair copper-blond in the sun, eyes blue fire.

"Got a light?" I ask.

He flicks the ash from his cigarette and holds it out to me. As I light my cigarette with his, he straightens as though he might head back inside.

"You don't have to leave on my account," I say with a grin.

He eyes me warily. "I don't have a death wish." His voice is low and raspy, like he has choked on enough smokes for a lifetime even if I would estimate that he is a few years younger than me. The voice fits the industry he is in, with just enough gravel to it to have an effect on anyone who hears it.

But his words make me pause. "What do you mean?"

"I know who you belong to," he says, taking back his cigarette with a raised brow. "My life may not mean much, but I'd like to keep it and not get shot for being near the boss's girl."

I can't help but laugh at his bluntness, the sound escaping before I can stop it. His frown deepens, unsure of how to react.

I laugh—sharp, unrestrained. His frown deepens, uncertain. "I don't belong to anyone."

He smirks, drags on his cigarette. "You keep telling yourself that."

The alley thickens with smoke and tension, the moment charged. His gaze roves, lingering, assessing. "Though, you don't seem the type to be easily kept."

I tilt my head, lips curving. "And what type is that?"

He shrugs, the smirk still on his face. "The kind who knows their worth and doesn't let anyone dictate their life."

The words dig under my skin, too close to truth. I grin, wicked. "Well, you're not wrong." I let the silence hang before I ask, "So do you drive or ride?"

He blinks. "Ride. Why?"

"Got your bike here?" I ask, my tone light.

He unzips his shorts pocket, pulls out a key, dangling it with a cocky smirk. "Why, doll, you wanna go for a ride?"

I laugh again, dark and amused, as I saunter closer to him, feeling the tension crackle between us. "Where would I find it if I did?" I drop my tone, making it more suggestive.

He gestures absently toward the carpark end of the alleyway. I smoothly slide the key from his fingers, brushing against him as I do. His lips part, stunned.

"Tell him I gave you no choice when he comes looking," I purr, voice deliberate, daring.

Fear flashes in his eyes. "Wait—shit—don't do this to me—"

But I'm already walking away, smoke trailing from my lips, his panic echoing behind me. I should feel bad. I don't. His words carved too deep.

No one dictates my life.

Not anymore.

Chapter 4

Rylan

It TAKES ME ALL of thirty seconds to pick out which bike belongs to the dancer. Sleek. Black. Mean as sin. The chrome winks at me like it's in on the joke, like it knows it's about to be stolen. I swing my leg over, the leather seat hot under me, the weight solid between my thighs. When the engine growls to life, it purrs deep and throaty, a vibration that hums through my bones. Oh, yes. Hello beautiful. God, I could almost come just from the rumble.

The city swallows me whole the second I hit the street. Wind claws at my hair, the chaos of the city bleeding into me, fueling me. Car horns, drunken laughter, sirens in the distance, the air tastes like gasoline and garbage. I can't help but grin. Chaos is comfort—it keeps the voices in my head occupied, drowns out the itch in my fingers that wants to carve answers out of someone's skin.

Fifth Street isn't far, but the closer I get, the heavier it presses on my lungs. By the time I roll to the curb, the smell of burned dreams hits me first—char, ash, wet soot. The once vibrant restaurant and offices above it are now nothing more than a burnt husk. The front façade has collapsed inward, and the roof is partially caved in. What's left of the building looms like a ribcage picked clean, jagged bones clawing at the sky.

I pocket the keys and step off, boots splashing through puddles streaked with ash. Every crunch of glass underfoot is a reminder: someone did this. Someone thought they could take what's mine.

I walk slowly toward the alleyway beside the building, each step heavy with a mixture of anger and sorrow. This was more than just a business—it was the first place that I rebuilt and developed after I took over the city. It was my building. My blood and sweat turned to blackened rubble.

As I round the back of the building, shadows clutching at me like greedy hands. And then—oh, there it is. Kai was right. Black paint, sloppy and deliberate, screaming a promise on the wall. A threat. My fists curl so hard my knuckles ache.

I stand there looking at it for a few moments, letting the rage settle in my bones. That's when I hear it—the shuffle of boots, the scrape of steel on concrete. I tilt my head, listening. Five of them. Heavy feet, different rhythms. Trying to creep, like cockroaches. They think they're hunting me. They've already wrapped the rope around their own necks and don't even know it.

"Look at this, boys," one sneers, trying so hard to sound cocky it almost makes me yawn. "A little mouse, scurrying into a trap."

I whip around, eyes wide, mouth open in a gasp. I stumble back, clutching my chest. "Oh noooo," I wail, trembling like a bad actress in a B-grade horror flick. Their steps falter, confusion tripping them.

Two in front, two flanking, one skulking in the rear like he's a puppet master. Classic. Predictable. I widen my eyes, step back, shrinking like a rabbit. "Five against one? That's hardly fair. What are you gonna do with me?" My voice trembles, all breathy fear—but my pulse is thrumming with delight.

He laughs, the sound thick as tar. "Pretty little thing like you? You'll make perfect bait. When your boys see you strung up, they won't keep ignoring our boss."

I whimper. Bend lower. Fingers curl around the blades in my boots. "Please," I croon, voice breaking into a high, shivering note. "Don't hurt me, Mister Bad Guys…"

The one who steps forward first doesn't even realize he's already dead. He leans in, trying to taste my fear. "You should never have come here. Things are about to get real ugly."

And that's when I laugh. A sharp, manic crack that echoes like gunfire. "Ugly?" I snarl, rising in a blur of motion. "Yeah, I can do ugly."

The blades sing as I bury them in his throat. Blood sprays, painting the alley red. His body hits the ground before the others catch up to what just happened. The sound he makes is wet, a dying rattle.

"Oh," I gasp theatrically, tilting my head at the corpse, "did I do that?" I giggle, high and sharp, before baring my teeth at the rest. "Three guesses who's next!"

Chaos detonates. The others howl, blades flashing, lunging. Perfect. It makes my blood sing.

The first lunges and swings wide, sloppy. But I saw his move from a mile away. I dance aside, giggling, and open him from hip to hip. He crumples. Another comes screaming, knife aimed at my ribs, but I'm already moving. I meet him steel-to-steel, sparks flying, and twist, burying my second blade in his throat. He gurgles, spraying red. "Shhh," I whisper, pressing a finger to my lips as he falls, "don't ruin the moment."

Three down. I wipe blood from my lip, eyes bright. Two left.

The next stumbles, fear in his eyes. Oh, I *love* that look. He tries to retreat but I kick his legs out and he hits the concrete hard. "Where you going, huh? We were *just* getting to the fun part." Before he can squeal, I straddle him, burying my blade in his chest, twisting until his body stills.

That just leaves the leader. Oh, he's shaking now, but desperate dogs bite hardest. And I want him alive.

He charges, desperate, a roar on his lips. I move to slip past, but he's better than I gave him credit for. He slams me hard against the bricks. My knives clatter to the ground, and cold steel presses into my throat.

"I'll cut you open," he hisses, spittle hitting my cheek, "and fuck what's left. Shove their knives in you one by one so they can join in from hell."

I laugh. Blood trickles down my neck from his blade, and I laugh in his face, sharp and jagged. "God, you're creative. I almost like you."

And then—bang.

The shot rattles the alley, warm spray splattering across me. His eyes go wide, his mouth opening in a silent *oh* before he crumples, knife dragging shallowly across my throat on the way down.

The leader's corpse is still twitching when Hudson storms into view, all broad shoulders and black fury. The alley is a slaughterhouse—bodies leaking red into dirty puddles, steel gleaming where it dropped, smoke still curling from his gun. And he looks like the executioner.

His eyes lock on me, and it's like being pinned by a thunderhead. Dark, electric, full of the kind of rage that makes men kneel. And his focus is solely on me. I tilt my head, grin splitting across my face, blood dripping down my neck.

"Aw," I rasp, voice ragged but amused, "you ruined my fun."

Hudson doesn't smile. Doesn't even blink. He advances, gun still raised, each step a promise of violence. "Fun?" His voice is molten iron, low and sharp. "You call this fun?"

I giggle, high and breathless, stepping over the twitching body at my feet. "I was *winning*." I sweep an arm wide, theatrically presenting the carnage. "Four down, one to squeal, and you—" I jab a bloodied finger at him—"you stole my encore."

The barrel of his gun dips as he closes the last steps between us. His free hand snaps out, fingers clamping around my arm hard enough to bruise. He jerks me forward, chest to chest, his face carved from stone and storm.

"You think this is a game?" he snarls, voice rough with barely restrained rage. "You think bleeding yourself out in alleys makes you untouchable?" His eyes flick to the thin line of blood still seeping down my throat, and for a second, the storm flickers into something else. Fear. Frustration. Then it's rage again, sharper. "You could've been dead before I got here."

I laugh in his face, sharp and feral, blood spattering his cheek. "But I'm *not*." I tilt my head back, lips curling wickedly. "And admit it—you love watching me dance with death. Makes your cock twitch, doesn't it?"

His jaw ticks, hard enough to crack teeth. "Get in the car," he growls, dragging me out of the alleyway and toward the waiting SUV.

I stumble once, laughing through it.

One of his men waits near the SUV, stone-faced, and Hudson doesn't hesitate—digging into my pocket for the bike key and tossing it to him like I'm a misbehaving child caught stealing candy.

I watch the man mount the stolen motorcycle, and it roars to life. "Hey!" I protest, my voice pitching high with mock outrage. "That's mine!"

Hudson whirls on me, jerking the SUV door open. His face is carved from fury. "Get. In."

For a beat, I almost laugh in his face again. Almost push him. But there's a line in his voice, one even I'm not stupid enough to cross right now. So I slide into the back seat, smirk curling back onto my lips as the cut on my neck throbs.

"You're mad because I had fun without you," I purr, stretching out across the leather like I own it. "Next time, Hudson, I'll save you a dance."

The door slams, hard enough to rattle the whole SUV.

Hudson slides into the driver's seat like a storm barely contained, slamming his own door. The engine growls when he turns the key, the sound a perfect match for the tension vibrating off him. He peels out, tires screaming against asphalt, and the silence that follows is heavy—thick enough to choke on.

His hands strangle the wheel, veins standing out across his forearms. His profile is cut in hard lines, jaw locked, eyes forward like if he looks at me too long, he might break something. Maybe me. Maybe himself.

The city blurs past until suddenly he jerks the SUV onto the shoulder, tires biting pavement with a sharp screech. We're outside a drugstore. The sunlight bouncing off the windows is blinding, obnoxious, ordinary. The kind of place people come for toothpaste and aspirin. Meanwhile, Hudson looks like he came here to bury a body.

I reach for the door handle. He's there before I can blink, yanking it open. "Stay." The word is a knife, sharp enough to skin me where I sit.

My hackles rise. I let out a sharp bark, feral and biting.

Hudson leans in, his shadow filling the doorway. His eyes are dark and lethal as they burn into mine. "Bark at me again and I'll put a collar on you and show you what I do to a *bad dog*."

His voice is a growl, his breath hot against my face. Then he slams the door, rattling my bones, and stalks inside.

My thighs squeeze together involuntarily. Jesus *fucking* Christ. What's wrong with me? I should hate that. I should claw his eyes out for daring. But instead, I'm left squirming in the seat, my pulse pounding. Yeah. Definitely fucked in the head.

When he finally emerges, his shoulders are still tight, but the edge is dulled. He tosses a plain bag onto the passenger seat and drops behind the wheel again, exhaling hard through his nose like he's trying to exorcise the fury.

For a long moment, he just stares at the dash. His fingers tap the wheel in a restless rhythm. Then his gaze flicks up, meeting mine in the rearview. His eyes are still dark, still dangerous, but there's something else now—something softer hiding under the cracks. "You okay?" His voice is quieter, almost human.

I grin, face stained with blood, and shrug. "Peachy."

"You're a fucking mess," he mutters, gravel dragging over every syllable. "Don't tell me you're fine when you're bleeding all over my car."

I wave him off like it's nothing. "It's just a scratch. Handled myself pretty damn well, in case you didn't notice."

His eyes narrow, disbelief sharp enough to cut. "That scratch looks like someone tried to cut your throat open."

I wince as I press a hand against it, feeling the sting deepen now that adrenaline's fading. "Relax. I've had worse. Still breathing, aren't I?"

He doesn't relax. Not even close.

I smirk, leaning forward just enough to let my voice curl around him like smoke. "You know, you sound like a grumpy old man with a hero complex. Next thing I know, you'll be waving a cane at me."

For the first time, his lips twitch. A shadow of a smirk. "Maybe I should get one. Use it to beat some sense into your ass."

Heat flushes low in my belly, and I fall back into the seat with a laugh. "Kinky."

The SUV lurches back onto the road, the silence no longer suffocating but humming, electric, strung tight between us. When we pull up outside the apartment, he kills the engine and just sits there. "You really know how to push my buttons."

I grin at him, baring my teeth. "What can I say? It's a talent."

His gaze meets mine, hard and unreadable. "That talent's going to get you killed." But there's that ghost of a smile curling at the corners of his mouth.

I lean back, eyes glittering. "Then I'll die keeping you young, old man."

Something dark flickers across his face. "There are better ways to make me feel young," he murmurs seemingly to himself, and the weight of it lingers in the air, heavy and hot.

Then it's gone. He grabs the bag, pushes his door open. "Come on. Let's get you cleaned up."

For almost two years I had built a wall between us. Ignoring the way my body reacted to him and the subtle undercurrent of tension that had slowly built over that time. The twins might make the occasional joke about that but I would never betray them by acting on anything. In the hours since the sun rose today, my whole world seems like it has tilted off its axis. It feels like I have taken a step in a direction I can't retreat from now but at the same time so did he. And I have a feeling the twins may have played a part in that.

Hudson nods to the guys stationed outside the Devil's Lair, and for a moment, my heart thuds in my chest. The thought of the twins being inside the club makes me suddenly uneasy; if they see me like this, I can only imagine their reactions. I can almost picture them locking me away in some tower to keep me safe. So, I sigh softly in relief when we walk through the club and only see the workers, with neither of my men in sight.

Inside the apartment, the silence is wrong. No twins. No laughter. No music. Just the thrum of my blood in my ears. Hudson's eyes sweep the room, sharp and clinical, muttering "Clear" like he's exorcising ghosts.

I almost stumble when he spins back on me at the bottom of the steps. His hand catches my chin, tilts my face up. His thumb drags the edge of the cut, and I growl low in my throat. He ignores it, eyes narrowing on the wound.

"You'll live," he says, finally releasing me. Then he thrusts the bag into my hands.

I frown at him, suspicious, tugging it open. My stomach drops when I see what's inside—hair dye. No box. No sticker. No way to know the color. That *asshole*.

I glare at him. "You didn't even ask me what I wanted."

His smirk is wolfish, pure sin. "Consider it payment. For me saving your ass."

I snatch the bag from him, stomping toward the bathroom with a muttered curse. The smile tugging at my lips betrays me anyway.

Chapter 5

Rylan

I'VE JUST WRAPPED A towel around my still wet hair when the bathroom door opens. Rev stands in the opening, his arms crossed over his chest and a scowl firmly on his face. My stomach dips a little because that look spells trouble for me. That look tells me that Hudson has already tattled.

"Are you fucking kidding me, Ry?" His voice is deadly quiet, which is always worse than when he yells.

I shrug, trying for nonchalance as I secure the towel better around my head. "What?"

His jaw ticks. "Don't play dumb. It doesn't suit you." He pushes off the doorframe, stalking into the bathroom. "Five men in an alley? Stealing some random dancer's motorcycle? A knife to your throat?"

I roll my eyes. "I had it under control."

"Under control?" He laughs, but there's no humor in it. "You call that under control? You could have died, Rylan."

"But I didn't," I counter, trying to step around him.

He blocks my path, his large frame filling the doorway. "That's not the point and you know it."

"Then what is the point, Rev?" I snap, frustration bubbling up. "That I should sit here and be a good little girl while you and Kai handle everything? That I should let Hudson babysit me like I'm some helpless princess?"

His eyes flash dangerously. "The point is that you were reckless. The point is that there are people in this city who want us dead, and you're making it fucking easy for them."

"I killed four of them," I remind him, chin tilting up defiantly.

"And the fifth almost killed you," he growls.

We stand there, tension crackling between us like a live wire. Finally, he shakes his head, a muscle jumping in his jaw. "We'll talk about this later."

Before I can respond, he turns and stalks out, leaving me alone in the bathroom. I rip the towel from my head, throwing it against the counter in frustration. Fucking Hudson. He didn't waste any time running to Rev with the story, did he?

I take a deep breath, trying to calm the storm brewing inside me. I examine the cut in the mirror. It's not deep, just a thin line that's already stopped bleeding. It'll heal without a scar—not that I care about one more mark on my body.

The dye has worked its magic, and I run my fingers through my still-damp hair, admiring the color. It's a rich teal, vibrant and bold, exactly like the color of the Devil's Playground sign. I style it quickly, letting it fall in loose waves around my shoulders.

The effect is striking against my pale skin, making my blue eyes pop even more.

I dress quickly in tight black jeans and a low-cut top that shows just enough skin to be distracting but not enough to be vulgar. Power isn't always about showing force—sometimes it's about commanding attention.

When I finally emerge from the bathroom, I can hear raised voices from the living room. I follow the sound, finding Rev and Kai facing off with Hudson, who stands with his back straight and expression neutral despite the twins' obvious anger.

"—could have called for backup," Kai is saying, his voice tight with barely controlled rage.

"She was gone before I could stop her," Hudson replies, his tone measured. "By the time I tracked her down, she'd already engaged."

"That's your fucking job," Rev snaps. "To stop her from doing stupid shit like this."

I lean against the doorframe, crossing my arms. "You know I'm standing right here, right? Maybe stop talking about me now that I'm in the room."

Three pairs of eyes snap to me, and I can't help the smirk that forms on my lips at their reactions. Kai's eyes widen slightly before his expression shifts to appreciation. Rev's scowl deepens, though I catch the flicker of heat in his gaze. But it's Hudson's reaction that interests me most—the slight parting of his lips, the way his eyes darken as they take in my new hair color.

"Well, don't you all look cozy," I drawl, pushing off the wall and sauntering into the room. "Having a nice chat about the troublesome little woman in your lives?"

Kai's lips twitch, fighting a smile despite his anger. "You're impossible, you know that?"

"Part of my charm," I reply, dropping onto the couch and stretching my legs out.

Rev hasn't moved, his eyes still locked on me. "This isn't a joke, Ry."

I sigh, some of my bravado fading. "I know it's not. But I'm fine. We're all fine. And now we know there are people bold enough to attack in broad daylight."

"That's not comforting," Kai mutters.

The elevator dings, cutting off whatever Rev was about to say. We all tense, hands moving toward weapons automatically, but relax when we see Camden step out—pushing a familiar figure before him.

My eyebrows shoot up. It's the dancer from the club, looking considerably less confident than he did this morning. His copper-blonde hair is disheveled, and there's a bruise forming on his cheekbone.

Camden is one of Hudson's most trusted men and probably the closest thing I have to a friend outside of my inner circle—he still isn't trusted to know who is really in charge though. Right now he has the dancer's arm twisted behind his back. Despite being in his mid-thirties, Camden moves with the agility of someone much younger. His face is all sharp angles and perpetual amusement, like everything in life is a private joke only he understands. We bonded over our shared appreciation for dark humor and our ability to find the absurdity in the most fucked-up situations. He's one of the few people who doesn't treat me like I'm made of glass, and for that alone, he became my friend.

"Special delivery," Camden announces, his lips quirked in that perpetual half-smile. "Stella over at the Playground rang to say he was going to the cops to report his stolen bike. Thought you might want to have a word."

The dancer's eyes widen when they land on me, a mixture of fear and resignation crossing his features.

Rev's attention shifts immediately, his predatory instincts kicking in as he stalks toward the newcomer. "So you're the one who let her steal your bike."

The dancer swallows hard. "I didn't exactly let her—"

"Shut up," Kai cuts in, moving to flank his brother. "You think we're stupid? You just happened to be there, just happened to leave your keys where she could take them?"

"I didn't—"

"Who do you work for?" Rev demands, getting right in the dancer's face.

The dancer's eyes dart around the room, looking for an escape that doesn't exist. "I don't work for anyone except the club. I'm just a performer."

Kai scoffs, pulling a gun from the waistband of his jeans and pressing it to the dancer's temple. "Try again. Who sent you?"

The dancer goes rigid, his breathing shallow. "My name is Oliver Hart. I'm from Portland originally. I moved here six months ago for the job at the club. I swear to God, that's all there is to it."

"Bullshit," Rev snarls. "The timing's too convenient. Fifth Street burns, and suddenly you're there, offering her a ride out?"

Oliver's eyes widen. "Fifth Street? I don't know anything about that. I was just taking a smoke break!"

I watch the exchange, the fear in Oliver's eyes seems genuine. While I'm no stranger to violence, something about this feels wrong.

"Camden," I say, my voice cutting through the tension. "Give us the room."

Camden raises an eyebrow at me, and I have to force myself to remember he doesn't know the truth. He looks to Hudson, who gives a short nod.

"You heard her," Hudson says. "Out."

Camden releases Oliver with a shove, shaking his head as he heads back toward the elevator. Disgust flickers across his face before the doors close.

As soon as he's gone, I stand up, moving between Oliver and the twins. "You can't kill him."

Rev's eyes narrow. "And why the hell not?"

"Because he's not involved," I say firmly. "I stole his bike because I was pissed off and wanted to make a point. He didn't offer it to me."

"You don't know that he's not involved," Kai argues, gun still trained on Oliver's head.

I roll my eyes. "What I know is that if he was sent to kill me or lure me into a trap, he did a piss-poor job of it. Besides, I'm the one who approached him, not the other way around."

Oliver's eyes are fixed on me, a mixture of gratitude and wariness in his gaze.

"Put the gun down, Kai," I say, my tone brooking no argument.

For a moment, I think he might refuse, but then he lowers the weapon, though he doesn't holster it.

"You don't know he's not involved," Kai shoots back. "Hell, I say we cut him up and bleed him a bit just for being prettier than me."

Oliver's head snaps to Kai, wide-eyed, frozen like a deer staring at the wrong set of headlights.

Something twists in me at the look. Fear, yes. But, I see it. A flicker in Oliver's gaze. Not terror. Something sharper. Hungrier.

Interesting.

Rev is still glaring at Oliver. "If I find out you're lying, I'll peel your skin off inch by inch," he growls, his voice dropping to that dark register that makes even me shiver. He leans in closer, blade suddenly in his hand, the tip pressing just beneath Oliver's eye. "See if there's anything worth keeping underneath."

I watch Oliver's reaction carefully. There it is again—that barely perceptible shiver that has nothing to do with fear. His pupils dilate, his breathing quickens, but not in the way of someone terrified. It's... anticipation. Desire, even.

Rev sees it too. His eyes narrow further, and he drags the blade down Oliver's cheek, not cutting, just threatening. "You'd like that, wouldn't you? Feel the bite of my knife?"

Oliver's lips part, his tongue darting out to wet them. "No," he whispers, but his body betrays him. His eyes follow the knife with fascination, not terror.

"Liar," Kai hisses, circling behind him. "I can see it in your eyes. You're just begging for us to make you bleed."

I step forward, placing a hand on Rev's arm. "I think our new friend might have some... interesting proclivities," I murmur, watching Oliver's face flush. "Might be useful."

Rev's eyes meet mine, a silent conversation passing between us. He lowers the knife slightly but doesn't put it away.

"Here's what's going to happen," I say, moving to stand directly in front of Oliver. "You're going to be a good boy for us."

The effect is immediate and unmistakable. Oliver's breath catches, his eyes widening before dropping submissively. There's no hiding the way his body responds to those words—the slight tremble in his hands, the flush creeping up his neck.

"You're going to keep your eyes and ears open at the club," I continue, my voice soft but firm. "If you see anything suspicious, anyone asking questions they shouldn't, you tell us immediately. Understand?"

He nods quickly, too quickly. "Yes. I understand."

"Good boy," I purr, watching with satisfaction as he nearly melts at the praise. "And if you're very, very good, maybe we'll let you find out exactly what Rev's knife feels like against your skin."

Hudson steps forward, his expression unreadable as he pulls out his phone. "Give me your number," he orders Oliver, who fumbles to recite it. Hudson types it in, then shows him his screen. "This is my number. You see anything, you call. Day or night. And if I find out you've been holding back information..."

He doesn't finish the threat. He doesn't need to.

"Your bike's in the parking garage," Hudson adds, his tone dismissive. "Don't make me regret returning it."

Oliver nods again, his eyes flicking between all of us as if he can't quite believe what's happening.

"You can go," I tell him, stepping aside. "For now."

He backs toward the elevator, nearly stumbling in his haste. Just before the doors close, I catch his expression—a mixture of relief, excitement, and something darker that makes me smile.

The moment the elevator doors close, Rev rounds on me. "What the fuck was that?"

I shrug, dropping back onto the couch. "That was me finding us a potential asset."

"An asset?" Kai scoffs. "He's a dancer with a death wish and a pain kink."

"Exactly," I reply, smirking. "Which means he's motivated by things that are easy for us to provide. Fear won't keep him loyal, but his... other interests might."

Hudson makes a sound that might be a laugh. "You're playing with fire."

I turn my gaze to him, letting my smirk widen. "When don't I?"

Rev drops into the seat beside me, his anger seemingly deflated. "You really think he's not involved?"

"No," I admit. "But I think if he is, we'll get more out of him this way than by cutting him open right away."

Kai holsters his gun finally, running a hand through his hair. "Fine. But I'm having Camden run a background check on him. If anything comes up suspicious, all bets are off."

"Fair enough," I agree, leaning back into the cushions. The adrenaline from earlier is fading, leaving me suddenly exhausted. The cut on my neck throbs, a reminder of how close I came to real trouble today.

Rev notices, his eyes softening slightly as they land on the wound. He reaches out, fingers gentle as they trace the edge of the cut. "You need to be more careful, little bit," he murmurs, but the heat has gone from his voice.

I lean into his touch, allowing myself this moment of vulnerability. "I know."

Kai drops down on my other side, his arm sliding around my shoulders. "We can't lose you, Ry," he says quietly. "Not again."

The weight of those words settles over us, heavy with memory. Not again. Never again.

"You won't," I promise, though we all know it's not entirely in my power to keep.

Hudson clears his throat, breaking the moment. "I should check in with the security team at the Playground. Make sure everything's in place for the opening since my earlier meeting was interrupted."

I nod, grateful for the shift in focus. "Good idea. We need everything to be perfect."

As Hudson heads toward the elevator, I can't help but notice the tension in his shoulders, the way his eyes linger on me for just a moment too long before the doors close.

"I see the way you watch him," Kai murmurs, lips brushing my ear.

I turn to him, raising an eyebrow. "Hudson? He's fine."

He snorts. "He wants to fuck you, Ry. Has since day one."

My cheeks heat despite myself. "That's not—"

"It is," Rev cuts me off, his voice low. "And we both know you're not exactly... uninterested."

I feel my face heat at Rev's words. "That's ridiculous."

"Is it?" Kai's fingers trace lazy patterns on my shoulder. "We've watched you two dance around each other for two years now, gorgeous. The tension's so thick I could cut it with my knife."

"It's getting painful to watch, baby girl," Rev adds, his dark eyes studying my face. "The way you snap at each other, the constant fighting—it's foreplay and you know it."

I pull away from both of them, standing up. "You're both delusional. Hudson works for us. That's it."

Kai laughs, the sound rich and knowing. "Keep telling yourself that. We see how your breath catches when he walks in a room. How your eyes follow him."

"And we see how he looks at you," Rev continues, his voice dropping lower. "Like he's one bad day away from pinning you against a wall and showing you exactly what he wants to do to you."

I stare at both of them, incredulous. "Are you two actually encouraging this? You do realize you're talking about me fucking another man, right?"

Kai's grin is all teeth and sin. "We're secure enough to know where your heart lies, gorgeous. Besides..." His eyes darken, flicking to Rev, who nods almost imperceptibly. "We've talked about it."

My mouth goes dry. "Talked about what, exactly?"

"About bringing Hudson in," Rev says simply, his voice steady but laced with heat. "About watching him lose that iron control. About sharing you."

The room suddenly feels too hot, too small. I can't breathe. My mouth falls open. Can't process what I'm hearing.

I blink rapidly, trying to process what they're suggesting. The twins have always been possessive—fiercely so. I know they seemed like they were pushing me toward Hudson, but for them to be so open about their intentions...

"I don't know what you're talking about," I manage to say, though the heat blooming across my skin betrays me.

Rev's lips curl into that knowing smirk that always makes my knees weak. He rises from the couch, stalking toward me with predatory grace.

"If you say so," he murmurs, his voice a dark rumble that vibrates through me.

I swallow hard, backing up until I hit the wall. Rev cages me in, one arm braced beside my head. His eyes hold mine, searching, seeing too much. I feel stripped bare under that gaze, all my defenses crumbling.

"We just want you happy, baby girl," he says softly, his thumb tracing my bottom lip. "Whatever—or whoever—that takes."

Rev's hand suddenly reaches for my hair, fingers twisting into the vibrant teal strands. He tugs just hard enough to make me gasp. "This is new. I like it."He steps back, leaving me breathless and confused. Kai stretches languidly on the couch, watching us with hooded eyes. "Teal suits you. Brings out those killer eyes." His lips quirk into a knowing smirk. "Funny thing, though. Isn't it Hudson's favorite color?"

My head jerks toward him. "What? How would you know that?"

Rev's chuckle is dark velvet. "He mentioned it a few months back when you were obsessing over the color scheme for the Playground. Said teal was always his favorite."

"He never told me that," I say, something odd fluttering in my chest. Hudson had been with me through every planning meeting for the club, offering opinions on security layouts, sight lines, exit strategies—but never once had he mentioned his color preference.

"Of course he didn't," Kai says. "The man's got walls thicker than a bank vault."

I don't admit that Hudson chose my hair dye for me. Instead, I roll my eyes dramatically, trying to ignore the warmth creeping up my neck. "What a coincidence," I mutter, though my mind is racing with implications.

Kai's grin widens. "Isn't it just?" His tone is dripping with suggestion, eyes dancing with mischief.

The moment hangs between us, heavy with implication.

I push off the wall, trying to steady my racing heart. "You two are impossible," I groan.

Rev's smirk deepens as he shares a look with Kai. "That's why you love us."

And damn them, they're right.

Chapter 6

Hudson

I HAD TO GET out of there. The sight of her—teal strands framing that face, that goddamn face—made something in my chest tighten until I couldn't breathe. Teal. My color. On her. I'd handed her the bag myself, played it casual like it meant nothing. But seeing it now, knowing those vibrant strands were there because of me... Christ.

It shouldn't matter. It can't matter. But the twins saw it. They always see everything. And the way they looked at me, like they knew exactly what was happening inside my head—I needed air before I did something stupid.

The Devil's Lair is already humming when I hit the ground floor. Staff move like cogs in a machine—bartenders restocking shelves, waitresses adjusting skirts, the DJ testing sound levels so the bass thunders through the floorboards. Camden's leaning against the far wall, arms crossed, eyes tracking the room with the lazy attention of a wolf who's already decided nothing here is worth the bite.

He notices me immediately, pushing off the wall and falling into step beside me as I cut across the club. No questions, no hesitation—just that familiar half-smirk that says he's about to run his mouth.

We step out into the sunlight. The noise of the club muffles behind the heavy doors, traded for the low thrum of the city—traffic, sirens, someone yelling two blocks over. Camden flicks a lighter, the flame catching, and soon the sharp bite of cigarette smoke curls into the air between us.

He takes a drag, exhales slow. "You know, Hud, I've been trying not to say it, but I'm struggling here." His tone is casual, but the words are edged. "Why the fuck are you stuck playing nanny to the girl when the twins are the ones who actually matter?"

My jaw tightens, but I don't answer. I keep walking, boots landing heavily on the sidewalk as we cut toward the SUV.

Camden doesn't take the hint. He never does. "Don't get me wrong, I like her. Funny as hell, good taste in liquor. I even think of her as a friend. But she's not the boss. Rev and Kai are. They're the ones who keep this city under control. And here you are, wasting the best talent we've got trailing after a woman who doesn't know how to stay put."

He takes another long drag, the cherry tip glowing. "It doesn't make sense. Not when we've got enemies lining up around the block waiting to take a shot at us."

We reach the SUV. I stop, turn to him. The air between us is thick with smoke and something sharper.

"Orders are orders." My voice is flat steel.

Camden arches a brow, his smirk tugging wider. "That all you've got? Orders?" He flicks ash onto the concrete. "Come on, Hud. Off the record. You really think this is smart? That girl is chaos wrapped in pretty skin. One day she's gonna drag you under with her, and when she does, don't expect me to say I told you so."

I step in close enough that he has to tilt his head back to keep my gaze. "You don't get to think off the record. You don't get to question. You follow orders. You keep your mouth shut. And you don't ever—ever—second-guess where I'm stationed."

Camden studies me through the smoke, his eyes calculating, that humorless grin tugging at the edge of his mouth. Then he chuckles low and shakes his head, flicking the cigarette to the ground and grinding it out beneath his boot.

"Fine," he mutters. "Your funeral."

I don't respond. I pull open the SUV door and climb in, the leather groaning beneath my weight. Out of the corner of my eye, I catch Camden watching me still, his expression unreadable.

The engine rumbles to life under my hands, and for a second, I let myself sit in the growl of it. Camden's words echo in my skull, but I shut them down with the same ruthless efficiency I use on everything else.

He doesn't understand. He doesn't need to. It's safer that no one knows who really runs this town.

Protecting Ry will always be my priority. It might even get me killed.

Something had felt off the moment she left my side at the Playground. I hadn't even gotten three minutes with the team there before I had to follow her outside. So, I followed. Slipped through the back entrance just in time to catch sight of the dancer—Oliver—babbling about being innocent. His hands were up, eyes darting, and for one second I thought maybe he had done something worse. Then the roar of an engine split the air.

Her.

I hit the lot just in time to see her tear out of the staff carpark, hair flying, as she leaned into the bike like she'd been born with it welded to her body. My stomach dropped like a stone.

Because I knew exactly where she was going.

Fifth Street.

By the time I caught up, adrenaline was a live wire under my skin. I knew I'd be too late to stop her. The only question was whether I'd be too late to save her.

The alley stank of smoke and rot when I rounded the corner, and my worst fear crystallized in front of me: her back pressed against brick, a blade at her throat.

For a heartbeat, my lungs refused to work. The world narrowed to her wide eyes and that thin line of blood already streaking down her neck.

And then the moment snapped. The gun was in my hand before I even registered pulling it. One shot. One body down.

I don't remember moving, only the weight of the trigger and the sound of my own blood pounding in my ears.

When she turned those laughing, blood-smeared lips on me, purring about how I'd ruined her fun, I felt rage and relief crash together so hard it nearly broke me. Because all I could see was how close I'd been to watching her die.

For a moment, I couldn't move. Couldn't breathe.

She was still laughing, blood dripping down her throat, blades slick with the lives she'd taken. She looked like sin incarnate standing there, hair wild, eyes bright, body thrumming with adrenaline.

And I was torn wide open.

I wanted to throttle her. Pin her against the wall and shake her until her teeth rattled for being so reckless, for making me feel that sick hollow fear in my chest.

I wanted to drag her over my knee, rip that cocky grin off her face with the flat of my hand until she remembered who the fuck kept her alive.

And worse—so much worse—I wanted to give into the madness clawing at me. I wanted to take her right there, in the blood and bodies, bury myself so deep inside her she forgot every name but mine. To claim her like she was already mine, to make sure every corpse in that alley was a witness to the truth I didn't dare speak.

Instead, I clenched my jaw until it ached. My hands shook around the grip of my gun, not from fear but from everything I was holding back. She was dangerous enough already. Me wanting her like this? That was suicidal.

She tilted her head, wiping the blood from her lip, and smiled at me like she knew. Like she could see every twisted thought crawling through my skull.

And maybe she could.

Chapter 7

Rylan

Night falls like a velvet curtain, and the Devil's Lair throbs beneath our feet. I stand at the edge of our penthouse, watching the city lights flicker like dying fireflies. The darkness calls to me—it always does. That sweet symphony of night and chaos that makes my blood sing.

"Ready?" Rev's voice slides over my skin, and I turn to find both twins watching me. They look predatory and perfect in their matching black pants and shirts open at the collars, showing off the tattoos crawling up their throats. Kai's hair is disheveled while Rev's is slicked back—two sides of the same deadly coin.

I grin, the expression feeling sharp on my face. "Born ready."

My reflection in the glass catches my eye—teal hair framing pale skin, the thin red line across my throat a reminder of how close I came to dancing with the reaper today. But death and I are old friends. We've been flirting for years. The cut I got from the asshole in the alleyway is healing nicely. I touch it, remembering the cold press of steel, the hot spray of blood when Hudson's bullet found its mark.

I feel electric tonight, like my skin is too small to contain whatever's building inside me. Like I could tear this city apart with my bare hands and laugh while doing it.

"You look like trouble," Kai murmurs, appearing at my side. His fingers brush the small of my back, tracing the curve of my spine through the thin material of my dress—black and tight, slashed low in the back, high on the thigh.

"Good," I purr, leaning into his touch. "That's the idea."

The elevator opens with a soft chime, and we step inside. Rev punches the button for the VIP level, and my stomach dips as we descend. The twins bracket me, their heat warming me on both sides, and I can feel the anticipation building in all of us. It's been weeks since we've taken a night for ourselves, too busy with the new club and the brewing trouble in our city.

The doors slide open to reveal the exclusive VIP section of the Lair. Music pounds through the floor, a heavy beat that vibrates in my bones. The space is dimly lit, plush couches arranged for maximum privacy while still allowing a view of the club below. Only a handful of people occupy the area—carefully vetted regulars who know better than to approach our private corner.

Camden stands near the entrance, eyes scanning the room. He nods once as we pass, and I catch the slight tightening around his eyes when they land on me. I blow him a kiss, just to watch him scowl.

The twins guide me to our usual spot—a curved booth in the corner with the best view of both the VIP area and the main floor below. A bottle of top-shelf bourbon already waits on the table, three glasses arranged beside it.

"Where's Hudson tonight?" I ask casually, sliding into the booth. The leather is cool against my bare thighs.

Rev pours the bourbon, the amber liquid catching the low light. "Down at the docks."

Ahh yes, the docks. We've had recent reports of rats of the human variety causing trouble down there. Some of our alcohol shipments have been tampered with, bottles going missing or being replaced with watered-down versions. Nothing too serious yet, but the kind of small-scale theft that grows into something worse if left unchecked. I've never allowed that kind of disrespect in my city.

"Anything I should be concerned about?" I ask, taking another sip of bourbon, letting it burn a path down my throat.

"Nothing Hudson can't handle," Kai replies, his fingers dancing along the rim of his own glass. "He's good at making problems disappear."

I nod, trying to ignore the slight twinge of disappointment. After our encounter earlier, I'd half expected Hudson to be shadowing me tonight. Below us, the club is packed, bodies writhing on the dance floor like a single organism, pulsing to the rhythm of the music.

The beat changes, something darker and heavier filling the space. I feel it in my chest, in the soles of my feet, and suddenly I'm restless. I need to move, to lose myself in the chaos for a while.

I down the rest of my drink in one swallow and stand. "I'm going to dance."

Kai's hand wraps around my wrist before I can step away. "No, you're not." His voice is soft but firm. "Not tonight."

I arch an eyebrow, challenge flaring. "Excuse me?"

Rev sets his glass down, his dark eyes fixed on mine. "We're keeping you close tonight, baby girl. After this morning's stunt, you don't get to wander off."

I open my mouth to argue, but Kai is already on his feet, tugging me against him and directing us to the mostly empty VIP dancefloor. "Dance up here," he murmurs, his lips brushing my ear. "You know I love how you move against me."

The heat of his body against mine sends electricity down my spine. Rev moves behind me, caging me between them, and suddenly dancing downstairs seems like a distant concern.

"Fine," I concede, letting my body relax against Kai's. "But you better make it worth my while."

Kai's laugh is a dark promise against my skin. "Oh, we will."

The music pulses around us as we begin to move. It's been too long since I've let myself go like this—too many responsibilities, too many threats to manage. I forget sometimes how good it feels to just exist in my body, to let the rhythm take over.

Kai's hands slide down to my hips, guiding my movements against him. Behind me, Rev presses closer, his chest a solid wall against my back. We move as one entity, three bodies perfectly in sync, and I feel the tension of the day melting away under their touch.

Kai's eyes are dark with hunger as they lock on mine. He leans in, capturing my lips in a kiss that tastes like bourbon and sin. When he pulls back, his smile is wicked. "I love watching you let go," he murmurs. "You never take enough time for yourself anymore."

It's true. Running an empire from the shadows—no matter how legitimate—leaves little time for simple pleasures. Dancing with my men, feeling their hands on my body, the music pounding through me—it's a luxury I rarely indulge in these days.

Rev's lips find the sensitive spot behind my ear, and I shiver. "Keep moving, baby girl," he growls, his hands spanning my waist. "Show us how that body works."

I laugh, the sound bubbling up from somewhere deep inside me, and let my head fall back against his shoulder. The music shifts again, something slower but no less intense, and I roll my hips in time with the beat. Kai's eyes darken as he watches, his grip tightening on my thighs.

We dance like this for what feels like hours, lost in our own world. The bourbon flows, and the music carries us, and for a little while, I forget about the threats looming over us. I forget about Fifth Street and mysterious enemies and the weight of ruling a city. I'm just a woman dancing with the men she loves, and it feels like freedom.

Until I notice her.

She's blonde and leggy, with a dress that leaves nothing to the imagination. Her eyes are fixed on Rev like he's the last meal she'll ever have, and she's moving closer to our corner with deliberate intent. I feel my hackles rise, the pleasant buzz of alcohol sharpening into something harder.

Rev hasn't noticed her yet, too focused on the way my body moves against his. But Kai has—I can tell by the way his eyes narrow slightly over my shoulder. He doesn't seem concerned, merely amused. After all, this isn't the first time someone's been stupid enough to try.

The woman sidles up to us, her smile practiced and predatory. "Mind if I join?" she purrs, eyes locked on Rev. "Looks like you could use another dancer."

I feel Rev stiffen behind me, his hands tightening on my hips. Before he can speak, I turn in his arms, facing the intruder with a smile that doesn't reach my eyes.

"Actually," I say, my voice soft and deadly, "we're good."

The woman's gaze flicks to me, dismissive at first, then wary as she catches the look in my eyes, but she doesn't back down. Brave. Stupid, but brave.

"I wasn't asking you," she says, chin tilting up defiantly. "I was asking him."

Something dark and vicious unfurls in my chest. I step away from Rev, closing the distance between myself and the blonde. Up close, I can smell her desperation, see the hunger in her eyes. She wants what's mine, and that simply won't do.

"Let me be very clear, sweetheart," I murmur, reaching out to straighten the strap of her dress with deliberate care. "These men belong to me. Touch them, look at them, even breathe too close to them, and I'll carve out your eyes with my nails and feed them to you. Do we understand each other?"

Her eyes widen, pupils dilating with fear. She swallows hard, nodding once.

I smile, patting her cheek with mock affection. "Good girl. Now run along before I change my mind about letting you leave with all your parts attached."

She backs away, nearly tripping over her heels in her haste to escape. I watch her go, satisfaction curling in my gut like a well-fed cat.

When I turn back to the twins, they're both watching me with identical expressions of heat and amusement.

"Possessive much?" Kai teases, pulling me back against him.

I shrug, unrepentant. "Mine."

Rev's laugh is dark as he moves to my side, his hand sliding possessively across my lower back. "Yes, you are," he murmurs, the double meaning clear. "And don't you forget it."

We return to our dance, the rhythm of the music seeping into my bones. I lose track of time, lost in the sensation of their hands on me, their bodies moving with mine. The moment is broken when I catch sight of something unusual on the main floor. A man near the bar is swaying oddly, his movements jerky and uncoordinated—not drunk, something else. My eyes narrow as I scan the crowd more carefully.

There—a woman in the corner, her head lolling back, eyelids fluttering. And another man near the stairs, scratching frantically at his arms like there's something crawling beneath his skin.

"Rev," I say, my voice suddenly sharp. "Look."

He follows my gaze, his body tensing as he spots what I've seen. Kai moves to my other side, his playful demeanor vanishing as he takes in the scene below.

"Drugs," he says, the word clipped. "That's not possible, we shut down every dealer in the city after we took over."

"Apparently not," I reply. I feel anger building, hot and vicious. I made the rules crystal clear when we took over: no dealing in our territory. The punishment for breaking that rule is swift and brutal.

"Camden," Rev calls, his voice commanding enough to carry over the music.

Camden is at our side in seconds, alert and ready. "Boss?"

"We've got users on the floor," Rev says, gesturing toward the increasingly obvious cases below. "Find out who's dealing."

Camden nods, already reaching for his radio, but before he can call it in, a scream cuts through the music. The crowd on the dance floor parts like the Red Sea, revealing a man convulsing on the ground, foam bubbling from his lips. Nearby, a woman collapses, her body jerking violently.

"Fuck," I breathe, already moving toward the stairs. "It's an overdose."

Rev's hand clamps around my arm, yanking me back. "Stay here," he orders, his voice brooking no argument. "Camden, lock this place down. No one leaves. Kai, with me."

The twins are already moving, cutting through the VIP section toward the stairs with Camden in tow. I watch them go, frustration burning in my veins, but I know better than to follow. Not when we don't know what we're dealing with.

Instead, I turn to the railing, gripping it so hard my knuckles turn white as I watch the scene unfold below. Security floods the main floor, but it's already too late. The overdoses are spreading like wildfire—more bodies dropping, some convulsing, others going frighteningly still. Panic erupts as reality dawns on the crowd. People stampede toward exits, trampling those who fall. Screams pierce through the pounding music, which cuts off abruptly, leaving only the cacophony of terror.

I scan the main floor, searching for the twins in the pandemonium. Rev's barking orders to security while Kai's already kneeling beside one of the victims, checking for a pulse. Even from here, I can see the grim set of his jaw. Not good.

My blood runs cold. This isn't just a few people getting high—this is a coordinated attack. In my city. In my fucking club.

Chapter 8

Rylan

I STAND FROZEN AT the railing, my knuckles white as I grip the metal bar. My vision narrows to the chaos below, where bodies continue to drop like dominoes. All I can hear is screams and the heavy thud of security boots as they try to control the panicking crowd.

White-hot rage builds in my chest, choking me. This is my territory. My fucking club. *This is fucking war.*

Below, Rev moves like a force of nature through the crowd, his face carved from stone as he directs security to block the exits. No one's getting out until we know what we're dealing with. Camden weaves between bodies, checking pulses, barking orders into his radio. Kai is helping load a convulsing woman onto a stretcher, his movements controlled despite the madness surrounding him.

In the distance, sirens wail, getting closer by the second. My jaw clenches. This is going to be a PR nightmare. The club is in the twins' names—all our businesses are—but this is my empire. My rules that someone just pissed on.

"Fuck," I hiss, slamming my palm against the railing.

Through the pandemonium, I see Rev catch Kai's eye, something passing between them in that silent twin language they've had since birth. He jerks his head toward the VIP section—toward me. Kai nods once, sharp and decisive, before breaking away from the medical team and heading for the stairs.

The sirens are screaming now, right outside. Red and blue lights flash through the windows, casting eerie shadows across the walls. We don't have much time.

Kai appears at my side, his face grim, eyes burning with the same fury I feel coursing through my veins. Without a word, he grips my elbow and steers me away from the railing.

"We need to go. Now," he growls, already guiding me toward the private elevator at the back of the VIP section.

"But—"

"Rev's handling it," he cuts me off. "We need to regroup."

I let him pull me into the elevator, my mind racing with all the ways I'm going to make whoever did this suffer. The doors slide shut just as uniformed officers pour into the club below.

The moment we reach the penthouse, I explode.

"Who the *FUCK* would dare?" I snarl, pacing across the living room like a caged animal. "In our club? Under our fucking noses? I want them found. I want them skinned alive."

Kai watches me, his eyes tracking my movements with predatory focus. His phone buzzes in his pocket, but he doesn't even glance at it.

"We'll find them," he says, his voice dangerously soft. "And when we do, they'll wish they'd never been born."

"This isn't coincidence," I snap, running a hand through my hair. "First Fifth Street, now this? Someone's testing us, Kai. Making a move against everything we've built."

"I know." His eyes darken as he stalks toward me. "And they'll pay for it. In blood."

"Damn right they will," I hiss. "I want to tear this city apart until we find them. I want to hunt them down and carve them open myself."

"I know." His voice is calm, but I can see the same rage simmering beneath his controlled exterior.

"We need to find whoever did this and make an example of them. I want their heads on pikes outside the club." I'm shaking now, anger and adrenaline coursing through me like electricity.

"I think that might cause more trouble than some overdoses," he mutters as his phone buzzes again. He pulls it out to look at it, his jaw tightening, but he makes no move to answer before his attention is on me again. "We will hunt them down. Every last one of them. I promise you that."

"When?" I demand, my voice cracking with fury. "I need blood, Kai. Tonight."

He tosses his phone onto the counter, ignoring the persistent buzzing. His eyes darken as they travel over me, taking in my flushed cheeks, the heaving of my chest, the murderous glint in my eyes.

"God, it's been too long since we've gone hunting together," he murmurs, closing the distance between us. "You have no idea how fucking hot you are like this. When you get that look—that killer gleam—it drives me insane."

His hand slides up my arm, fingers wrapping around my throat, just tight enough to make my pulse jump.

"The way you move when you've got a blade in your hand," he continues, voice dropping to a husky whisper. "The look on your face when you draw blood... makes me hard just thinking about it."

Before I can respond, his mouth crashes into mine. The kiss is brutal, all teeth and tongue, and I taste blood where his teeth catch my lip. I don't care. I need this—need the violence, the release.

His hands tear at my dress, the sound of ripping fabric loud in the quiet apartment. I should be angry—it was expensive—but instead, I help him, clawing at the material until it falls away in tatters.

Kai lifts me in one fluid motion, carrying me to the dining table. He sweeps his arm across it, sending papers flying to the floor before setting me down on the cool surface.

"I need to fuck you," he growls against my mouth. "Need to feel you come apart."

I reach for his belt, desperate to feel him against me, inside me. He bats my hands away, making quick work of his own clothes until he stands before me, naked and hard.

"Spread your legs," he commands, and I obey without hesitation, my thighs falling open for him. He hooks his fingers into the waistband of my lace underwear, yanking until the delicate fabric tears with a satisfying snap. I growl at him, the sound primal and warning, though we both know I won't stop him.

He drags a finger through my slick heat, his eyes never leaving mine. "Already wet for me. Always so ready."

I arch against his touch, needing more. "Fuck me, don't tease me, Kai."

With one powerful thrust, he buries himself inside me, and I cry out, the sensation overwhelming. He doesn't give me time to adjust, setting a punishing pace that has the table creaking beneath us.

"This is what you need," he pants, one hand braced beside my head, the other gripping my hip hard enough to bruise. "To be fucked until you can't think about anything else."

"Fuck, yesssss," I moan.

He's right. With each thrust, the rage inside me transforms into something else—something just as primal but infinitely more pleasurable. My nails rake down his back, leaving red trails in their wake, and he hisses in approval.

"That's it, gorgeous. Mark me. Claim me."

I'm close already, the adrenaline and anger pushing me toward the edge faster than usual. Kai senses it, his movements becoming more deliberate, hitting exactly where I need him.

"I can feel your pussy clenching around me," he growls, his voice rough with exertion. "So tight—"

The elevator dings.

My eyes snap open, my body freezing like a startled animal as Hudson steps into our apartment. His expression shifts from urgent to shocked to carefully blank in the space of a heartbeat.

"Fuck," Hudson curses, turning his back to us. "I sent you a message saying I was coming up."

Kai doesn't even slow his pace, his grip on my hips tightening as he continues to drive into me. "I know," he pants, not bothering to look over his shoulder.

The interruption has sent my impending orgasm retreating, leaving me suspended in a state of frustrated arousal. I bite back a whimper of disappointment. My face burns, but my body betrays me, still responding to his relentless rhythm despite—or perhaps because of—our audience.

"We need to go to the Playground," Hudson says, his voice tight with barely controlled irritation. "Now. Your pretty boy dancer sent a message. There's trouble."

Kai laughs, low and dark. "Well, you see, we have a problem." His hips snap forward, making me gasp. "We're not going anywhere until she comes, and she's nowhere near doing that now." He glances over his shoulder, his smile all teeth. "So you better fucking help if you want us to go anywhere."

Hudson's shoulders go rigid.

"Tick tock, Hudson," Kai taunts, his rhythm never faltering.

He growls, a sound so feral it sends a shiver down my spine and has me clenching around Kai again. "You're a fucking asshole, Kai."

I SHOULD WALK OUT. That would be the smart move. The professional move.

Instead, I'm frozen, my back to them but unable to erase the image already burned into my eyes—Rylan spread out on the dining table, her body flushed and trembling as Kai drives into her. That fucking teal hair I chose for her spilled across the wooden surface like some exotic ocean. Her perfect mouth open in a silent gasp.

Two fucking years I've kept my distance. Two years of iron control while I watched the twins possess her in every way imaginable. And now Kai has the audacity to invite me in like it's nothing.

"Last chance, Hudson," Kai calls out, his voice strained with exertion. "Either help or wait outside like a good boy."

My resolve shatters like glass. I turn slowly, my eyes immediately finding hers. She's watching me, those blue eyes wide with shock and something darker, hungrier. Her chest heaves with each of Kai's thrusts, her skin glistening with sweat.

"What's it gonna be?" Kai asks, slowing his pace deliberately, drawing a frustrated whimper from Rylan.

I don't answer him. Instead, I stalk forward, my boots heavy against the floor as I approach the table. Kai's lips curl into a triumphant smirk that I want to punch off his face, but I ignore him. My focus is entirely on her.

I reach the edge of the table and lean over her, my face hovering inches from hers. "Is this what you want?" I ask, my voice rough with need. "Tell me, Rylan."

Her lips part, but no sound comes out. Kai thrusts hard, making her gasp.

"Use your words," I command, letting her see the hunger I've been hiding for years.

"Yes," she whispers, the single word loaded with desire.

That's all I need. I wrap the fingers of one hand around her throat, applying just enough pressure to make her pulse jump beneath my palm. My other hand moves lower, seeking the place where she and Kai are joined. I find her clit, swollen and slick, and begin to circle it.

Her reaction is immediate and intoxicating—back arching, eyes widening, a choked moan escaping her lips. Kai resumes his rhythm, matching his movements to the pace of my fingers.

"Look at you," I murmur, watching her face contort with pleasure. "So fucking beautiful like this. I've imagined this for years—touching you, watching you come apart under my hands, around my cock."

I increase the pressure on her throat slightly, feeling her pulse quicken. Then I release it, allowing her a full breath before tightening again. The alternating pressure sends her higher, her eyes rolling back.

I tighten my grip on her throat, feeling her pulse jump wildly beneath my palm. Then I release, letting her drag in a desperate breath before squeezing again. The rhythm of it matches the movement of my fingers on her clit, and I can feel her body responding, tensing with each cycle. Her eyes are locked with mine, pupils blown wide with desire. Those fucking blue eyes, burning into me like they can see every filthy thought I've ever had about her.

Kai continues his relentless pace, his chuckle is like gravel, knowing and smug. I ignore him. He doesn't matter right now. Nothing matters but her—the way she writhes beneath my touch, the flush spreading across her skin, the soft, choked sounds she makes when I allow her to breathe.

"I've thought about making you come so hard you forget your own name," I confess, my voice rough with need. "Thought about watching your face when you fall apart. Dreamed about how you would taste on my tongue."

Her hips buck, seeking more pressure, more friction. I give it to her, increasing the speed of my circles, pressing harder.

"You're going to come for me," I demand, leaning closer until our lips are almost touching. "I want to see it, every second of it. Want to watch those pretty eyes roll back. Want to feel you shatter."

She whimpers, her body trembling on the edge. I loosen my grip on her throat, letting her gasp for air.

"Please," she begs, the word barely audible.

"Please what?" I press, needing to hear her say it. "Tell me what you need."

"Make me come," she gasps. "Please, Hudson."

My name on her lips is almost enough to undo me. I redouble my efforts, fingers working her clit while my other hand alternates pressure on her throat. Kai keeps up with my rhythm, driving into her with deep, powerful thrusts that have the sound of skin slapping against skin echoing through the apartment.

"That's it," I murmur, watching her face contort with pleasure. "Let go for me. I want to see everything—every expression, every tremor. Give it to me, sweetheart."

I pinch her clit and she breaks beautifully. Her back arches off the table, her mouth open in a silent scream as her body convulses. I don't miss a second of it—the way her eyes widen then flutter closed, the deep flush that spreads across her chest, the pulse of her throat beneath my fingers. I memorize every detail, burning it into my mind in case this is the only time I ever get to witness her coming undone.

Kai follows her over the edge with a guttural groan, his rhythm faltering as he empties himself inside her. For a moment, the three of us remain frozen, the only sound our ragged breathing.

Then reality crashes back in. I step away from the table, my hands falling to my sides. The loss of contact is physical pain, but I force myself to move back, to give her space.

Kai recovers first, pulling out of her with a satisfied sigh. He glances at me, that knowing smirk playing on his lips before he heads to the bathroom. I hear water running as he presumably gets a cloth to clean her up.

Rylan lies still for a moment longer, her chest heaving as she catches her breath. Then she sits up slowly, wincing slightly as she slides off the table without waiting for Kai. Her legs are unsteady beneath her, and I resist the urge to reach out and steady her.

She glances at me, a flush still coloring her cheeks. "Well," she says, her voice husky from my grip on her throat, "who knew the old man was so good with his fingers? Good thing too, since at your age, I'm guessing that's all that still works reliably."

The taunt snaps me out of my daze. I move faster than she expects, stepping into her path as she tries to walk toward the bedroom. Her eyes widen in surprise, but there's no fear—only challenge and a lingering heat.

I grab her wrist and press her palm firmly against the hard length straining against my pants. Her breath catches audibly, and the flush that had been fading returns with a vengeance, spreading across her smooth skin.

"Does this feel unreliable to you?" I growl, leaning in until my lips brush her ear. "Next time you want to test what works, I'll bend you over and show you exactly how well everything functions. And you won't be walking straight for days after."

Her pupils dilate, and for a moment, I think she might call my bluff. Part of me hopes she will. But Kai chooses that moment to return, cloth in hand.

"As much as I'd love to see where this goes," he drawls, "we've got trouble at the Playground."

I release her reluctantly, stepping back. "Get dressed," I order, my voice still rough with desire. "We need to move. Now."

She holds my gaze for a beat longer, something unreadable flickering in those blue depths, before nodding, snatching the cloth from Kai and heading for the bedroom. I watch her go, wondering what the hell I've just gotten myself into and knowing there's no going back now.

Kai's chuckle draws my attention. "Well," he says, looking far too pleased with himself while he pulls his clothes back on, "that was interesting."

I glare at him. "Fuck you."

Chapter 9

Kai

I CAN'T HELP BUT grin wider at Hudson's discomfort. "You're not my type. Besides, we've got work to do." I watch him adjust himself, the big man suddenly awkward as a teenager. It's fucking delicious. I've always known Ry would unravel him—she has that effect on everyone. Even me, after all this time.

The bedroom door opens and Ry emerges, transformed back into the deadly creature I know so well. Black jeans hugging those curves, hair pulled to the base of her head, severe and tight. I catch the way Hudson's breath hitches, the way Ry deliberately avoids his gaze.

"Let's go," she commands, voice steady but I hear what others don't. "Tell me what Oliver said."

I follow them to the elevator, watching the space between them—electric, dangerous. In the confined space, I observe how they both press against opposite walls, how Hudson stares straight ahead while Ry's fingers tap restlessly against her thigh. I've seen her kill men without blinking, but now her hands tremble.

I smile to myself.

"Oliver didn't say much," Hudson finally breaks the silence as the elevator descends. "Just that there was trouble at the Playground and we needed to get there immediately."

"That's not very fucking helpful," Ry mutters, still not looking at him.

I lean against the elevator wall, enjoying the tension radiating between them. "Maybe our pretty dancer just misses us already."

The look Ry shoots me could cut glass, but I just wink back at her. The elevator reaches the basement, and the doors slide open to reveal the private garage. My bike sits next to Rev's, both gleaming under the fluorescent lights. The SUV Hudson usually drives is parked in its designated spot.

I stride over to my motorcycle, swinging my leg over and starting the engine with a satisfying rumble. I flash a wicked grin at Hudson and Ry, already imagining them trapped together in the SUV after what just happened upstairs.

"See you there," I call over the engine's roar.

But before Hudson can shepherd Ry toward the SUV, she's moving—quick and determined—straight for me. She slides onto the bike behind me, her arms wrapping around my waist, her body pressing against my back.

I scoff, though I can't deny the pleasure of having her pressed against me. "I thought you two should have some quality time."

"Drive," she says, her voice brooking no argument.

Hudson curses, loud enough that I hear it over the engine. Then, to my surprise, instead of heading to the SUV, he grabs a spare helmet from the rack along with Ry's and stalks over to us.

"What do you think you're doing?" I demand as he shoves Ry's helmet onto her head, buckling it under her chin with quick, efficient movements.

"Making sure she doesn't crack her skull open," he growls, then swings his leg over Rev's bike.

I can't help but laugh. "Oh, Rev is going to fucking murder you when he finds out you touched his baby."

Hudson ignores me, starting the engine with practiced ease. The bike roars to life, and I can see the satisfaction on his face. Rev keeps that thing in pristine condition—it probably runs better than my own.

I'm still laughing as I kick up the stand and guide my bike toward the exit.

We tear out of the garage, the cool night air hitting us like a slap. Outside the Devil's Lair, chaos reigns—ambulances with flashing lights, police cars forming a perimeter, confused patrons milling about while being questioned by officers. We weave through the emergency vehicles, Ry's arms tightening around my waist as I take a corner too sharply.

Hudson follows close behind, handling Rev's bike with surprising skill. The streets blur as we speed toward the Playground, the city a kaleidoscope of neon and shadow. Ry's heartbeat pounds against my back, her grip never loosening. I can feel her tension, the barely contained rage vibrating through her. Whoever's behind this mess is going to wish they'd never been born. I've seen what Ry can do when she's truly angry, and it's both terrifying and fucking beautiful.

We reach the Playground in record time, pulling into the staff parking lot at the back of the club. The place is quiet, not yet open to the public. The grand opening is three nights away, but right now the place is meant to be empty, the staff only preparing during the day.

I kill the engine, and Ry immediately slides off, pulling her helmet free and brushing a hand over her teal hair. Hudson parks beside us, his movements stiff as he dismounts Rev's bike.

We approach the back entrance together, a united front despite the complicated dynamics between us. Hudson steps forward, knocking solidly on the metal door. There's a pause, then the sound of a bolt sliding. The door opens just a fraction at first, then widens to reveal Oliver.

The dancer looks almost fearful, his eyes darting between the three of us like he can't decide who to be more afraid of. I'm not sure if it's whatever he saw that has him spooked, or if it's just us. Maybe both.

"Thank god you're here," he says, voice low and urgent as he ushers us inside. "They're gone now, but they'll be back. I heard them talking about opening night."

"Who? Start from the beginning," Ry commands, all business despite the fact that less than thirty minutes ago she was coming apart on my dining table with Hudson's hand around her throat. "Tell me exactly what you saw and heard."

His words start tumbling out so fast I can barely keep up.

"So I was practicing earlier but then that big guy—" he shoots a nervous glance at Hudson, "—one of your men grabbed me and hauled me out like I was trespassing even though I work here and I tried to explain but he wouldn't listen and I left my bag with all my stuff in it and I really needed it so I came back after everyone was gone because I wanted to get some extra practice in for opening night because I want to be perfect for you—for the club, I mean—and make sure I do my absolute best and I was just about to put on the harness to practice the aerial routine from the ceiling platform when I heard voices and I didn't want to get in trouble for being here so late especially after what happened earlier so I hid behind the—"

We've been following him through the darkened club, the only illumination coming from the emergency lights that cast long shadows across the space. As we start up the stairs to the mezzanine level, I reach out and grab him by the collar, yanking him to a halt.

"Hey, Puppy, take a breath and slow it down," I order, keeping my grip firm on his shirt.

Oliver rolls his eyes but when he starts speaking again, his pace is noticeably slower.

"I hid behind one of the curtains near the VIP section," he continues, leading us toward the area. "Even though I was hidden, I could still see them. Three men I've never seen before. Not workers, definitely not supposed to be here."

"And?" I prompt when he pauses.

"They were working on something near the ceiling. Looked like they were messing with something in one of the panels."

Hudson growls low in his throat, and I don't need to be a mind reader to know why. Security is his department and if they touched one of the panels then they messed with his systems. Someone touching his systems is like someone touching his woman.

I suppress a grin at that thought.

"Can you describe them?" Hudson demands, voice tight.

Oliver nods eagerly, leading us toward the back of the club. "One was tall, maybe six foot, buzzed hair, scar across his right eyebrow. Another was shorter, stocky build, with a full beard. The third guy was thin, nervous-looking. He kept watching the doors while the others worked."

I frown for a moment but we reach a section of wall near the stairs leading to the aerial platform. Hudson immediately drops to his knees, examining the paneling with practiced hands. His fingers trace the outline of a small access panel, and when he pries it open, his entire body goes rigid.

"Motherfuckers," he growls, examining the wiring inside. "They've tampered with the fire suppression system."

Ry curses, checking her watch. "The fire marshal inspection is in six hours. If they find this..."

She doesn't need to finish. We all know what happens if the Playground fails inspection. The grand opening gets delayed, our reputation takes a hit, and whoever's behind this wins the first round.

"Oliver," Ry says, "did you check the security cameras?"

He shakes his head, copper-blonde hair falling across his face. "I don't know where they are or how to access them."

"Follow me," Hudson commands, already stalking toward the administrative offices down on the main floor at the back of the club.

The security room is small but state-of-the-art, with monitors covering one wall and a control panel that looks like it belongs in a military installation. Hudson slides into the chair, his fingers flying across the keyboard as he pulls up footage from earlier in the night.

"Fuck," he mutters, clicking through empty frames. "The system's been wiped clean. All footage from after Stella left is gone."

"Can you recover it?" I ask, already knowing the answer from his expression.

"No. This wasn't amateur hour. They knew exactly what they were doing." He pulls out his phone. "I need to check every system in the building. This could be just the beginning."

As Hudson starts making calls, I watch Ry. Her face has shifted into what I privately call her boss mode—eyes sharp, jaw set, fingers already tapping messages into her phone. She's beautiful like this, all cold calculation and deadly intent. It reminds me of the Dead Devil's Night years ago when we saw her alive after thinking she was dead—that perfect blend of fire and ice.

But then she does something that catches me off guard. She pauses, slides her phone into her pocket, and approaches Oliver, who's hovering uncertainly by the door.

"You did well," she says, her voice softening in a way I rarely hear directed at anyone but me and Rev. "Coming back here alone was risky, but you were very brave to call us right away."

Oliver practically melts under her praise, his eyes widening with naked adoration. "I just wanted to help," he says, voice small.

"And you did. You're such a good boy, Oliver." She reaches up, brushing his hair back from his face in a gesture so intimate it makes my teeth clench.

The look he gives her is exactly why I called him Puppy. His eyes are wide and worshipful, hungry for more praise, more attention. He'd probably roll over and show his belly if she asked. I hate it. I hate the way he looks at her like she's his salvation and his destruction all wrapped in one perfect package.

But I can never deny Ry anything, not even this. If she wants to keep this pretty little dancer as a pet, so be it.

I turn away, focusing on Hudson instead. "How bad is it?"

"Bad enough," he replies, still on the phone. "I'm bringing in a team to check everything. If they messed with the fire suppression system, they could have tampered with other safety measures too."

Ry rejoins us, her hand lingering on Oliver's arm for a moment before she lets go. "We have six hours to fix this before the inspector arrives. Whatever it takes, the Playground opens on schedule."

Her voice brooks no argument, and I find myself nodding along with Hudson. When Ry gets like this—all iron will and cold determination—it's impossible not to follow her lead.

"I'll call Rev," I say, pulling out my phone. "He needs to know what's happening."

As I dial, I glance back at Oliver, who's watching Ry with those puppy-dog eyes. Yeah, he's going to be a problem. But maybe he'll be a useful one.

If anything, at least I know he likes pain so I can get some knife practice if he ever even thinks of hurting her.

For now, we have more pressing concerns. Like finding the fuckers who dared to sabotage our club and making them regret the day they were born.

Chapter 10

Rylan

The fire marshal is a short man with a permanent scowl etched into his weathered face. He adjusts his glasses, squinting at the clipboard in his hands as he makes another check mark. His khaki uniform is pressed to perfection, the badge on his chest catching the light as he turns to examine another section of the sprinkler system.

"Everything appears to be in order so far," he mutters, more to himself than to us.

I follow a few steps behind, my heart hammering against my ribs despite my casual expression. If he only knew how close we came to disaster.

Six hours of frantic work. Six hours of Hudson's team tearing apart the club, finding and repairing every bit of sabotage those bastards left behind. They'd done a thorough job—disabling sprinklers, tampering with emergency lighting, even rigging some of the electrical systems to fail under stress. It would have been impressive if it wasn't aimed at destroying us.

"The spacing on these sprinkler heads is good," the marshal mutters, making another mark. "And these emergency exit signs?" He gestures toward the glowing red signs above each door.

"All connected to the backup generator," Hudson replies smoothly. "In the event of power failure, they'll remain illuminated for a minimum of ninety minutes."

The marshal nods, making another notation. "Good, good. And the capacity limits for each area?"

I step forward, handing him the laminated charts we had prepared. "All clearly posted at the entrance to each section. We've also trained our staff to monitor the numbers and redirect patrons if necessary."

He examines the charts, his expression unreadable. I feel sweat gathering at the small of my back, but I keep my smile firmly in place. We can't fail this inspection. The grand opening is in two nights, and I'll be damned if I let some saboteurs derail everything we've worked for.

Around us, workers are already starting to file in, carrying tools and materials for the final touches. They keep their distance from the inspection, but I can feel their curious glances. News travels fast in this city, and I'm sure they've all heard about the overdoses at the Devil's Lair by now. The timing couldn't be worse.

The fire marshal continues his methodical inspection, checking every extinguisher, every emergency exit, every last inch of the sprinkler system. Each moment that passes feels like an eternity, but finally, he closes his clipboard with a decisive snap.

"Well, Ms. Coal, it seems everything is up to code," he announces. "You're cleared to open as scheduled."

I release the breath I didn't realize I was holding. "Thank you. We appreciate your thoroughness."

He narrows his eyes slightly. "Just make sure it stays that way. I'll be back for a follow-up inspection."

With that, he turns and heads toward the exit, his boots clicking against the polished floor. I wait until the door closes behind him before allowing my shoulders to slump in relief.

"That was too close," I mutter, running a hand through my hair.

Hudson nods, the tension in his jaw finally relaxing a fraction. "We got lucky. If Oliver hadn't found those men when he did..."

"We made our own luck," I counter. "Your team worked miracles."

He accepts the compliment with a slight nod, but I can see the pride in his eyes. His security team is hand-picked, trained personally by him, and their loyalty is absolute. They worked through the early morning without complaint, understanding exactly what was at stake.

I straighten, really looking around for the first time in hours. I had been so focused on the pending disaster that I hadn't noticed where Oliver was in all the chaos. "Where is our puppy, anyway?"

"Sent him home a few hours ago," Hudson replies. "Kid was dead on his feet after staying up all night. Thought it was best to get him out of the way before the inspector arrived."

"Good call," I agree. Rev had needed Kai back at the Lair to help with damage control for the overdoses and since I was surrounded by Hudson's team it was more logical that Kai return to the Lair. The mess there needed to be handled carefully. The last thing we need is the police digging too deeply into our operations.

The club manager, Stella, approaches us, her eyes wide with surprise. She arrived only minutes before the fire marshal, clearly shocked to find us already here.

"I still can't believe you beat me here," she says, glancing between us. "Is everything okay?"

Hudson steps forward, smoothly intercepting her concerns. "Just some last-minute adjustments to the security systems," he explains, his voice calm and reassuring. "Nothing to worry about."

She doesn't look entirely convinced, but she nods anyway. "Well, I'm glad we passed inspection. The staff is prepped and ready for opening night."

"Good," I say, forcing a smile. "Make sure everyone gets plenty of rest. We want them at their best."

Stella nods again, turning to address one of the workers who's calling for her attention. As she walks away, I feel the weight of exhaustion pressing down on me. I haven't slept in over forty-eight hours, and the events in that time have left me drained.

Hudson studies my face, those green eyes missing nothing. "You should get some rest," he says quietly.

"Not yet," I reply, watching as workers begin installing the final decorative elements around the club. "We still have too much to do."

We stand in silence for a moment, both of us surveying the space. The Playground is truly magnificent—a fantasy brought to life with silk drapes cascading from the ceiling, intimate alcoves nestled along the walls, and the performance stages positioned for maximum impact. It's everything I envisioned and more.

And someone tried to burn it all down before it even opened.

"The repairs aren't our real problem," Hudson says finally, his voice low enough that only I can hear. "We need to find whoever is behind this."

I nod, feeling the anger that's been simmering since last night rise to the surface again. "The attack on the Lair was a distraction," I say, the realization crystallizing as I speak it aloud. "They wanted us focused there while they sabotaged the Playground."

"And they probably think they succeeded," Hudson adds. "I doubt they knew the Fire Marshal was due for the final inspection today. Which means they'll have something planned for opening night."

I turn to face him fully, my voice hardening. "I want names, Hudson. I don't care what it takes. Someone in this cesspit of a city knows something, and I want to speak to whoever does."

His expression darkens, something dangerous flickering in his eyes. "I'll put out feelers. My contacts on the street and even some of my old military connections. If there's chatter, we'll hear it."

"Good." I feel my lips curl into something that's more snarl than smile. "*Nobody* fucks with what's ours."

For a brief moment, the professional mask slips, and I catch a glimpse of the same fierce possessiveness in his eyes that I feel burning in my chest. It reminds me of last night—his hand around my throat, his breath hot against my skin as he demanded I come for him. The phantom sensation of his fingers sends a shiver down my spine that I try desperately to hide.

But as quickly as it appears, the moment passes, and we're back to business. Hudson has been nothing but professional since what happened at the apartment, as if he's determined to pretend it never occurred. Part of me is relieved; the other part is... disappointed? Frustrated? I'm not sure, and I don't have time to examine the feeling too closely.

I glance around the club, noticing for the first time that the bar shelves are still half-empty. "What happened down at the docks?" I ask, remembering that Hudson was supposed to investigate the tampering with our alcohol shipments before everything went to hell.

His jaw tightens, a muscle ticking beneath the skin. "The latest shipments weren't just tampered with," he says grimly. "They were stolen. The containers were completely empty when they arrived."

I curse under my breath. Sourcing quality alcohol in this dead city is nearly impossible—the local stuff is more likely to kill you than get you drunk. It's one of the reasons our clubs are so popular; we import everything from outside the city, using connections that took years to establish.

"That's not a coincidence," I say, my mind racing. "First the overdoses, then the sabotage, now this. It's all connected."

Hudson nods, his expression grim. "Someone's trying to hit us from all angles. Weaken us before delivering the knockout punch."

I straighten my spine, ignoring the way my body screams for sleep, a cold determination settling over me. "Take me there," I demand. "To the docks. I want to see it for myself."

He hesitates, clearly weighing the risks. "Ry, it might not be safe—"

"I don't care," I cut him off, my voice dropping to a growl. The exhaustion burns behind my eyes, but anger burns hotter. "This is my city, my business they're fucking with. I need to see it."

For a moment, I think he might argue, but then he gives a short nod. "Alright. But we do this my way."

I brush past him, letting my shoulder graze his chest. "Whatever you say, old man," I murmur, letting a hint of a smile play at my lips. "I know how you security types get all worked up about protocols."

His eyes flash with something that isn't entirely professional as I walk toward the exit. Despite everything that's happened, despite the threats closing in from all sides, there's a part of me that feels alive with anticipation. Whoever is behind this has made a critical mistake.

They've underestimated just how far I'll go to protect what's mine.

The docks are a different world from the glittering clubs in the entertainment district—gray, grimy, and reeking of fish and diesel. Shipping containers are stacked like massive building blocks, creating a maze of metal corridors that could hide any number of threats. I've studied the shipping manifests for years, looked at blueprints, approved the security protocols, signed off on every detail of our operation here, yet being here in person among the stacked containers feels different.

Hudson slows Rev's bike to a halt at the main gates. He flips his visor up, revealing his face to the guard who steps forward with a nod of recognition. The guard's eyes shift to me, his hand making an upward motion. I hesitate before reluctantly lifting my own visor, the cool air hitting my exposed skin. A fleeting thought crosses my mind: this constant verification, this suspicion—it would all be unnecessary if I hadn't spent two years ruling from the shadows, my face a mystery even to those who serve me.

The motorcycle engine growls beneath us as Hudson guides us through the labyrinthine paths between towering metal containers. His voice crackles through the intercom in our helmets.

"Our shipments come in through the northeast section. Private dock, minimal traffic, maximum security—or so we thought."

I watch the scenery blur past, noting the increasing isolation as we move deeper into the dock complex. "How many people know about the route?" My voice sounds tinny in the confined space of my helmet.

"That's the problem." Through the intercom, I can hear the edge in his voice even over the wind. "The list should be very short. Me, the twins, our top security personnel, and the shipping company we contract with."

"So either someone talked, or we have a leak," I conclude, feeling heat rise in my chest. Two years of careful anonymity, of ruling through proxies and paperwork, and now this enemy threatens everything.

Hudson slows the bike near a nondescript warehouse with a single loading bay, the tires crunching on loose gravel as we come to a stop. "This is it."

We dismount, pulling off our helmets. I immediately notice the additional security—four of Hudson's men positioned strategically around the perimeter, all armed and alert. They nod respectfully as we approach, but their eyes continue to scan the surroundings.

Inside, the warehouse is cavernous and mostly empty. A few shipping containers sit in various stages of unloading, but it's the one at the far end that catches my attention. Its doors stand open, revealing nothing but empty space where crates of premium liquor should be.

I follow Hudson to the empty container, my boots echoing against the metal floor. The hollow sound matches the emptiness in my chest—rage filling the void where our merchandise should be.

"Look at this," Hudson says, crouching down near the container's edge. His fingers trace something I can barely see—small scratch marks around the lock. "These aren't from crowbars or bolt cutters. This was done with precision tools."

I kneel beside him, squinting at the barely visible markings. "They could have just broken it."

"But they didn't," he says, his voice low. "They wanted to get in and out without anyone noticing until it was too late." He stands, moving to the container's interior. "No fingerprints, no boot prints, nothing left behind. They even knew about our security cameras."

He points to a corner where a small camera should be recording everything. "They didn't destroy it—they looped the feed. Made it look like nothing was happening while they emptied the container. That's not amateur work."

"Professionals," I mutter, the word tasting bitter on my tongue.

"Military grade," Hudson confirms. "Or ex-military at least." His eyes meet mine, and I see the same cold fury I feel burning in my chest. "This wasn't a random theft. This was targeted. Planned. They knew exactly what they were looking for and how to get it without leaving a trace."

My hands curl into fists so tight my nails bite into my palms. "They have to be storing it somewhere," I snap, my voice rising with each word. "A shipment that size doesn't just vanish. Someone's housing it, distributing it, something."

Hudson watches me carefully, his face impassive.

"*Someone* in this fucking city knows who's behind this," I continue, pacing the empty container. "I don't care what it takes. I want names. I want locations. I want whoever did this strung up as a fucking example."

"We'll find them," Hudson says evenly.

"When?" I whirl on him, fury bubbling over. "After they burn down another building? After they poison more of our customers? After they completely destroy everything?"

I'm shouting now, my voice bouncing off the metal walls of the container. The exhaustion of the past forty-eight hours fuels my rage, making it burn hotter, brighter.

Hudson moves faster than I expect. One moment he's standing a few feet away, the next he's right in front of me, backing me against the container wall. His hands plant on either side of my head, caging me in.

"Enough," he growls, his face inches from mine. "This isn't helping."

"Don't tell me what helps," I snarl back, refusing to be intimidated even as my body reacts to his proximity. "This is *my* city. *My* business they're fucking with."

"And you won't be able to protect any of it if you burn yourself out," he counters, his voice dropping lower, vibrating with authority.

I try to duck under his arm, but he shifts, blocking my escape. "Move," I demand.

"No." The single word is absolute. "Not until you take a breath and think clearly."

Our eyes lock in silent battle. I refuse to back down, even as I feel the weight of his presence pressing against me. His body radiates heat, his scent—cedar and that underlying scent that's just *him*—filling my senses. My heart hammers against my ribs, but whether from anger or something else, I can't tell anymore.

"We will find them," Hudson says again, each word deliberate and weighted. "And when we do, you'll have your revenge. But right now, you need to focus."

His eyes are impossibly green in the dim light of the container, intense and unwavering. I watch as his gaze drops briefly to my lips before snapping back up to meet mine. The air between us thickens, charged with something beyond anger. Something that makes my body hum.

My phone chimes suddenly, the sound shattering the moment. Hudson doesn't move immediately, his breath still mingling with mine, his eyes still holding me captive. Then, slowly, he steps back, allowing me space to reach for my phone.

I pull it from my pocket, glancing down at the screen. The message is from Rev, and as I read it, I feel a slow, dangerous grin spread across my face.

'We found someone with information. Get back here now.'

Chapter 11

Rylan

I HOLD MY PHONE up, my grin turning feral. "Rev's got someone who knows something."

Hudson's eyes darken as he reads the message. "Let's go."

I practically bounce on my toes as we head back to the bike, adrenaline pushing back the exhaustion that's been clawing at me. My limbs feel weightless, almost disconnected, like I'm floating rather than walking. The world around me seems to blur at the edges, colors too bright, sounds too sharp. I know this feeling—this manic energy that comes when I've pushed my body far past its limits—but I embrace it.

Sleep is for the weak. I can rest when whoever's responsible is bleeding out at my feet.

After putting on our helmets Hudson swings his leg over Rev's motorcycle, the leather seat creaking beneath his weight. I slide on behind him, my body fitting against his like we've done this a thousand times. His back is a wall of muscle against my chest, solid and unyielding. I wrap my arms around his waist, feeling the heat of him even through his jacket.

"Hold tight," he warns, revving the engine.

We tear out of the docks, the wind whipping at my clothes as Hudson navigates through the labyrinthine pathways. Once we hit the main road, he opens up the throttle, and the bike surges forward with a roar that vibrates through my entire body.

The city becomes a blur of light and shadow as we weave through traffic. My heart pounds in rhythm with the engine, and I find myself pressing closer to Hudson's back, seeking his warmth. His body is like a furnace, radiating heat that seeps into my bones, chasing away the chill of fatigue.

Hudson takes a corner sharply, and I instinctively tighten my thighs around the bike, around him. The friction sends a jolt of heat straight to my core, and I bite my lip to suppress a gasp. The combination of his body against mine, the powerful machine between my legs, and the danger coursing through my veins is intoxicating.

Another sharp turn, another squeeze of my thighs, and I feel my body responding in ways that are entirely inappropriate for the situation. Each vibration of the engine thrums through me, settling low in my belly, between my legs. I shift slightly, trying to alleviate the pressure, but it only makes things worse.

Hudson's muscles flex beneath my hands as he maneuvers the bike through a particularly tight gap between cars. The display of control, of power, sends another wave of heat through me. I can't help but remember those same hands on my throat, on my skin, demanding and precise.

Not the time, Ry. Not the *fucking* time.

But my exhausted brain isn't listening to reason. My body has its own agenda, responding to the proximity, the danger, the thrill of the hunt ahead. I press my cheek against his back, inhaling his scent.

Hudson accelerates suddenly, the bike surging forward with unexpected force. The burst of speed hits me like a drug, and a wild laugh escapes me, high and unrestrained. I throw my head back, cackling into the wind as buildings fly past us.

The helmet's comm crackles to life. "You're insane," Hudson's voice comes through, intimate in my ear despite the roar of the engine. There's a smile in his voice that sends heat down my spine.

"Faster!" I demand through my own mic, squeezing his waist until my fingers dig into the leather of his jacket.

He obliges, pushing the bike to its limits as we race through the streets toward the Devil's Lair. The world becomes nothing but streaks of color and sound, my laughter mingling with the scream of the engine.

By the time we pull into the parking garage beneath the club, my body is humming. Hudson kills the engine, and the sudden silence rings in my ears. For a moment, neither of us moves. I'm still pressed against him, my arms around his waist, my breath coming in short gasps.

Slowly, reluctantly, I slide off the bike. My legs feel unsteady beneath me—from the ride or from something else, I'm not sure. Hudson dismounts with fluid grace, pulling off his helmet and running a hand through his hair.

"You good?" he asks, eyes tracking my face.

I nod, not trusting my voice. The exhaustion I've been fighting hits me again, a wave of dizziness that I push back through sheer force of will. I refuse to be weak. Not now. Not when we're so close to answers.

Hudson leads me through the dimly lit garage, toward a nondescript door at the far end. Anyone else would walk right past it, assuming it's a maintenance closet or electrical room. But we know better.

He punches a code into the keypad beside the door, and it slides open silently. The hallway beyond is grey, polished concrete. My boots echo against the floor as we make our way deeper into what we jokingly refer to as our "special conference room."

Who doesn't have a secret torture room in their building, right?

At the end of the hall is another door, heavier than the first. Hudson presses his palm against a scanner, and after a brief pause, the door unlocks with a metallic click.

The room beyond is spacious and meticulously clean. The walls are soundproofed, the floor sealed concrete for easy cleanup. Various implements hang from hooks along one wall—tools designed for one purpose only: to extract information from unwilling subjects.

Rev and Kai are already there, standing close together, speaking in hushed tones. They look up as we enter, their identical faces breaking into predatory smiles that mirror my own.

"About time," Rev drawls, pushing away from the wall he was leaning against. "We were starting to think you got lost."

"Or distracted," Kai adds, his eyes flickering between Hudson and me with knowing amusement.

I ignore the implication, my attention already fixed on the room's other occupant. A man sits bound to a metal chair in the center of the room, his head hanging forward limply. Blood matts his hair, trickles from his nose, stains the collar of his shirt. But he's conscious—I can see the rapid rise and fall of his chest, the tension in his shoulders.

"Who is he?" I ask, approaching slowly, circling him like a shark scenting blood.

"Name's Marcus, or at least that's what he told us," Rev says, following my movement with his eyes. "One of the new bartenders working last night. Cam caught him trying to slip something into a bottle behind the bar after the overdoses started."

I stop in front of the man, bending slightly to look into his face. He raises his head, and our eyes meet. His are bloodshot, one swollen nearly shut. A split lip, bruises forming along his jaw. He's been roughed up, but not broken. Not even close to what I have in mind.

"He hasn't been very forthcoming," Kai continues, voice deceptively casual. "We thought maybe you'd have better luck, gorgeous."

My lips curve into a smile that makes the man flinch. "Awwwwww. Did you save him for me?" I ask, not taking my eyes off our prisoner.

"Consider it a gift, baby girl," Rev says, stepping closer. "We know how much you enjoy this part."

I feel a rush of affection for the twins, for how well they know me, how perfectly they understand what I need right now. After too many sleepless hours, after watching our empire being attacked from all sides, after feeling helpless and reactive instead of in control—this is exactly what I need. Someone to make bleed. Someone to make pay.

"You shouldn't have," I murmur, reaching out to touch Marcus's bruised face with mock tenderness.

He tries to jerk away, but there's nowhere to go. His eyes dart frantically between the four of us, wide with terror. "I already told them everything I know," he rasps, voice cracking. "I was just following orders. I didn't know people would die—"

My hand moves faster than thought, the crack of my palm against his cheek echoing in the room. His head snaps to the side, a fresh trickle of blood spilling from his reopened lip.

"I didn't say you could speak," I say softly, dangerously.

I turn to the wall of tools, considering my options. Each one promises a different kind of pain, a different path to the truth. My fingers hover over the selection, caressing handles, testing edges. Behind me, I hear the man's breathing quicken, panic setting in as he realizes what's coming.

"Who gave you the drugs?" I ask without turning around. "Who told you to poison my customers?"

"I-I don't know his name," Marcus stammers. "He approached me outside the club a few nights ago. Offered me money to slip something into the drinks when he gave the signal."

I select a thin-bladed knife, testing its weight in my hand. "Not good enough, Marcus. I need a name. A face. Something I can use."

"I swear, I never got a name! He wore a hood, kept his face hidden. All I know is he had this accent, like he was from way outside of the city."

I turn back to him, knife glinting in the harsh light. "That's still not good enough."

I take a step toward Marcus, twirling the knife between my fingers. The blade catches the light, sending little rainbows dancing across his terrified face. I'm so tired that the colors seem to leave trails in the air, like shooting stars streaking across the night sky. Beautiful. I giggle at the thought.

"An accent," I repeat, tapping the flat of the blade against my lips. "That's what you're giving me? An accent?" I lean in close enough that my breath stirs the hair matted with blood against his forehead. "Do better, Marcus."

His eyes dart frantically between me and the twins standing behind me. "I swear! He kept his face covered! All I know is he paid in cash—old bills, like they'd been stored somewhere for years. And he knew things about the club, about the security. Said he used to work here, back before—"

Hudson's phone rings, cutting through Marcus's babbling. He steps away to answer it, but I can still hear his sharp intake of breath, the low curse that follows.

"When?" he demands, his voice tight with controlled fury. "How bad?"

I turn, knife still in hand, watching as Hudson's face darkens. The room suddenly feels too small, too hot, the walls pulsing in time with my heartbeat.

"I'll be there in fifteen," he says finally, ending the call. His eyes meet mine, and I know before he speaks that it's bad.

"The coffee shop on Seventh," he says, jaw clenched so tight I can see the muscle ticking. "Someone set it on fire. It's still burning."

The coffee shop. Another one of my first legitimate business-es. One of the first truly good places I created in this dead city to bring it to life again.

"I'm coming with you," I say immediately, already moving toward the door.

Rev's hand clamps around my arm, yanking me back with enough force that I stumble. "No, you're not."

"Let go of me," I snarl, trying to wrench my arm free. The room tilts slightly, exhaustion making my movements clumsy. "That's my fucking coffee shop!"

"And this," Rev says, shoving me roughly toward Marcus, "is our only lead. Hudson can handle the fire. You're staying here."

I whirl on him, knife still gripped in my white-knuckled fist. "You don't give me orders, Rev."

His eyes flash dangerously, but instead of backing down, he steps closer, towering over me as his voice drops low. "Tonight I do, little bit. You haven't slept in days. You're running on fumes and rage, which makes you sloppy. And we can't afford sloppy right now."

Hudson is already moving toward the door, phone to his ear as he barks orders to his security team. I take a step to follow, but Kai blocks my path this time, immovable as a mountain.

"Get out of my way," I hiss.

"No," he says simply. "You're staying here. With us." He nods toward Marcus, who's watching our exchange with growing terror. "Finish what you started."

Hudson pauses at the door, his eyes finding mine across the room. Something passes between us—concern, understanding, maybe even longing. Then he's gone, the door closing with a final-sounding click.

Chapter 12

Rylan

"Fuck!" I scream, hurling the knife. It embeds itself in the wall with a satisfying thunk, quivering from the force. The room spins, and for a moment, I think I might collapse. I press my palms against my eyes, willing the world to stop tilting.

"Hey," Kai's voice is suddenly closer, his hand warm on the small of my back. "We've got this. Let Hudson handle the fire. You focus on getting answers out of our friend here."

I drop my hands, blinking rapidly to clear the black spots dancing at the edges of my vision. Marcus stares up at me, eyes wide with renewed fear. The sight of his terror centers me, brings everything back into sharp focus.

"Right," I say, a smile stretching across my face that feels too wide, too sharp. "Where were we, Marcus?"

I retrieve my knife from the wall, testing its edge with my thumb. A bead of blood wells up, bright red against my pale skin. The pain is clarifying, grounding. I suck the blood away, never taking my eyes off Marcus.

"Please," he whispers as I step closer. "I told you everything I know."

"I don't think you did," I murmur, circling behind him. The knife's tip presses against his shoulder, enough to make him flinch but not to draw blood. "I think you're holding out on me, Marcus. And I don't like that."

With a sharp flick, I slash through the fabric of his shirt, opening a shallow crease across his back. He jerks against the straps, a strangled cry escaping.

"That was just a taste," I breathe, leaning in so only he can hear. "Again. Who hired you?"

His shoulders shake. "I—I swear, I told you—"

I slice again, parallel to the first cut. Warm blood puddles at the edge of his shirt. "Not good enough."

Marcus gasps, but before he can beg, something in his eyes shifts. The panic drains away. He straightens, lifts his chin. The air around him seems to crackle.

"How was my acting? I took drama in school. You think that hurts?" he says, voice calm and cold. "You think this little dance matters?" A slow smile twists his lips. "I watched them all die. Your precious customers, writhing and choking on what I sold them. Their screams... music for the cause."

I freeze, knife hovering. His voice is steady now, devoid of fear. "You're dead devils," he continues softly. "All of you. Just lie down and die already."

Blood pulses at my fingertip where I grip the blade. My heart hammers—rage, betrayal, something darker—surging through me. I plunge the knife back in without thinking.

Time fractures into a brutal rhythm: question, cut, his laughter, grime and gore painting my hands. I drive each stroke to hear his voice crack, to prove he bleeds, to force something more from him. Skin parts, muscle yields, and he still smiles, drenched in his own poison.

Rev's shifts out of the corner of my eye, silent witness to my fury. Kai's low chuckle floats from behind me, warm against my back. Their presence hammers my fury into focus.

I carve deeper and his grin falters, replaced by a stunned whisper: "I'll... never... tell... you..."

"Of course you won't," I snap, and the knife sings through his skin. Blood arcs across concrete in slow motion, the scent—metallic and sacred—filling my lungs.

I twist the blade, watching bone and tissue split. His eyes flicker, glassy, as the world narrows to this dance of steel and blood.

Then at last, he goes still. I blink, coming back to myself slowly. The knife handle is slippery in my grasp, tacky with drying blood. I look down at the corpse that was Marcus, at the masterpiece I've carved into cooling flesh, and feel nothing but frustration.

"Fuck," I mutter, wiping the blade clean on what remains of his shirt. "He was never going to talk."

Kai laughs behind me, the sound rich with appreciation. "Worth it to watch you work," he murmurs, sliding his arms around my waist. His body is hard against my back, his arousal evident. "The way you move when you've got a knife in your hand... it's like watching art in motion."

Rev steps closer, his eyes dark with desire as they rake over my blood-spattered form. "Nothing hotter than watching you lose control like that," he agrees, voice dropping to that register that makes my skin prickle.

I'm covered in blood, most of it not mine. It's warm and sticky between my fingers, drying in flakes on my forearms. The crimson puddle beneath the chair reflects the harsh overhead lights, making the floor look like it's covered in rubies.

"The coffee shop—" I start, but Rev's hand slides into my hair, yanking my head back.

"Hudson's handling it," he growls against my ear, his breath hot on my skin. "Right now, you're ours."

The exhaustion that's been clinging to my bones suddenly feels like electricity, like lightning crackling through my veins. I should be horrified at how quickly my body responds—at how the sight of blood and death makes me ache every time with need instead of recoil with disgust—but I'm beyond caring. Beyond shame.

I turn in Kai's arms, pressing my blood-slick palms against his chest. "I need—" I don't have to finish. They always know what I need.

Rev's hands find my hips, spinning me around to face him. His pupils are blown wide, only a thin ring of color remaining. "We know exactly what you need, baby girl."

His mouth crashes into mine, teeth scraping my bottom lip hard enough to draw blood. The coppery taste mingles with the scent of Marcus's blood, creating a heady cocktail that makes my head spin. Kai presses against my back, his hands already working at my clothes.

Between them, I'm stripped bare in seconds, my skin prickling with goosebumps in the cool air of the room. The concrete is cold beneath my feet, but I barely notice, too consumed by the heat of their bodies surrounding me.

"So beautiful," Kai murmurs, trailing kisses down my neck as Rev drops to his knees before me. "All covered in blood and violence."

Rev's hands grip my thighs, pushing them apart. I brace myself against Kai's solid chest as Rev's mouth finds me, his tongue insistent and demanding against my already slick flesh. A moan tears from my throat, my head falling back against Kai's shoulder.

"That's it," Kai encourages, one hand sliding up to cup my breast, pinching my nipple between his fingers. "Let us hear you."

Rev works me with his mouth, skilled and relentless, bringing me to the edge too quickly. Just as I'm about to fall, he pulls back, leaving me gasping and desperate.

"Not yet," he says, rising to his feet, his lips glistening. "On your knees."

I obey without hesitation, sinking to the cold concrete. Blood seeps into my knees, warm at first, then cooling rapidly against my skin. I look up at them through my lashes, watching as they strip with practiced efficiency.

They're beautiful, my twins. Identical and yet so different in the ways that matter. Both covered in tattoos. Rev's body is a canvas of discipline, each muscle defined and controlled. Kai's frame carries the same strength but with a fluidity that speaks of barely contained chaos. Both are hard with need, their cocks standing proud against their abdomens.

"Open, little bit," Rev commands, his hand fisting in my hair again.

I part my lips, taking him deep into my mouth. The weight of him against my tongue, the stretch of my lips around his girth, grounds me in this moment. Kai moves behind me, his hands roaming over my back, my ass, dipping between my thighs to find me wet and ready.

"So eager," he murmurs, sliding a finger into me. "Always so fucking eager."

I moan around Rev's cock, the vibration making him hiss with pleasure. His grip tightens in my hair, setting the pace as he fucks my mouth with measured thrusts. Kai adds another finger, curling them just right to hit that spot inside me that makes my vision blur.

"Enough," Rev grunts after a few minutes, pulling away. "I need to be inside you."

He drops to his knees in front of me, pushing me back until I'm lying in the blood pool, my teal hair soaking up crimson. The contrast must be striking—pale skin, teal hair, red blood. A macabre artwork they've created with me as the centerpiece.

Rev settles between my thighs, the blunt head of his cock pressing against my entrance. He watches my face as he pushes in slowly, savoring every inch, every gasp that escapes my lips.

"Fuck, you're tight, little bit," he groans, fully seated within me. "So perfect."

Kai moves to kneel beside my head, his cock heavy in his hand. "Open for me too, gorgeous."

I turn my head, taking him into my mouth as Rev begins to move inside me. The dual sensation—Rev's cock stretching me, Kai's filling my mouth—is overwhelming. I'm caught between them, used by them, cherished by them in the only way that matters to monsters like us.

Rev's pace quickens, his thrusts becoming more forceful. Each one pushes me further into the blood, my skin sliding against the slick concrete. The metallic scent fills my nostrils, mixing with the musk of sex and sweat.

"That's it," Kai urges, his voice strained as he watches Rev take me. "Fuck her harder. Make her scream around my cock."

Rev complies, his hands bruising my hips as he slams into me. The pleasure builds, sharp and insistent, a coiling tension at the base of my spine. Kai's hand finds my breast again, pinching and twisting my nipple in time with Rev's thrusts.

I'm close, so close, teetering on the edge of oblivion. The world narrows to the three of us, to the blood beneath us, to the primal rhythm of bodies moving together in ancient harmony.

"Come for us," Rev demands, his voice a rough command that brooks no argument. "Now, Ry."

The orgasm crashes through me like a tidal wave, my body arching off the floor as every muscle tenses. I cry out around Kai's cock, the sound muffled but no less intense. Rev continues to pound into me, prolonging the pleasure until it borders on pain.

Just as the aftershocks begin to subside, they switch. Rev pulls out, and Kai takes his place between my thighs. He enters me in one smooth thrust, filling the emptiness Rev left behind.

"My turn," he grins, setting a pace that's different from his brother's—more erratic, more desperate. Where Rev was controlled power, Kai is wild abandon.

Rev moves to my mouth, his cock slick with my arousal. The taste of myself on him is intoxicating, a reminder of the pleasure he's given me. He feeds himself into my mouth, groaning as I suck him clean.

"Look at you, baby girl," he murmurs, brushing blood-soaked hair from my face. "Covered in blood and taking both of us. Most beautiful thing I've ever seen."

Kai's rhythm falters, his movements becoming jerky as he nears his climax. "Fuck, Ry, I'm gonna come. Where do you want it?"

I release Rev with a wet pop. "Inside," I gasp, already feeling another orgasm building. "Both of you. Inside me."

Kai grunts, his hips snapping forward one final time as he empties himself into me. The warmth of it, the knowledge that he's marking me from the inside, pushes me over the edge again. My second orgasm ripples through me, gentler than the first but no less satisfying.

Before I can recover, they're moving again. Kai pulls out, and Rev takes his place once more. He's close—I can see it in the tension of his jaw, the tightness of his shoulders. He pounds into me relentlessly, chasing his release.

"Mine," he growls, his eyes locked with mine. "Ours. Always."

"Yours," I agree breathlessly. "Always yours."

That's all it takes. With a final thrust, he buries himself deep and comes, his cock pulsing inside me. I feel the warmth of his release joining his brother's, filling me completely.

For a long moment, we stay like that, a tangle of limbs and blood and satisfaction. Then Rev carefully pulls out, moving to lie beside me. Kai settles on my other side, his arm draping across my waist.

"You need to sleep," Rev murmurs, pressing a kiss to my temple. "You're running on empty."

I know he's right. The adrenaline is fading, leaving me hollow and exhausted. The concrete is hard beneath my back, but I can't find the energy to move.

"Can't," I mumble, fighting to keep my eyes open. "Too much happening. The fire, the club..."

"Hudson's handling the fire," Rev repeats, more gently this time. "And the club is secure for now. You're no good to anyone if you collapse."

Kai's hand strokes my hair, careful to avoid the places where blood has matted it into clumps. "Just a few hours, gorgeous. We'll wake you if anything changes."

I want to argue, to insist that I'm fine, but my body betrays me. My eyelids grow heavier with each blink, the world blurring around the edges.

"Promise?" I whisper, already drifting.

"Promise," they say in unison, their voices the last thing I hear before darkness claims me.

I dream of fire. Of buildings crumbling to ash. Of shadowy figures watching from the sidelines, their faces obscured by smoke and malice. In my dream, I'm running, always running, never fast enough to catch them, never strong enough to stop the destruction.

Chapter 13

Rylan

I WAKE WITH A gasp, heart hammering against my ribs like it's trying to escape. The nightmare clings to me, images of fire and smoke still burning behind my eyelids. For a moment, I'm disoriented, unsure where I am until my eyes adjust to the darkness.

Our bedroom. Not the interrogation room. Not surrounded by blood and concrete.

My body aches pleasantly, reminding me of what happened before I fell asleep. I turn my head slowly, finding the twins on either side of me, their breathing deep and even. They look peaceful in sleep, dangerous faces softened, all sharp edges temporarily blunted.

I reach for my phone on the nightstand, checking the time. Not even two hours have passed since we returned to the apartment. The twins must have cleaned me up and carried me to bed in the brief time I was out. No trace of blood remains on my skin or under my nails.

But the memory of Marcus's last words echoes in my mind, an insidious whisper that refuses to be silenced. Dead devils. Just lie down and die already.

Carefully, I slide out from between the twins, holding my breath when Kai stirs. He mumbles something unintelligible before settling back into sleep, one arm reaching across the space where my body had been.

My legs are unsteady as I pad across the floor to the closet. I grab the first things my fingers touch—a fitted black top and a flared leather skirt—pulling them on with clumsy movements. A small, hysterical giggle bubbles up in my throat as I recognize the skirt. I wore it on a Dead Devil's Night almost two years ago, right before we'd consolidated our power.

The coincidence feels like an omen.

I stumble through the darkened apartment, my exhausted brain barely registering where I'm going. My body moves on autopilot, guided by an urgency I can't fully articulate. I need to see it—need to see the destruction with my own eyes.

I pull on a pair of boots by the door, not bothering with socks. The leather jacket hanging on the hook is the final piece. I slide it on, the familiar weight settling across my shoulders like armor.

The elevator ride to the parking garage is a blur. I lean against the wall, fighting to keep my eyes open as the numbers count down. The doors slide open with a soft ping that sounds too loud.

Kai's motorcycle gleams under the harsh fluorescent lights, a sleek predator waiting to be unleashed. Hudson's voice echoes in my head, lecturing me about helmets and safety protocols. I mentally send him a hearty fuck you as I throw my leg over the seat, ignoring the helmet hanging from the hook nearby.

The engine roars to life beneath me, the vibration traveling up through my body, reminding me I didn't grab underwear in my haste but too tired to care. I guide the bike up the ramp and out into the night.

The city is still alive despite the hour, streets busy with people heading to clubs and bars. The Devil's Lair is already open again, the twins' efficiency evident in how quickly they managed damage control. The line outside stretches around the block, people desperate to be part of the story, to say they were there the night after the infamous overdoses.

I weave through traffic, the wind whipping my hair around my face as I aim the bike toward Seventh Street. To what was once my coffee shop, that served actual good coffee, not the bitter sludge most places in this city pass off as caffeine. A place where people could sit and read and pretend for a few hours that they didn't live in a cesspool.

I can smell the smoke before I see it, acrid and heavy in the air. When I turn the corner onto Seventh, my heart sinks. The building is just a blackened shell, still smoldering in places despite the firefighters' efforts. Emergency vehicles create a perimeter, their lights painting the scene in surreal flashes of red and blue.

I kill the engine, letting the bike coast to a stop across the street. For a long moment, I just sit there, staring at the ruins of something I created. Something good. The rage that bubbles up is different from what I felt at the club or the docks—this is deeper, more personal.

Dismounting, I cross the street. A firefighter spots me approaching the barricade and moves to intercept.

"Sorry, princess," he says, holding up a hand. "Nothing to see here. Area's closed off."

Princess. The condescension in his tone makes something snap inside me. I'm about to tell him exactly who he's talking to when a hand clamps down on the collar of my leather jacket, yanking me backward.

"She's with me," a familiar voice growls. "Now fuck off."

The firefighter backs away, hands raised in surrender. Before I can react, Hudson hauls me back to the motorcycle. He shoves me into its curve, then swings himself up in front of me. The engine roars to life under his grip, and I wrap my arms around his waist as we tear away from the chaos.

The city lights blur in our wake. My heart hammers, adrenaline still screaming through my veins. Hudson steers us through a tangle of side streets, the night air whipping at my face. I try to speak, but the wind steals my words.

After what feels like an eternity, he cuts the engine at a deserted overlook, kicking down the stand. He dismounts in one fluid motion, stalking away from the bike. His boots kick up gravel as he paces, hands clenched into fists at his sides. Below us, the town's lights glitter, oblivious to the fury building in my chest.

"Why the fuck were you there?" he demands, whirling to face me, his voice low and dangerous.

Something in me cracks. Maybe it's the exhaustion, or the accumulation of blows we've taken over the past days, or the way he's looking at me like I'm a child who needs protection.

Whatever it is, I feel myself fracture, control slipping away like water through cupped hands.

"Why the fuck was I there?" I repeat, my voice rising hysterically as I leap off the bike and storm toward him. "That's my fucking coffee shop, Hudson! Mine! Another piece of what I built burning to the ground while I'm supposed to, what, sit at home and wait for you to handle it?"

He steps closer, crowding me but I stand my ground. "You're dead on your feet," he hisses. "Look at you—you can barely stand. When was the last time you fucking slept? What exactly were you planning to do there besides collapse?"

"I don't know!" I shout, shoving at his chest. "Something! Anything! I'm so fucking sick of being reactive, of watching everything burn while we scramble to catch up!"

My hands connect with his chest again, but this time he catches my wrists, jerking them behind my back which only draws me closer to him. His body presses against mine, trapping me in place.

"You think I don't understand that?" His voice drops to a dangerous whisper. "You think I like watching you run yourself into the ground? Watching you take risks that could get you killed?"

"Let go of me," I demand, struggling against his grip. But there's no real force behind it. I'm too tired, too strung out on adrenaline and grief and rage.

"No," he says simply. "Not until you listen to me." His face is inches from mine, his breath warm against my skin. "We are going to find who's behind this. We are going to make them pay. But not like this—not with you half-dead from exhaustion, making yourself an easy target."

"I'm not—" I start to protest, but he cuts me off.

"Yes, you are," he insists, his grip tightening on my wrists. "You're running on fumes and fury, and that makes you vulnerable. And I can't—" His voice breaks slightly, something raw and unguarded flashing in his eyes. "I can't protect you if you won't let me."

The sincerity in his voice, the naked concern in his eyes, disarms me more effectively than any physical restraint. My body sags in his grip, the fight draining out of me.

"I hate this," I whisper, my voice cracking. "I hate feeling helpless. I hate watching everything burn."

His expression softens marginally. "I know," he says, loosening his grip on my wrists but not releasing them entirely. "But this isn't the way. You need rest. Real rest, not just passing out for an hour or two."

"I can't," I argue, though with less conviction. "Every time I close my eyes, I see fire. I see everything we built crumbling to ash."

Hudson's eyes narrow. "You think you're the only one who sees destruction every time you close your eyes? I've been a soldier. I know what it's like to have nightmares that feel more real than waking life."

"Oh, spare me the war stories, old man," I snap, the words flying out before I can stop them. "I don't need your PTSD therapy session."

Something dangerous flashes in his eyes. His jaw tightens, a muscle jumping beneath the skin. "Old man?" he growls, and the sound sends an involuntary shiver down my spine. "I'll show you old."

Before I can react, his mouth crashes against mine. The kiss is brutal, all teeth and tongue and barely controlled rage. I want to push him away. I want to slap him. Instead, I find myself responding with equal ferocity, my body arching into his as if it has a mind of its own.

He walks me backward, his hands still gripping my wrists behind my back, until my ass hits the motorcycle. The cool metal against the backs of my thighs makes me gasp into his mouth.

"You're such an asshole," I pant when he finally breaks the kiss, my chest heaving.

His lips curve into something too predatory to be called a smile. "And you're a spoiled brat who doesn't know when to quit." His voice is rough, like gravel wrapped in velvet. "But I know what you need right now."

"Oh yeah?" I challenge, tilting my chin up defiantly. "And what's that?"

"Something to burn away the images in your head," he murmurs, his lips brushing my ear. "Something to exhaust you so completely you can't think, can't dream, can't do anything but surrender."

I hate that he's right. I hate that he can read me so easily. Most of all, I hate how much I want what he's offering.

"You think you're up to the task?" I taunt, my voice deliberately mocking. "At your age, I'm surprised you can still—"

His hand wraps around my throat, cutting off my words. Not hard enough to restrict my breathing, just enough to make his point.

"Keep talking," he dares me, his eyes glittering in the moon-light. "Give me another reason to show you exactly what this old man can do."

In one fluid motion, he releases my throat and swings himself onto the motorcycle. Before I can process what's happening, his hands are on my waist, lifting me onto the bike in front of him. He positions me so my back is against the tank, my legs hooked over his own.

"What are you doing?" I ask, though it's perfectly obvious.

"Shutting you up the only way that works," he replies, his hands already pushing my skirt up around my waist. His eye-brows rise when he discovers I'm not wearing anything under-neath. "Were you planning this?"

"No," I admit, heat rising to my cheeks. "I was in a hurry."

His laugh is dark and knowing. "Lucky me."

His fingers find me already wet, and he makes a sound of satisfaction low in his throat. "All that fight, all that rage, and look at you," he murmurs, circling my clit with his thumb. "So fucking ready for me."

My head falls back against the motorcycle tank, a moan es-caping my lips as he slides two fingers inside me. The stretch burns in the best way, my body clenching around the intrusion.

"That's it," he encourages. "Let me hear you."

His fingers work me with devastating precision, finding spots inside me that make my vision blur. The cool night air against my exposed skin, the hard metal beneath my back, the stars spinning overhead—it all blends into a surreal backdrop for the pleasure building inside me.

"Hudson," I gasp, my hips rocking against his hand. "Please—"

"Please what?" he asks, slowing his movements deliberately. "Tell me what you need, Rylan. I want to hear you say it."

I hate him for making me ask. Hate him for the knowing look in his eyes. But the need burning through me is stronger than pride.

"Fuck me," I whisper, the words barely audible over the distant sound of the city below us.

"I didn't quite catch that," he says, removing his fingers entirely. "Louder."

I grab his wrist, trying to guide his hand back where I need it. "Fuck me, Hudson. Now."

He smirks, satisfied with my surrender. I hear the rasp of his zipper, and then he's positioning himself between my thighs, the blunt head of his cock pressing against my entrance.

"Is this what you wanted?" he asks, pushing in just enough to make me gasp. He has a goddamn fucking piercing. "To be filled by this old man's cock?"

"Shut up and fuck me," I growl, wrapping my legs around his waist to pull him closer.

He enters me in one smooth thrust, filling me so completely that the air rushes from my lungs. For a moment, we both freeze, adjusting to the sensation, and I can't help but register the subtle friction of not one but three little barbells sliding inside me. Then he begins to move, setting a pace that's just shy of punishing.

"Look at you," he murmurs, his hands gripping my hips hard enough to bruise. "Taking me so well. So fucking perfect around my cock."

Each thrust pushes me back against the motorcycle tank, the metal warming beneath my body. The position is precarious, the bike rocking slightly beneath us, but the danger only heightens every sensation.

"You want to know why I'm angry?" he asks, his rhythm never faltering. "Because every time you put yourself in danger, I see you lying broken and bleeding. Every time you push yourself past your limits, I imagine finding you collapsed somewhere I can't reach you."

His words cut through the haze of pleasure, touching something raw and vulnerable inside me. I open my mouth to respond, but he changes the angle of his thrusts, those tiny barbells rubbing a spot that makes coherent thought impossible.

"And the worst part," he continues, his voice strained with effort, "is knowing that if anything happened to you, it would destroy them. It would destroy me."

He punctuates this confession with a particularly deep thrust that has me crying out, my nails digging into his shoulders through his jacket.

"Hudson," I gasp, feeling the tension coiling tighter inside me. "I'm close—"

"Not yet," he growls, slowing his pace to a maddening crawl. "Not until I'm done telling you exactly what I think of you."

I whimper in frustration, trying to move my hips to increase the friction, but his grip is unyielding.

"You're reckless," he says, pulling almost completely out before slamming back in. "Stubborn." Another thrust. "Infuriating." And another. "And the most magnificent creature I've ever seen."

The last words are softer, almost reverent, and they hit me harder than the accusations that came before.

"I've wanted you since the first moment I saw you," he confesses, his pace quickening again.

His hand wraps around my throat suddenly, fingers pressing against my carotid arteries. The pressure builds gradually, cutting off blood flow rather than air. My vision swims almost immediately, the edges darkening as my pulse pounds against his palm.

"This is what you need," he growls, his hips never slowing. "To let go completely."

The pressure increases, and stars burst behind my eyes—brilliant pinpricks of light dancing across my darkening vision. My body responds instantly, pleasure spiking savagely as oxygen deprivation heightens every sensation and the subtle scrape of his piercings inside me intensifies every thrust.

"Look at those stars," he murmurs, his voice coming from somewhere far away. "I'm causing those. I'm giving you the universe right now."

I try to speak but can only manage a strangled moan. My fingers scrabble against his wrist, not to pull him away but to anchor myself as the world tilts and spins. The weight and stretch of his cock, the scrape of those barbells inside me, the pressure of his hand on my throat, the cool metal of the motorcycle against my back—everything narrows to these points of contact.

"Come for me," he commands, and it's as if my body has been waiting for permission.

The orgasm tears through me with savage intensity, my vision going completely black for a moment as every muscle tenses. I'm dimly aware of Hudson's rhythm faltering, of his groan as he empties himself inside me, joining me in the blissful oblivion of release. My body continues to pulse around him, aftershocks rippling through me as the world slowly comes back into focus.

His hand remains on my throat, though the pressure has lessened. I blink up at him, still dazed from the intensity of my orgasm. His green eyes are dark, unreadable as they lock with mine. Something shifts in his expression.

"I'm sorry," he whispers, and before I can process his words, the pressure on my throat increases again. Not the gentle, pleasurable pressure from before, but something more deliberate, more calculated.

My eyes widen in surprise, hands flying up to clutch at his wrist. "Hudson—what—" I try to say, but the words die in my throat as darkness creeps in from the edges of my vision.

I struggle weakly, but my body is spent, exhaustion and post-orgasmic lassitude making my movements sluggish. His grip is unyielding, professional—he knows exactly what he's doing.

"I'm sorry," he murmurs again as my hands fall limply to my sides, and the world goes black.

Chapter 14

Rev

I GRIP THE STEERING wheel so hard my knuckles turn white, foot pressing the accelerator closer to the floor. The SUV roars down the empty road, streetlights flashing past in rhythmic pulses. Beside me, Kai stares out the window, his profile sharp against the darkness, one leg bouncing with barely contained energy, his fingers drumming an erratic rhythm against his armrest.

"Slow down before you kill us both," he mutters, but there's no real force behind it. He's just as worried as I am.

"She wasn't there when we woke up," I say through gritted teeth, taking a curve too fast. "She hasn't slept properly in days. What the fuck was she thinking?"

The text message had come through twenty minutes ago—coordinates to the overlook with a simple message: She's safe. I'm with her.

No explanation. Just those coordinates and five words that did nothing to calm the rage building inside me since I woke to cold sheets where our girl should have been.

"Hudson said she's safe—"

"Safe now, maybe. But going out alone, in her condition? After everything that's happened?" I cut him off, fear gnawing at my gut.

"You know how she gets," Kai replies, running a hand through his hair. "When she's like this, she can't sit still. Can't process from a distance. She has to see, has to touch."

I know he's right, but it doesn't make me any less furious. The past few days have been a nightmare—the overdoses, the sabotage at the Playground, the fire at the coffee shop. Someone's systematically targeting everything we've built, and Rylan's response is to throw herself headfirst into danger.

The road winds upward as we approach the overlook. It's a secluded spot with a view of the entire city, far enough from civilization that we've used it for private conversations that couldn't happen elsewhere. In the distance, I can see the lights of our empire spread out below, beautiful and vulnerable.

"There," Kai points as we round the final bend. His motorcycle is parked near the edge, gleaming under the moonlight.

I pull the SUV alongside it and kill the engine. We're both out of the vehicle before the echo of the engine dies, scanning the area. The bike is empty, no sign of Hudson or Rylan.

"Where the hell—" I begin, but Kai grabs my arm, pointing toward a cluster of trees about twenty yards away.

That's when I spot them. Hudson is sitting with his back against a large oak, looking out over the city. And cradled in his arms, head resting against his chest, is Rylan. Even from this distance, I can see the steady rise and fall of her chest as she sleeps.

Something in me unclenches at the sight, anger giving way to relief so profound it's almost dizzying. I approach them quietly, Kai following close behind.

Hudson looks up as we near, his expression guarded. He doesn't move, careful not to disturb Rylan's sleep.

"Thanks for sending us the message," I say, keeping my voice low as I crouch down beside them. I brush a strand of teal hair from Rylan's face, noting the peaceful expression that's been absent for too long. "How'd you manage this miracle?"

Hudson's mouth quirks in what might be a smile. "I may have helped her reach the end of her rope."

I notice the faint bruising around her throat then, the small marks peeking out from beneath her chin. The scent hits me next—sex and sweat, them, mingled together. I'm not surprised. We've seen this building for years, the tension between them thick enough to cut with a knife.

"She's going to be furious with you when she wakes up," I observe, running my thumb lightly over her cheek.

Hudson gives a half-shrug that speaks volumes. "Don't care. As long as she gets some fucking sleep, I can take her fury."

I grin, unable to help myself. "I bet you can." My eyes flick meaningfully to the marks on her skin, the rumpled state of her clothes, the way her body fits against his like she belongs there. Not that we care—hell, we were the ones to encourage it in the first place. Some things need to burn themselves out, and the fire between these two has been smoldering for too long.

Kai crouches on Hudson's other side, his expression a mix of amusement and concern. "How long has she been out?"

"About half an hour," Hudson replies, his arm tightening slightly around her sleeping form. "Dead to the world the moment she went under."

"You know she's going to try to kill you for that little trick," Kai says, though there's no heat in his voice. "She hates feeling vulnerable."

"Let her try," Hudson murmurs, his eyes dropping to Rylan's face with an expression that makes my chest tighten. It's the same way Kai and I look at her—like she's the center of our universe, like we'd burn the world to ash to keep her safe.

"Did she see the coffee shop?" I ask, settling more comfortably on the ground.

Hudson nods grimly. "That's where I found her. She was about to cross the police line when I intercepted her."

"And you brought her here instead of home?" Kai raises an eyebrow.

"She needed to break," Hudson says simply. "Somewhere away from everything. Somewhere she could let go without worrying about appearances."

I understand immediately. Rylan never allows herself to be weak in our territory—not where others might see, not where it might undermine the image we've carefully constructed. Out here, miles from the city, she could finally surrender to the exhaustion that's been dogging her for days.

"Smart," I acknowledge. "We should get her home, though. She'll be more comfortable in her own bed."

Hudson hesitates, looking down at her sleeping form. "I don't want to wake her. She needs this."

There's a protectiveness in his voice that I recognize—it's the same fierce devotion that drives Kai and me. It should make me jealous, this man holding what's ours, but instead, it feels right. Like a piece clicking into place that we didn't know was missing.

"We'll carry her to the car," I decide, standing up. "You can ride with her in the back seat. Kai will take his bike."

Kai nods his agreement, already heading toward the motorcycle. Hudson rises carefully, cradling Rylan against his chest. She stirs slightly but doesn't wake, her face pressing into his neck as if seeking his warmth even in sleep.

As we walk back to the SUV, I can't help but study them. The way his arms cradle her so securely, the way her body fits against his like she was made to be there. She is so tiny against him. There's something primal in the sight, something that satisfies a part of me I didn't know needed satisfying.

"You did good," I tell him as he slides into the back seat, still holding her. "With her. And with all of this. We couldn't have handled it without you."

He looks up, surprise flashing across his face before his expression settles back into its usual stoic mask. "Just doing my job."

I laugh softly, shaking my head. "No, you're not. And we all know it."

I close the door before he can respond, circling around to the driver's side. Through the window, I can see him adjusting his position, making sure Rylan is comfortable against him. His hand strokes her hair in a gesture so tender it makes my chest ache.

As I start the engine, I catch Kai's eye in the side mirror. He's already on the bike, watching the scene in the back seat with the same knowing expression I feel on my own face.

We've been sharing Rylan for years, Kai and I. But something tells me our duo is about to become a trio, and I'm okay with that. More than okay.

Because anyone who looks at our girl the way Hudson does—like she's simultaneously the most precious and most dangerous thing in his world—deserves a place in our fucked-up little family.

I put the SUV in drive, heading back toward the city that's tried so hard to break us. Let them try. With the four of us united, they don't stand a chance.

As we descend from the overlook, Rylan stirs in Hudson's arms, her eyes fluttering open briefly. She looks disoriented for a moment, then her gaze locks with Hudson's. I watch in the rearview mirror as confusion gives way to recognition, then anger.

"You bastard," she murmurs, but there's no real heat behind it. Her voice is thick with sleep, her movements sluggish as she tries to sit up.

"Go back to sleep, sweetheart," Hudson says softly, his hand continuing its gentle stroking of her hair. "We're taking you home."

She blinks slowly, her gaze drifting to the front seat where she spots me watching her in the mirror. "Rev?"

"Right here, little bit," I confirm. "Kai's on the bike behind us. Everything's under control. Just rest. Please."

She seems to consider arguing for a moment, but at my 'please' she lets the exhaustion win out. Her eyes drift closed again, her body relaxing back against Hudson's chest. The last thing I hear before she succumbs to sleep again is a whispered, "Still gonna kill you when I wake up."

Hudson's soft laugh fills the car. "I'm counting on it."

Chapter 15

Rylan

CONSCIOUSNESS RETURNS TO ME slowly, like I'm swimming up through dark water. My body feels heavy, weighted down with exhaustion finally satisfied. I stretch languidly beneath soft sheets, reaching instinctively for the warmth of bodies that should be there.

Nothing. Empty space.

My eyes fly open. Sunlight filters around the closed curtains—curtains we rarely use—casting the room in a muted golden glow. I'm naked, my skin clean and fresh, no trace of blood or sweat or... other activities. Someone bathed me while I slept. Again.

I try to piece together fragmented memories: the coffee shop in ruins, Hudson on the motorcycle, his hands on me, his fingers around my throat—that bastard choked me out. After I came. The absolute fucking audacity.

I sit up, scanning the room for my phone, but it's nowhere in sight. Typical. They're always hiding it when they think I need to rest. As if I'm some child who can't manage my own sleep schedule.

"Fuckers," I mutter, but without real heat. I hate to admit it, but I do feel better. My mind is clearer, the exhaustion that's been dogging me for days finally receding.

I slide out of bed, my muscles protesting slightly—a pleasant ache that reminds me of Hudson's hands, his cock, those surprising barbells. A flush rises to my cheeks at the memory. Bastard.

The bathroom tile is cool under my feet as I splash water on my face and brush my teeth. I study my reflection in the mirror—the faint bruises around my throat, the clarity returning to my eyes. I look... rested. Centered. Ready.

I pull on a black silk robe hanging on the bathroom door, cinching it tightly around my waist before padding toward the bedroom door. Voices drift from the main living area, too low to make out words but familiar enough to recognize. The twins. Hudson. And... someone else?

"—reliable source?" That's Hudson, always the skeptic.

"I know what I heard." This voice is younger, eager, with an undercurrent of anxiety. Oliver?

I push open the door to the living area and four heads turn in my direction. Rev and Kai are lounging on opposite ends of the sofa, looking like mirror images in black jeans and fitted t-shirts. Hudson stands by the window, arms crossed over his chest, expression unreadable as ever. And perched awkwardly on a barstool at our kitchen counter is Oliver, looking like he's afraid the furniture might bite him.

"Well, look who's rejoined the land of the living," Kai drawls, his eyes raking over me with open appreciation.

"How long was I out?" I ask, tightening the sash on my robe when I notice Oliver's wide-eyed stare. Poor puppy looks like he might spontaneously combust from embarrassment.

"Just about nine hours," Rev answers, checking his watch. "It's early afternoon."

"The day before Dead Devil's Night," Hudson adds pointedly, his gaze heavy on mine. The unspoken message is clear: we're running out of time.

I ignore him for the moment, still not ready to forgive the stunt he pulled last night. Instead, I focus on Oliver, whose presence in our private sanctuary is unexpected, to say the least.

"What's he doing here?" I ask, not bothering to be subtle.

Oliver shrinks slightly under my direct attention, and I feel a twinge of something like guilt. He's been nothing but helpful so far, and here I am, making him uncomfortable in a space where he's clearly already out of his depth.

"He called Hudson with information," Rev explains, his tone neutral but his eyes sharp on my face, gauging my reaction. "We thought it was important enough to bring him up, and we didn't want to leave you alone while you slept."

"I'm sorry if I'm intruding," Oliver says quickly, his hands fidgeting in his lap. "I wouldn't have—I mean, I know this is your private space, but I heard something at the Playground this morning and I thought—"

"It's fine," I cut him off, softening my tone. "What did you hear?"

He straightens, eager to be useful. "I was at the club early, getting in some practice before the opening. I was in the dressing room when I overheard two people talking. They didn't know I was there and they were in the main area so I couldn't see them, but I could hear them." He leans forward, voice dropping conspiratorially. "They were discussing something happening at the docks this afternoon. A shipment coming in. They mentioned containers specifically."

My interest sharpens immediately. "Our containers?"

Oliver nods, a strand of copper-blonde hair falling across his forehead. "They didn't say whose, but they mentioned something about 'finishing what was started' and 'hitting them where it hurts.'"

I look to Hudson, whose jaw is tight with tension. "Could be nothing," he says, but I can tell he doesn't believe that any more than I do.

"Or it could be exactly what we've been looking for," I counter. "A lead. A chance to catch these fuckers in the act instead of always being one step behind."

Kai stands, stretching like a cat. "Either way, worth checking out. We can set up surveillance, see if anything happens."

"I can go back to the club," Oliver offers quickly, sliding off the stool and taking a step toward me. "Try to get more information from them."

I notice how he gravitates in my direction, like a satellite caught in my orbit. His eyes follow my movements with that puppy-like devotion that's becoming familiar. It should be annoying, but there's something endearing about his eagerness to please.

"No need," Rev says, his gaze flicking briefly to Oliver before settling on me. "I think you've earned the right to ride along with us to the docks. If you want to."

Oliver's eyes widen, genuine surprise and pleasure lighting up his face. "Really? I mean—yes, absolutely. I want to help however I can."

"It's settled then," I decide, ignoring the way Hudson's eyebrows rise at my easy acceptance of Oliver's inclusion. "We'll go tonight, see what's happening at our docks."

I move toward the kitchen, suddenly ravenous. Nine hours of sleep has awakened an appetite I've been ignoring for days. As I pass Oliver, he shifts slightly, unconsciously moving closer to me, his eyes tracking my movements with that same desperate need for approval.

"Thank you," he says softly, just for me. "For trusting me with this."

I pause, studying him. There's something in his expression—a hunger that goes beyond simple admiration. It reminds me of how I felt years ago, desperate to belong, to be seen, to matter.

"Don't make me regret it," I tell him, keeping my voice low enough that only he can hear.

He shakes his head vehemently. "I won't. I promise."

I believe him, which is rare enough these days to be noteworthy. There's something about Oliver that feels genuine, despite—or perhaps because of—his obvious fixation.

"Ry," Hudson calls from across the room, his voice deliberately casual. "A word?"

I turn to find him watching me with an intensity that sends heat racing down my spine. Memories of last night flash through my mind—his hands on my throat, his voice in my ear, the stars bursting behind my eyes.

"Sure thing, old man," I reply, deliberately provocative.

His eyes narrow at the nickname, but he says nothing as he leads the way to the other end of the room past the dining area. I follow, aware of the twins watching us with identical knowing smirks.

The moment we have an illusion of distance and privacy, Hudson turns to face me. "Are you sure about bringing the dancer?"

"His name is Oliver," I correct, leaning against the glass wall. The city stretches out below us, bathed in afternoon sunlight that does nothing to disguise its grime and decay. "And yes, I'm sure. He's proven himself useful so far."

"He's a liability," Hudson argues softly, stepping closer. "Untrained, unpredictable, and completely infatuated with you. That's a dangerous combination."

I arch an eyebrow. "Jealous?"

His expression doesn't change, but I see the muscle in his jaw jump. "Concerned. We don't know enough about him."

"We know he's risked his own safety twice now to bring us information," I point out. "That counts for something in my book."

Hudson sighs, running a hand through his dark hair. "Just... be careful. There's something about him that doesn't sit right with me."

I study his face, noting the genuine concern in his eyes. "I'm always careful," I say, softening my tone. "But I need allies right now, Hudson. I need people I can trust."

"And you trust him?" he asks, incredulous.

"I trust that he wants to impress me," I reply honestly. "That's useful."

He shakes his head, a reluctant smile tugging at his lips. "You're dangerous, you know that?"

"So I've been told." I step closer, invading his personal space deliberately. "Speaking of dangerous, we need to talk about last night."

His body tenses, but he holds his ground. "I'm not apologizing for making sure you got some sleep."

"By choking me unconscious?" I hiss, jabbing a finger into his chest. "After fucking me senseless on a motorcycle?"

"It worked, didn't it?" he counters, unrepentant. "You're rested. Clearer. Ready to face whatever's coming."

He's right, damn him, but I'm not about to admit it. "Do it again, and I'll gut you in your sleep."

His smile is slow and knowing. "No, you won't."

"No," I concede, my own lips curving upward despite myself. "But I'll make you wish I had."

His laugh is unexpected—a deep, rich sound that makes something warm unfurl in my chest. "I'm sure I'll enjoy you trying."

The tension between us shifts, transforming into something different but no less intense. For a moment, I consider leaning in, tasting that laugh on his lips. But we have an audience, and more importantly, we have work to do.

"Let's head to the docks," I say, stepping back to a safer distance. "I want to catch these bastards in the act. End this game they're playing."

Hudson's expression sobers, all traces of humor vanishing. "Agreed. But we do it smart. No unnecessary risks."

"Since when do I take unnecessary risks?" I ask innocently.

His look of sheer disbelief is answer enough.

"Fine," I concede. "Be boring. We play it your way. For now."

We rejoin the others, finding that in our absence, Oliver has somehow managed to relax slightly. He's sitting on the couch now, listening intently as Kai explains something about the club's security systems.

"—so if anything happens, the silent alarm triggers automatically," Kai is saying. "Hudson's team can be there in under three minutes."

Oliver nods, absorbing the information with obvious fascination. When he notices me, he straightens immediately, that eager-to-please expression returning to his face.

"We leave at sunset," I announce to the room at large. "I want to be in position before anything happens."

Rev stands, stretching lazily as he checks the time on his watch. "I'll make sure everything's ready."

"I need food," I announce, suddenly aware of the gnawing emptiness in my stomach. Nine hours of sleep after days of running on fumes has left me ravenous. "I'm starving."

I pad barefoot to the kitchen, opening the refrigerator to survey the contents. There's not much—we rarely cook, preferring to order in when we're home, which isn't often. I spot some leftover containers from what must be yesterday and grab one without checking what's inside.

Cold pad thai. Not ideal, but it'll do. I hop onto one of the bar stools and dig in, not bothering to heat it up. The first bite hits my empty stomach like a revelation, and I close my eyes momentarily in satisfaction.

"You should probably eat something with actual nutritional value," Hudson comments, leaning against the counter next to me.

I point my fork at him threateningly. "Don't push your luck, old man. I'll decide what I eat and don't eat."

His lips quirk up slightly at the corners before he murmurs, "Does that include my cock?"

Heat rushes to my face, but I refuse to give him the satisfaction of seeing me flustered. Instead, I shovel another forkful into my mouth, chewing with deliberate slowness while maintaining eye contact.

Behind him, I see Kai roll his eyes before returning his attention to Oliver, who's now looking at a map of the docks on Kai's tablet. Rev has disappeared, probably to call Camden.

I finish the pad thai in record time, then raid the fridge again, grabbing a yogurt I find hiding behind some beer bottles. As I eat, I mentally catalog what needs to be done before we leave. Shower. Clothes. Weapons.

"I'm going to get ready," I announce to no one in particular, depositing my empty containers in the garbage.

Kai glances up. "Want company?" he asks, his tone suggestive.

I consider it for a moment, then shake my head. "Not enough time."

"Spoilsport," he mutters, but there's no heat behind it.

I head back to our bedroom, mind already shifting into preparation mode. Tonight could be the breakthrough we need—a chance to finally see who's targeting us, to go from reactive to proactive. The anticipation sends a thrill through me that's almost as good as sex.

Almost.

Chapter 16

Rylan

THE RHYTHMIC HUM OF the SUV's engine provides a steady backdrop to my thoughts as I sit in the back seat, my body swaying gently with each turn. I've dressed for the occasion—a fitted black top paired with a pair of dark green booty shorts that's short enough to draw attention but not so revealing that I can't move if I need to. My teal hair is pulled back tightly, emphasizing the sharpness of my features. Add in my thigh high boots and I look like any other girl heading to a club for the night—sexy, maybe a little silly, definitely not someone who could kill you six different ways before you hit the ground.

The weight of concealed knives presses against my thighs, my lower back, nestled against my ribs—accessories more essential to me than the small purse sitting between Oliver and me. I've learned that playing the harmless party girl is the perfect cover for getting close to people who would otherwise keep their distance. They never see the danger until it's too late.

Instead of watching the city slide past the tinted windows, I turn my attention to Oliver. He's dressed simply—dark jeans, a shirt that shows off the lean muscles of a dancer. He must have been kitted by Hudson because I can still make out the subtle bumps and ridges that I assume are weapons. His gaze flicks nervously between the road ahead and Hudson's eyes in the rearview mirror.

"So," I begin, breaking the silence that's settled over us since we left the penthouse, "what brought you to this cesspool of a city in the first place?"

He seems startled by the question, like he wasn't expecting conversation. "Job opportunities, mostly," he answers after a moment's hesitation. "There's not much out there beyond the city anymore—just dying towns and empty promises. Here, at least, there's a chance at something better."

"Family?" I press, curious about the background checks Hudson ran that seemed to satisfy him enough to let Oliver tag along.

A shadow crosses his face. "Estranged," he says shortly. "My dad died a couple years back." He doesn't elaborate, and something in his expression warns me not to push.

"Sorry to hear that," I offer, not entirely sure if I mean it. Everyone has their ghosts in this city.

He shrugs, the movement fluid and graceful even in the confined space. "It is what it is." His eyes meet mine, and I see a flash of that confidence I noticed when we first met—before Rev and Kai terrified him for letting me steal his bike. "Things started looking up when I landed the gig at the Playground. Felt like my luck was finally changing."

"Do you still feel lucky?" I ask, genuinely curious given everything that's happened since.

A smile spreads across his face—open, genuine. "Yes. More than ever."

Something about his certainty makes me pause. Most people would be running in the opposite direction by now, especially after witnessing the chaos in my life. But Oliver seems to be leaning into the danger, drawn to it—or maybe drawn to us.

"Even after everything that's happened?" I press, studying his reaction closely. "The sabotage at the club, the overdoses?"

"Especially after all that," he replies without hesitation. "I've spent my whole life being invisible, just another nobody trying to survive. But now..." He glances toward Hudson, then back to me. "Now I'm part of something important. Something real."

There's an intensity in his eyes that I recognize—the desperate need to belong, to matter. I've seen it before in the twins when we were at the foster home together, that hunger for connection that goes beyond the ordinary.

"We'll see if you still feel that way after tonight," I say, keeping my tone light despite the weight of what might be waiting for us at the docks.

The SUV takes a sharp turn, and Oliver slides slightly closer to me on the seat. I notice Hudson's eyes flick to the rearview mirror, watching the movement with that predatory focus he never quite manages to hide.

"Can I ask you something?" Oliver says, his voice dropping lower as if sharing a secret.

I raise an eyebrow. "You can ask. Doesn't mean I'll answer."

He hesitates, his fingers fidgeting with the hem of his shirt. "How did they do it? The twins. How did they take control of everything? Make people fear them?"

The question surprises me. It's not what I expected from him—not a question about our relationship, or any of the rumors that swirl around us. Instead, he's asking about power. About control.

"What makes you think they want people to fear them?" I counter, curious about his perception.

He looks at me like I've said something absurd. "I've seen how people react when they realize who they are. Fear is... useful. Powerful."

There's something in his tone—a hunger, an admiration—that makes me reassess him. Maybe there's more to our pretty dancer than I initially thought.

"Fear is a tool," I agree carefully. "But it's not the only one. Respect is more valuable in the long run."

"And how do they earn that?" he asks, leaning closer, hanging on my every word.

I study him for a moment, weighing how much to reveal. "Consistency," I finally say. "People need to know exactly what happens when they cross certain lines. No exceptions, no surprises. Break the rules, there are consequences. Keep your word, deliver what you promise, and you'll have protection."

Oliver nods slowly, absorbing this like it's gospel. His eyes drift to my neck, lingering on the marks there. His fingers twitch like he wants to reach out.

"How did you come to belong to them? The twins, I mean. How did they earn you?" he asks, voice dropping to just above a whisper.

I say nothing, my face going carefully blank as I feel Hudson's eyes on me. I let the silence stretch between us until Oliver shifts uncomfortably.

"And the violence?" Oliver pivots when I don't respond. "The... enforcement?

Hudson's eyes meet mine in the mirror, a silent warning that I ignore.

"Sometimes necessary," I admit. "But never random, never without purpose. Violence for its own sake is wasteful. It should always serve a greater goal."

"Like tonight?" he asks, gesturing vaguely toward the road ahead, toward the docks waiting for us.

"Exactly like tonight," I confirm, a cold smile spreading across my face. "If we find who's been targeting us, they'll learn exactly why crossing us was their last mistake."

Rather than being disturbed by this, Oliver looks... excited. His pupils dilate slightly, his breathing quickens. It's subtle, but I notice these things—I've spent years reading people's reactions, looking for signs of deception or fear.

"I want to learn," he says suddenly, earnestly, as he shifts closer again. "Everything they are willing to teach me. I can be useful to them—and you—not just as a dancer."

I tilt my head, considering him. "And what exactly are you offering, Oliver?"

His gaze doesn't waver. "Whatever any of you need. Eyes and ears in places you can't always be. Someone who doesn't look like a threat until it's too late." He gestures to himself with a self-deprecating smile. "People underestimate me. Always have. Could be an advantage."

He's not wrong. With his pretty face and dancer's grace, most would see him as harmless. A perfect spy in plain sight.

"We'll see," I say noncommittally, though I'm intrigued by the possibility. "Let's get through tonight first, shall we?"

He nods eagerly, settling back in his seat but still watching me with that same intensity. I can feel Hudson's disapproval radiating from the front seat, but I ignore it. I make my own decisions about who to trust, who to use.

The SUV slows as we approach the outskirts of the dock area. Through the windshield, I can see Rev and Kai ahead of us on their bikes, sleek and dangerous in the fading light. Behind us, Camden follows with another SUV full of Hudson's men—insurance in case things go sideways.

"Almost there," Hudson announces unnecessarily, his voice tight with the tension we all feel.

I check my weapons one last time—the knife at my thigh, the one nestled against my spine, the garrote wire disguised as a stylish bracelet. I've played this role before—the lost party girl who took a wrong turn, stumbling into places she shouldn't be. Men always underestimate a pretty face, always want to help the damsel in distress. It's their last mistake.

"Remember," Hudson says, his eyes finding mine in the mirror, "the goal is to observe. We need to know who we're dealing with before we make a move."

"I know how to do my job," I reply, a hint of sharpness in my tone that makes Oliver glance between us curiously.

Hudson's jaw tightens, but he says nothing more as we turn onto the access road that leads to the docks. The sun has nearly set, casting long shadows between the towering stacks of shipping containers. Perfect hiding places for whatever—or whoever—might be waiting.

"Ready?" I ask Oliver, watching his face carefully for any signs of doubt or fear.

He nods once, determined. "Ready."

The SUV rolls to a stop, and I take a deep breath, sliding into the character I'll need to play—just another silly girl who's about to be in way over her head. Unless, of course, they're the ones who are already drowning.

The docks spread before us like a metal labyrinth, shipping containers stacked three high creating corridors of steel and shadow. Hudson kills the engine, and for a moment, we sit in silence, listening to the distant sound of waves lapping against the pier and the occasional metallic groan of settling containers.

Rev and Kai have already dismounted from their bikes, moving with predatory grace as they secure the perimeter. Through the windshield, I watch them signal to each other—all clear so far.

"If they make a move the activity would be centered around the northeast section," Hudson reminds us, his voice low. "That's where our containers are."

I nod, my mind already mapping out approach routes and escape paths. "Oliver stays with you," I decide. "I'll go in alone."

Hudson's head whips around, his eyes narrowing. "Like hell you will."

"This isn't up for debate," I say, my voice hardening. "I can get closer playing the lost party girl if I'm alone. A group draws attention."

"Then I'll go with you," Oliver offers quickly. "We could pretend to be a couple who got lost looking for a rave or something."

I consider his suggestion. It's not terrible—two people might actually sell the story better than one. And if things go south, having someone to watch my back could be useful.

"Fine," I concede, ignoring Hudson's deepening scowl. "Oliver and I will approach from the east. You, Rev, and Kai coordinate with Camden to cover the other access points. If we spot anything, we signal and wait for backup. No heroics."

The last part is directed at Oliver, who nods solemnly. I know the twins will ignore that directive if they think I'm in danger, but it's worth saying anyway.

"I don't like this," Hudson mutters, but he doesn't object further.

"You don't have to like it," I remind him, the words leaving my mouth with a sharpness I know I'll regret later when we're alone. "You just have to do your job."

His eyes meet mine in the mirror one last time, something unspoken passing between us—a warning, a promise, the certainty that we'll revisit this conversation when the night is over. Then he's opening his door, the cool night air rushing in to replace the SUV's climate-controlled atmosphere as he disappears into the darkness.

Chapter 17

Rylan

"Let's move," I say to Oliver, gathering my small purse, already calculating what Hudson's retribution might cost me. "And remember—you're just a clueless kid looking for a good time, got it?"

He nods, a slow smile spreading across his face that transforms him completely. Suddenly he looks younger, more carefree—the sharp intelligence in his eyes replaced with wide-eyed excitement. It's an impressive transformation, and I make a mental note of his acting skills.

We exit the SUV, and I immediately adopt my own disguise—shoulders slightly slumped, steps less precise, giggling slightly.

"Are you sure this is the right way?" I ask loudly, making my voice carry just enough to be heard by anyone nearby. "I thought Jax said the party was by the water."

Oliver plays along beautifully, his arm sliding around my waist as he guides me deeper into the maze of containers. "Trust me, babe. I know where I'm going."

"We need to head east," I mumble under my breath, directing him with subtle pressure against his side.

The tiny earpiece nestled in my ear crackles to life, Hudson's voice low and controlled. "Keep a leash on the puppy, Ry. Don't do anything stupid. I'm going to make you regret this later."

I suppress a smile, maintaining my vapid party girl expression while replying through the nearly invisible mic concealed in my necklace. "Looking forward to it, old man."

Oliver glances at me, confusion flickering across his face at words that seem directed at him but don't make sense in context. I wink, playing it off as flirtation while listening to Rev's voice now in my ear.

"What exactly is she going to regret, Hudson?" Rev sounds amused, the smirk evident in his tone even through the static.

"Ask her yourself," Hudson growls.

I let out a high-pitched giggle that would make a sorority girl proud while muttering through gritted teeth, "If you three don't stop this pissing contest, I'll personally ensure none of you can piss standing up ever again. Any movement that isn't my patience leaving my body?"

Oliver's eyes widen like I've grown a second head, but he adapts quickly, wrapping his arm around my waist as we careen around a corner with all the grace of two tequila-soaked college freshmen.

"Ooh, she's feisty tonight," Kai's voice crackles in my ear. "Rev, think Hudson would look good in your bathrobe? The purple one with the hearts? Are we going to have to play scissors paper rock to decide who shares their side of the bed?"

I pretend to trip, using the moment to scan for threats while dramatically clutching Oliver's surprisingly firm chest. "Christ on a cracker, I'm out here risking my ass while you three plan your throuple honeymoon. If I get shot because you're comparing dick sizes, I'll haunt you so hard your grandchildren will need exorcisms."

"Northeast quadrant showing activity," Camden reports. "Multiple heat signatures around the containers."

It's obvious that Camden can't hear the conversation between me and the guys, or I'm sure I would have heard a smart ass comment or two by now about getting myself killed.

I steer Oliver down a narrow passage between two rows of containers, deliberately taking a zigzagging path that would make sense for lost drunk kids but also keeps us out of direct sightlines of anyone watching the main pathways.

"Perimeter established," Hudson confirms in my ear. "We're closing the circle. ETA three minutes to your position. Do not engage until we're in place."

"Wouldn't dream of it," I reply sweetly, loud enough that Oliver raises an eyebrow.

"Is there someone else here?" he whispers, playing his part but genuinely confused.

I tap my ear subtly, and understanding dawns on his face. He nods, continuing our charade with renewed enthusiasm, wrapping his arm more securely around my waist as we stagger forward.

The sounds of activity grow louder as we approach the northeast section—men's voices, the clang of metal, the low rumble of engines. I mentally catalog each noise, building a picture of what we're walking into. Whoever is behind this didn't expect company tonight. They think they're operating under cover of darkness, safe from prying eyes.

I hope they've gotten comfortable in that assumption. Complacency makes people careless.

"I think I hear music!" I exclaim loudly as we round the final corner, clinging to Oliver's arm. "See? I told you we were going the right way!"

The scene before us is exactly what I feared. Our shipping area is alive with activity—men in black clothing and balaclavas moving between containers. A freshly arrived shipment sits open, its contents being transferred to two boats moored at the small dock adjacent to our warehouse. The boats explain how they've been bypassing our security—coming in by water instead of through the main gates.

I press my lips to Oliver's ear as if whispering something flirty, using the moment to murmur into my mic. "Look at all those helpful workers moving our party favors to those pretty boats. At least a dozen friends with toys. Jax should have said it was a costume party."

"Fuck," Kai hisses in my ear. "That's the premium stock for the opening."

"Hold position," Hudson orders. "We're almost in place."

I scan the area, looking for whoever might be in charge, when Oliver stumbles deliberately, sending us both tumbling against a container with a loud clang. My heart stops as several heads turn in our direction.

"Shit, sorry babe," Oliver slurs loudly, playing his part. "Told you those last shots were a bad idea."

I giggle, clinging to him and trying not to be distracted by the muscles under my hands while positioning myself to reach the knife at my thigh if needed. "You're such a lightweight!"

For a moment, I think we might pull it off—just two drunk kids who took a wrong turn. But then one of the men breaks away from the group, his hand moving to his waistband as he approaches.

"Hey! You two! What the fuck are you doing here?"

I stumble forward, putting myself slightly in front of Oliver as he shrinks back. "Oh my god, is this not the rave? Jax said it was by the water and there'd be boats and—" I break off, squinting dramatically at the man. "Wait, this doesn't look like a party."

"You need to leave. Now." The man's voice is hard, his hand still hovering near what I'm certain is a concealed weapon.

"Thirty seconds," Hudson's says in my ear. "Stall."

I pout dramatically at the masked man. "But we came all this way! And Jax said there'd be molly, you know how tight those assholes in the city are about that stuff, and—"

"I said leave!" The man steps closer, and now I can clearly see the gun tucked into his waistband. Behind him, the others have stopped working, their attention now focused on us.

"Ten seconds," Rev's voice promises in my ear.

I'm calculating our chances—whether to maintain the charade or drop it and go for my weapons—when the decision is made for me. A second man approaches, this one already holding his gun at his side.

"Who the fuck are they?" he demands, gesturing at us with the weapon.

"Just some kids looking for a party," the first man replies, his tone dismissive. "I'm handling it."

The second man steps closer, studying us with narrowed eyes. "How'd they get past security?"

A chill runs down my spine. That's a very good question—one that suggests they know exactly what security measures should have stopped us. Which means they know our protocols.

"In position," Hudson's voice confirms in my ear. "On your signal."

"Wait, wait," I slur, holding up my hands in what I hope looks like drunken panic. "We'll just go, okay? No harm, no—"

The cold press of metal against my forehead stops my words instantly. The second man has moved faster than I anticipated, his gun now digging into my skin. His eyes—the only part of his face visible through the balaclava—are cold, calculating.

"Too late for that," he says, voice muffled by the mask. "Grab them both."

Strong hands seize my arms from behind—a third man I didn't see approaching. I let my body go slack, playing up the terrified party girl while my mind races through escape scenarios. Oliver struggles briefly beside me before another masked figure subdues him.

They drag us forward, my boots scraping against concrete as I pretend to stumble. The gun never leaves my forehead, the pressure constant and threatening. I count our captors—four handling us directly, at least eight more by the containers and boats. Twelve against four of us, plus Oliver. Not great odds, but we've faced worse.

As we're pushed toward the dock, I realize this might actually work in our favor. Their leader must be waiting on one of those boats. If we can get close enough, we might identify whoever's behind all this.

"Please," I whimper, making my voice break. "We didn't see anything. We won't tell anyone."

"Shut up," growls the man behind me, fingers digging painfully into my bicep.

Through my earpiece, I hear Hudson's voice, tight with controlled fury: "We're moving in. Wait for my signal."

The wooden planks of the dock creak beneath our feet as they march us forward. Water laps gently against the pilings below, the sound almost peaceful compared to the hammering of my heart. The boats—sleek, expensive speedboats that could disappear quickly into the night—wait at the end of the pier, their engines idling.

I stumble deliberately, using the moment to assess my weapons. The knife at my thigh is closest, but the one at my back would be easier to reach with my arms restrained. I just need the right moment.

"Oliver," I whisper, making it sound like a frightened plea rather than a command. "Stay down when it happens."

His eyes flick to mine, wide but understanding. He gives me the barest of nods.

We're halfway down the dock now. The boats bob gently on the water, their sleek hulls gleaming in the moonlight. Through my earpiece, I can hear the soft sounds of movement as the twins and Hudson close in.

"Now," Hudson's voice commands.

I drop my weight suddenly, throwing the man holding me off-balance. As he stumbles, I twist, driving my elbow into his solar plexus. He doubles over with a grunt, and I use the momentum to pull the knife from my back.

Gunfire erupts around us as Hudson's team engages the men by the containers. The man with the gun whirls toward the sound, his weapon no longer pressed against my forehead.

"Oliver, hide!" I shout, slashing at the hand of another guard who reaches for me. Blood sprays across the wooden planks as my blade finds flesh.

The night explodes into chaos. I catch glimpses of the twins moving like shadows between the containers, their movements fluid and deadly. Hudson's team advances from multiple directions, boxing in the thieves.

I spin, blade flashing, as another masked man charges me. He's fast, but I'm faster, ducking under his wild swing and driving my knife into the soft spot beneath his ribs. He collapses with a wet gurgle.

"Oliver, stay down!" I yell again when I spot him crouched behind a stack of ropes, his eyes wide with something that looks almost like exhilaration.

A bullet whizzes past my ear, too close for comfort. I drop and roll, coming up with my second knife in hand. Three men are retreating toward the boats, firing wildly to cover their escape. I recognize the opportunity—if they get away, we lose our chance to find out who's behind this.

I sprint after them, dodging between bullets, aware that I'm exposing myself but unwilling to let them escape. One of the men turns, taking aim directly at me. Time seems to slow as I register the barrel pointed at my chest, too far to reach him before he pulls the trigger.

Then something—someone—barrels into me from the side, knocking me off my feet. Oliver. He's tackled me out of the bullet's path, his body covering mine as we hit the dock hard.

"Stay down!" I hiss, trying to push him off me, but he's already scrambling to his feet.

"They're getting away!" he shouts, and before I can stop him, he's running toward the men at the boat.

"Oliver, no!" I scream, lunging after him.

The world narrows to this single moment—Oliver charging forward, unarmed, as the men by the boat turn in unison. Their weapons rise. The sound of gunfire is deafening.

I watch in horror as Oliver's body jerks with the impact of the first bullet. Then another. And another. At least five shots, center mass. His momentum carries him forward two more steps before he staggers, his body turning half way as though instinctively trying to protect itself too late.

Our eyes meet across the distance. His are wide with shock, mouth forming a perfect O of surprise. Then he topples backward, his body arcing gracefully—a dancer's fall—before disappearing off the edge of the dock with a splash.

"No!" The scream tears from my throat as I race to where he fell. The dark water below reveals nothing—no movement, no body, just the gentle ripple of disturbed water already fading.

Rage, white-hot and all-consuming, erupts through me. I turn toward the men who shot him, my vision tunneling until all I see are targets. The knife leaves my hand before I consciously decide to throw it, burying itself in the throat of the nearest shooter. He drops, clutching at the blade, blood spurting between his fingers.

The boats' engines roar louder as the remaining men try to flee. I grab the fallen man's gun, taking aim at the pilot of the nearest vessel. The recoil vibrates up my arm as I empty the magazine, satisfaction blooming as the windshield shatters and the driver slumps over the controls. The boat veers wildly, crashing into the dock with a splintering of wood and fiberglass.

"Rylan!" Hudson's voice cuts through the fog of my rage. He appears beside me, his own weapon raised as he scans for threats. "Are you hit?"

I shake my head, unable to form words past the knot in my throat. My eyes remain fixed on the spot where Oliver disappeared, searching desperately for any sign of movement in the black water.

"He's gone," Hudson says, following my gaze. "The current's too strong."

"We have to find him," I insist, my voice breaking. "He might still be—"

"We need to secure the area first," Hudson cuts me off, his hand gripping my arm. "There could be more of them."

The rational part of my brain knows he's right, but everything in me rebels against leaving Oliver to the cold, dark water. He was trying to protect me. He took those bullets because of me.

"We got one," Kai's voice calls from behind us. "Alive. The rest are dead or escaped on the second boat."

I turn to see Kai dragging a struggling man across the dock, blood streaming from a gash in the captive's forehead. Rev follows close behind, his expression grim as he takes in the carnage.

"Oliver?" Rev asks, his eyes meeting mine.

I shake my head, gesturing helplessly toward the water. "He—they shot him. He fell in."

Rev's jaw tightens. Without a word, he strips off his jacket and boots, then dives cleanly into the water where Oliver disappeared. Kai shoves our captive to his knees, pressing a gun to the back of his head to ensure compliance, before turning his attention to me.

"You okay, gorgeous?" he asks, his eyes scanning me for injuries.

"I'm fine," I reply automatically, though I'm anything but. The image of Oliver's wide, shocked eyes as the bullets hit him plays on repeat in my mind. "He was trying to help me."

Hudson's hand comes to rest on the small of my back, a solid, grounding pressure. "He made his choice," he says quietly. "A brave one, and we will forever be grateful to him."

I want to rage at him, to scream that it shouldn't have happened, that we should have protected him better. But the words die in my throat as Rev resurfaces, gasping for air.

"Nothing," he calls, treading water. "Current's already taken him. It's too dark to see."

My heart sinks. Even if by some miracle Oliver survived the gunshots, the cold water and strong current would finish what the bullets started. He's gone.

I need a distraction. I turn my attention to our captive, cold fury replacing the shock. This man—this piece of human garbage—has answers. And I'm going to extract every last one of them, no matter what it takes.

"Take him to the warehouse," I order, my voice steady despite the storm raging inside me. "I want to know everything. Who they're working for, how they knew our security protocols, all of it."

Hudson studies my face for a long moment before nodding. "We'll get answers," he promises, his voice low and dangerous. "For Oliver."

"For Oliver," I repeat, the name tasting like ash in my mouth.

As Hudson's men secure the area and begin the cleanup, I stand at the edge of the dock, staring into the black water that claimed our dancer. I should feel guilty—he died trying to protect me, after all. But all I feel is a cold, calculating rage. Whoever is behind this has just made their final mistake.

They thought they could break us by destroying what we've built. Instead, they've reawakened something far more dangerous: a devil out for revenge.

"We've got work to do," I say finally, turning away from the water. "And someone is going to pay."

Chapter 18

Kai

The warehouse feels like a sauna with the metallic tang of blood hanging heavy in the air. I lean against the wall, watching Ry work with a precision that's both terrifying and beautiful. The look in her eyes is wild, unhinged in a way I haven't seen since Dead Devil's Night two years ago.

Our captive whimpers as she circles him, her knife dancing between her fingers. She's been at this for hours now, methodically taking him apart piece by small piece. His face is barely recognizable beneath the blood and swelling, his shirt in tatters, skin a canvas of her rage.

"One more time," she says, her voice deceptively soft. "Who hired you?"

"I told you," he sobs, words slurring through broken teeth. "Just a guy. Called himself Bren Cade. Paid cash. I never saw his face."

Ry sighs, as if disappointed in a child who keeps making the same mistake. Then she presses the tip of her blade against his eyelid, just enough pressure to dimple the skin without breaking it.

"I don't believe you," she whispers.

I shift my weight, adjusting myself discreetly. I really shouldn't be rock hard watching her like this, but fuck if her crazy doesn't turn me on. Always has. The way she moves when she's like this—all deadly grace and controlled fury—makes my blood burn.

Rev catches my eye from across the room, the ghost of a smirk playing on his lips. He knows exactly what I'm feeling. He's probably in the same state.

"Please," the man begs, blood bubbling from his lips. "I swear I don't know anything else."

I didn't realize how close Ry had gotten to the puppy in such a short time, but watching her now, it makes perfect sense. She saw something of herself in him—that same desperate need to belong, to matter. Now he's gone, and she's channeling all that grief into the man strapped to the chair before her.

"I think," she says, pressing just a fraction harder until a bead of blood wells up beneath her blade, "that you're holding out on me."

The man screams, the sound bouncing off concrete walls as Ry makes another precise cut along his collarbone. Not deep enough to kill, just enough to maximize pain. The manic energy just below her surface threatens to break through with every slice.

Camden stands by the door, his face carefully neutral, but I catch him flinching every time the captive screams. He's been watching for hours, probably wondering when one of us will step in and stop her. Earlier, he actually asked Rev if he was going to control her. Rev just gave him a bland look and asked, "Why would I?"

The memory almost makes me laugh. Camden has seriously underestimated our girl if he thinks we'd ever try to leash her fury. We've learned long ago that Ry is at her most magnificent when she's unleashed.

Our captive jerks against his restraints, a strangled sob escaping him."Please," he begs, "I don't know anything else. I swear to god."

"God isn't here," Ry whispers, leaning in close. "Just me."

I glance at the clock on the wall and shudder. It's past midnight—officially Dead Devil's Night. Before we took over tonight would be the night when all the monsters come out to play, when the city descends into its annual chaos of violence and mayhem. The night that made us what we are.

"We're running out of time," I say, loud enough for Ry to hear.

She doesn't acknowledge me, too focused on her prey. We've been at this since we brought him back from the docks, and while he's given up some information, I'm not convinced it's enough to matter. Whoever is targeting us is smart—too smart to leave an obvious trail. They've built layers to safeguard themselves. This guy we're torturing likely doesn't know anything beyond the man who hired him. But what bothers me most is how our attackers knew all the ins and outs of our operation. The security protocols, the shipment schedules, the weak points in our defenses. That kind of information only comes from the inside.

If I had to guess, the guy who hired this poor bastard won't know more than whoever hired him, and so forth up the chain. But I guess we have to start somewhere, right?

But Ry isn't thinking clearly. She's running on rage and grief, determined to make someone pay for Oliver's death. I understand. I do. But I'm also worried about what happens when she burns through that rage and has nothing left.

Hudson left a while ago to personally hunt down the guy our captive gave up during Ry's "interrogation." She insisted it be him or me or Rev who went, but there was no way in hell Rev and I were going to leave her like this. Not when she's balanced on the knife-edge of control.

The captive screams again as Ry makes another precise cut, and I see Camden flinch once more. Hudson really needs to reevaluate who he has as his second.

"Please," our captive gasps, blood bubbling from his split lip. "I've told you everything I know. I gave you the only name I know and the warehouse on Fifteenth where we were supposed to deliver what we stole."

Ry steps back, wiping the blade clean on a rag as she considers his words. "And who would you have delivered it to?"

"I don't know!" he wails. "I swear to god, I don't know!"

"But you've heard things," she presses, her voice dangerously soft. "Rumors. Whispers. Tell me what people are saying."

He hesitates, his one good eye darting between Ry and the door as if weighing his options.

"You're not leaving here," she informs him calmly. "But how you leave is up to you. In a body bag, or in pieces. Your choice."

Something in her voice must convince him because he swallows hard and nods.

"There's talk," he begins, voice trembling, "on the streets. People saying this year's Dead Devil's Night will be different. That it'll be returned to the way it used to be. That something will happen at the new club to kick it off."

Before we took control, Dead Devil's Night was a nightmare—a purge where the worst elements of the city ran free, where murder and rape and torture were just part of the celebration. We changed that, imposed our own order on the chaos. Made rules. Consequences.

"Who's saying this?" Rev asks, stepping closer.

The man licks his bloody lips. "Everyone. It's spreading through the ranks. People who've been waiting for the old days to come back. When there were no rules, when it was every man for himself."

"And who," Ry asks, her knife tracing idle patterns in the air, "is going to make this happen?"

The captive's eye widens, fear making him hesitate again. Ry sighs dramatically, then plunges her knife into his thigh. His scream echoes off the walls as she twists the blade.

"I asked you a question," she says pleasantly.

"Silas!" he screams. "They're saying Silas is back! That he's going to bring back the true Dead Devil's Night!"

We all freeze at that name. I feel like someone's dumped a bucket of ice water down my spine. Beside me, Rev has gone completely still, his face a perfect mask of control that doesn't fool me for a second. I can feel the rage radiating off him in waves.

"Silas," Ry repeats, her voice eerily calm.

The man nods frantically. "That's what they're saying. That he's been planning his return for years. Waiting for the right moment to take back what's his."

There's no way. No fucking way that Silas is back. Our father—if you could call that monster a father—is dead. Rev and I killed him ourselves two years ago. I remember the way his blood felt on my hands, the sound he made when Rev cut his throat. The satisfaction of watching the light fade from his eyes and knowing he couldn't return to hurt us.

"You're lying," I say, pushing off the wall and approaching the chair. "Silas is dead."

"I'm just telling you what people are saying!" he protests, shrinking back as far as his restraints will allow. "I don't know if it's true! Please, I'm just repeating what I heard!"

The door to the warehouse slams open, cutting off whatever bullshit our captive is about to spew next. Hudson strides in, his expression grim and posture rigid—the way he gets when things have gone sideways. Blood spatters his jacket, none of it his from what I can tell. His eyes lock with Ry's immediately, a silent conversation passing between them.

"Well?" Ry asks.

Hudson's jaw tightens. "Camden," he says instead of answering her, "finish this." He nods toward our bloody captive.

Camden straightens, already pulling his sidearm. "Yes, sir."

"Wait," Ry protests, stepping between Camden and the captive. "I'm not done with him."

Hudson's hand wraps gently around her upper arm. "Yes, you are. We need to talk." His voice drops lower as he adds, "All four of us. Now."

Something in his tone makes her relent. She tosses her bloody knife onto the metal table with a clatter, then follows as Hudson leads her toward the small office at the back of the warehouse. Rev and I exchange glances before falling in step behind them.

The office is barely more than a closet—a desk, a few chairs, and walls thin enough that we'll hear the gunshot when Camden executes our captive. Hudson closes the door behind us, then runs a hand through his hair, leaving streaks of someone else's blood in the dark strands.

"Bren Cade is dead," he announces without preamble. "Someone got to him before I did. Professional hit—two to the chest, one to the head. Whoever did it knew exactly what they were doing."

"Fuck," Rev mutters, leaning against the wall.

"The warehouse on Fifteenth?" Ry asks, her voice unnervingly calm.

Hudson shakes his head. "Empty. Cleared out. Not a fingerprint, not a shell casing, nothing. Whoever we're dealing with is thorough."

I slam my fist into the desk, sending papers scattering. "So we've got nothing. Again." The frustration burns in my chest, made worse by the ghost of a name that shouldn't be possible. Silas. Just thinking it makes bile rise in my throat.

"Sixteen hours until the Playground opens," Hudson says, checking his watch. "Whatever they're planning, it'll happen there."

Ry says nothing for a long moment, her face unreadable as she stares at a point somewhere past Hudson's shoulder. When she finally speaks, her voice has that deadly calm that always precedes her most vicious moments.

"Fine," she says with a casual shrug that doesn't match the cold fury in her eyes. "Let them come."

Rev pushes off the wall, moving closer to her. "Ry—"

"No," she cuts him off. "We've been chasing shadows for days. Let's stop running and let them come to us. We know the battlefield now. We know when they'll strike."

"I can increase security at all properties," Hudson offers. "Double the men at the Playground, put snipers on the surrounding buildings—"

"No," Ry interrupts again, and now I see the plan forming behind her eyes. "Don't change anything. Don't show them we're scrambling. We rule this fucking city, and we're not going to roll over and show our belly for someone pretending to be a dead man."

The gunshot from the main floor punctuates her words, marking the end of our captive. None of us flinch.

"You want to use the Playground opening as bait," I realize, a slow smile spreading across my face. "Let them think we're vulnerable."

She nods, a matching smile curving her lips. "It's about time they knew who really rules this city. I'm not running anymore. Not from ghosts, not from shadows." She looks between the three of us, her eyes gleaming with that beautiful madness I love so much. "We're going into Dead Devil's Night fully fucking armed. And if the Devil himself shows up looking for a fight, we'll send him back to hell wearing his balls as a necklace."

Rev laughs, the sound dark and appreciative. "That's my girl."

Hudson studies her face, something like admiration flickering in his eyes. "It's risky," he says finally. "But it could work. Draw them out on our terms, on our territory."

"Exactly," Ry agrees. "We've been reacting. It's time to force their hand."

The second gunshot makes us all turn toward the door. Camden must be making sure our captive is really dead. Thorough, at least.

"What about Oliver?" I ask quietly, watching Ry's face closely.

Pain flashes across her features before she locks it down. "We need to find his body," she says, voice tight. "Give him a proper burial. He deserves that much."

"He saved your life," Hudson says softly. "That means something."

Ry nods, a muscle jumping in her jaw. "It means everything. And whoever is behind this will pay for taking him. For taking all of it." She straightens, rolling her shoulders back. "But first, we have a club to open."

The door opens and Camden steps in, his expression carefully professional despite the blood spatter on his sleeve. "It's done," he reports. "Clean-up crew is on the way."

"Good," Hudson says. "Have them be thorough. Then I want you to coordinate with the team at the Playground. Business as usual, but I want eyes on everyone who enters that club."

Camden nods and retreats, closing the door behind him.

"So what now?" Rev asks, cracking his knuckles. "We just wait?"

"We prepare," Ry corrects. "We rest. We get ready for war." She moves to the small window, staring out at the city lights in the distance. "And tomorrow, we remind this city why they call us the current devils."

I cross to her, wrapping my arms around her waist from behind. Rev joins us, his hand sliding into her hair, grounding her between us. After a moment, Hudson steps closer too, not quite touching but part of our circle nonetheless.

"Whatever happens," I murmur against her ear, "we face it together."

She leans back into me, her body finally relaxing slightly. "Always," she whispers.

The night stretches before us, full of shadows and ghosts and impossible names. But for the first time since this all began, I feel like we're finding our footing again. Whatever comes for us, they'll find us ready.

And if by some miracle it really is Silas somehow back from the dead? Well, I'll just enjoy killing him a second time.

Chapter 19

Rylan

THE DAY OF THE Playground's opening passes in a blur of preparations and contingency plans. After the warehouse, we'd grabbed a few hours of sleep before diving headfirst into finalizing every detail for tonight. Hudson's men have been discreetly armed and stationed throughout the club, their weapons concealed but ready. The twins have spent the day memorizing every exit, every hiding spot, every potential ambush point. And I've been everywhere at once, overseeing it all while maintaining the facade that nothing is wrong.

Replacing Oliver proves more challenging than expected. Not just because of the physical skills required, but because every time I see the aerial apparatus, I remember his body jerking with the impact of bullets before disappearing into dark water. Stella, suggests another dancer named Malik who can handle the routine with minimal practice. I approve without really seeing him, too distracted by the memory of Oliver's wide, shocked eyes.

"He'll be fine," Stella assures me, mistaking my distraction for concern about the performance. "Malik's been understudy for weeks."

I nod, forcing myself to focus. "Make sure he understands the importance of tonight. No mistakes."

As the day wears on, the tension builds. We've set our trap, baited it with ourselves, and now we wait for our enemies to spring it. The thought should terrify me, but instead, I feel eerily calm. After days of reacting to shadows, it's a relief to finally have a plan.

By eight o'clock, we are back at the apartment to prepare. I stand before the full-length mirror, my body still damp from the shower, and begin the ritual of arming myself.

First, the basics. Black lingerie, practical but still laced with enough detail to make me feel like myself. Then the leather corset, tight enough to hold weapons but not so constrictive that I can't move. I lace it methodically, my fingers working on muscle memory while my mind runs through scenarios for the night ahead.

The fitted black pants come next, hugging my curves but stretchy enough for fighting if necessary. I slide knives into hidden sheaths at my lower back, along my ribs, and my hips. A garrote wire disguised as a bracelet circles my wrist. Small throwing knives slide into my boots.

I'm applying the finishing touches—dark eyeshadow, blood-red lips, teal hair pulled back severely from my face—when I sense him rather than hear him. Rev stands in the doorway, watching me with an intensity that would unnerve anyone else.

"You look ready for war," he says, voice low and appreciative.

"That's the idea." I meet his eyes in the mirror. "How's security?"

"In place. If anyone tries anything, we'll be ready." He pushes off from the doorframe and approaches, his reflection growing larger in my mirror. "But that's not what I came to talk about."

I turn to face him, raising an eyebrow. "Oh?"

Rev steps closer, until I can feel the heat radiating from his body. His hands come up to frame my face, thumbs brushing gently across my cheekbones. The tenderness of the gesture contrasts sharply with the weapons strapped to both our bodies.

"Be careful tonight," he says, his voice dropping to a near-whisper. "I know you, little bit. I know you'll throw yourself into danger without a second thought if you think it'll protect what's ours. But remember that we need you."

I start to make a flippant remark, to brush off his concern with bravado, but the intensity in his eyes stops me. Instead, I lean into his touch, allowing myself this moment of vulnerability before the storm.

"I'll be careful," I promise.

He shakes his head slightly, not satisfied. "Promise me you won't take unnecessary risks. That you'll let us protect you as much as you protect us."

"Rev—"

"Promise me," he insists, pressing his forehead against mine. "We can't lose you again, little bit. Not after last time."

The pain in his voice reaches something deep inside me. I know what he's remembering—the night Silas nearly destroyed us all. The night I almost died.

"I promise," I whisper, meaning it despite the danger I know lies ahead. "We face it together. All of us."

He kisses me then, deep and claiming, like he's trying to imprint himself on my soul. I surrender to it, letting the connection ground me, remind me what I'm fighting for.

When we break apart, the warrior has returned to his eyes. "Let's go remind this city who rules it."

The ride to the Playground passes in tense silence. Hudson drives, his knuckles white on the steering wheel. Kai sits in the passenger seat, unusually quiet. Rev and I occupy the back, our hands linked between us.

By the time we arrive at the club, the transformation is complete. I've locked away the vulnerability, the fear, the grief. My face is a mask of cold confidence as we enter through the rear entrance.

"Showtime," I murmur, and the twins nod in unison.

Hudson peels off to check in with his security team one last time, while we make our way to the VIP mezzanine that overlooks the main floor. From this vantage point, we can see everything—the bar areas, the dance floor, the performance spaces. The perfect place to spot trouble before it finds us.

At precisely ten o'clock, the doors open, and the crowd streams in. The Devil's Playground comes alive in a sensory overload of lights, smoke, and sound. The Arabian Nights theme transforms the space into a fantastical realm of luxury and excess. Silk curtains shimmer down from the mezzanine, creating the illusion of tents in a desert oasis. Dancers twist in elevated cages, their bodies painted gold and draped in strate-gically placed jewels. The lighting shifts constantly, bathing everything in rich teals, deep blues, and warm golds.

"Impressive," Kai murmurs beside me, his eyes tracking the flow of guests. "No one would guess we've been under attack for days."

He's right. The club is perfect—a testament to our power and resilience. Guests from every stratum of society fill the space, from known criminals to politicians to celebrities, all mingling under the illusion of civility that our rule provides. They're drawn to the danger, to the edge of chaos we control, like moths to flame.

Hudson rejoins us, his tall frame instantly recognizable as he moves through the crowd. He's dressed in black from head to toe, somehow managing to look both formal and ready for com-bat. His eyes meet mine across the distance, a silent question that I answer with a slight nod. All good. So far.

He makes his way up to the mezzanine, positioning himself slightly behind me. "Security is running smoothly," he reports. "Camden has the crowd flow under control. No red flags yet."

"Early still," Rev comments, his gaze never stopping its con-stant sweep of the club below.

Another hour passes, I force myself to circulate, to play my role as one of the gracious hosts. Hudson remains my shadow, never more than a few steps behind me. The twins work the crowd separately, their identical faces causing the usual dou-ble-takes and whispers. To most of the city, the Draven twins are myths, dangerous legends rarely seen together in public. Tonight, they're making an exception, a show of force disguised as celebration.

The night progresses without incident. The crowd grows larger, louder, more intoxicated. The music pulses through the floor, vibrating up through my boots. Dancers perform increasingly elaborate routines. Drinks flow freely. By all appearances, the opening is a spectacular success.

But beneath the surface, tension coils like a serpent. My nerves are strung tight, anticipating an attack that hasn't yet materialized. Hudson's men report nothing suspicious. The twins find no threats among the guests. It's all going too smoothly, and that makes me more uneasy than any obvious danger.

"Midnight," Hudson murmurs behind me, checking his watch.

I nod, scanning the crowd below. It's the witching hour, the true height of Dead Devil's Night. The moment when—

The club plunges into absolute darkness.

The music cuts off abruptly, leaving a vacuum immediately filled by confused murmurs that quickly escalate to frightened shouts. The darkness is complete, oppressive—even the emergency lights haven't activated. This isn't a simple power failure.

"Hudson," I hiss, reaching out blindly. His hand finds mine instantly, steady and reassuring.

"Stay close," he orders, his voice tight with controlled tension.

Screams erupt from the dance floor as panic spreads through the crowd. My other hand moves to the knife at my back, fingers closing around the familiar handle.

Then, suddenly, a single spotlight cuts through the darkness, illuminating the central performance platform. The crowd's panic subsides to confused murmurs as Malik appears in the beam of light, his body painted gold, suspended from silk curtains that cascade from the ceiling.

Music begins again—not the pulsing club beats from before, but something haunting and ethereal. Malik's body twists gracefully through the silks, his movements fluid and precise.

I watch as Malik performs Oliver's aerial routine, his body twisting gracefully through the silk curtains suspended from the ceiling. He's good—very good—but not Oliver. The thought sends a pang through my chest that I quickly suppress. There will be time for grief later. Tonight is about survival.

But something's wrong. This isn't how we planned it. This isn't the way we had it all set up and what had been checked over and over again. The lights were never meant to go completely dark, and more than just the central spotlight should have come back up for the performance.

I scan the rest of the club, my eyes now adjusted enough to make out vague silhouettes in the darkness. My heartbeat accelerates as instinct screams danger.

Something is *very* wrong.

I turn to where Hudson stands beside me, the realization striking like a knife to the gut.

"Where are Rev and Kai?" I hiss, gripping his arm so tightly my knuckles whiten. My eyes dart frantically across the darkened club, searching for the familiar silhouettes of the twins. "Hudson, where the fuck are they?"

His head snaps toward me, then he scans the club. The muscle in his jaw tightens as he realizes what I already know—they're gone.

THE MOMENT THE LIGHTS cut out, I feel the shift in the air. Years of surviving have honed my instincts to razor sharpness—this isn't part of the plan.

"Kai," I mutter, immediately reaching for my brother in the darkness. His fingers brush against mine, a silent confirmation that we're thinking the same thing.

"Gentlemen," Camden's voice materializes beside us, unnervingly calm amid the rising chaos. "Security protocol Blackout is now in effect. I need you to come with me immediately."

"Where's Ry?" I demand, already scanning the darkness for her silhouette.

"Hudson has her," Camden assures me, his hand firm on my shoulder. "He's taking her to the designated meeting point. We need to move now."

Something feels off, but with the club descending into panic and the spotlight suddenly illuminating the performer, I can't afford to hesitate. If there's an attack coming, we need to regroup.

"This way," Camden urges, guiding us toward the staff exit at the back of the VIP section. "My team is securing the club. The patrons will be fine."

Kai and I exchange a glance, a silent conversation passing between us. We've known Camden for years—he's Hudson's right hand, practically family. If he says this is protocol, we follow.

We move swiftly through the darkness, Camden leading us through service corridors I recognize from the building plans. The sounds of the panicked crowd fade behind us as we push through an emergency exit into the alley behind the club.

The night air hits my face, cool compared to the heat of bodies packed inside. The alley is dimly lit by the ambient glow from the club's exterior lights and the distant neon of the city skyline. Camden's SUV sits idling at the end of the narrow passage, its dark outline barely visible.

"Where's the rest of your team?" I ask, the unease growing stronger with each step toward the vehicle.

"Securing the perimeter," Camden replies, his pace quickening. "We need to get to the safe house before they make their move."

"Who's 'they'?" Kai demands, his voice sharp with suspicion. "What exactly are we dealing with here, Camden?"

Camden reaches the SUV and pulls open the rear door. "Get in. I'll brief you on the way."

My instincts are screaming now, but before I can act on them, I hear the softest whisper of movement behind us. I start to turn, reaching for the knife at my belt—

Pain explodes at the base of my skull. My vision splinters into fragments of light and shadow as my knees buckle beneath me. I hear Kai grunt beside me—he's been hit too.

I fight to stay conscious, to reach for my brother, but my limbs won't obey. The ground rushes up to meet me, rough asphalt scraping my palms as I try to push myself up, but my arms give out. The world spins, my senses dulling as Camden's boots appear in my narrowing field of vision. He crouches down, grabbing a fistful of my hair to lift my face toward his.

"You will listen to me now, won't you?" he sneers, his face twisted with contempt I've never seen him display before. "Not so powerful anymore."

I try to speak, to ask why, but my tongue feels swollen in my mouth. Blood trickles warm down the back of my neck from where I was struck. Through blurring vision, I see Kai face-down on the asphalt beside me, his body unnaturally still.

My brother. I need to reach him.

"Get them in the vehicle," Camden orders someone I can't see. "And make it quick. We need to be gone before Hudson realizes what's happening."

Rough hands grab me under the arms, dragging me toward the SUV. I struggle weakly, fighting to maintain conscious-ness, but it's like swimming through tar. My weapons are still on me—they haven't bothered to disarm us yet, which means they're either stupid or extremely confident.

Or they don't plan on us waking up again.

As darkness closes in, I hear footsteps approach and another voice—cold, emotionless, devoid of any human feeling—says, "Kill them quickly. No loose ends."

Camden's response fades as consciousness slips away from me, but I cling to one thought as the darkness claims me:

Rylan.

They've separated us from her. And that means whoever is behind this has just made their fatal mistake.

Because nothing on this earth is more dangerous than Rylan when someone takes what's hers.

Chapter 20

Rylan

"FIND THEM," I SNAP, already moving toward the hidden staircase that leads to the security room. "Now."

Hudson follows close behind, his body a solid wall between me and the panicked crowd as we navigate through the darkness. The music continues to play, the spotlight still focused on Malik's performance—a distraction, I now realize. A deliberate one.

We burst into the security room to find it empty. The bank of monitors shows nothing but static, the communications system dead. Hudson tries the backup generator switch—nothing.

"This was planned," he growls, slamming his fist against the console. "Whoever did this knew exactly what they were doing."

He pulls out his radio, trying to reach Camden. "Camden, do you copy? Camden!" Nothing but static. He tries again with the same result before hurling the useless device against the wall.

"Our radios are being jammed," he says, running a hand through his hair. "We're blind and deaf."

I reach for my phone, a cold calm settling over me as adrenaline clears the fog of panic from my mind. "Not completely."

Hudson watches as I unlock my phone and open an app that looks like a simple game. When I enter a specific code, it transforms into a tracking system.

"After what happened to us years ago," I explain, my voice steady despite the storm raging inside, "I made sure there was never a moment when I couldn't find them. The first thing I did after we took over was to get trackers."

I wave a hand in his direction, the rings on my fingers catching what little light filters into the room. "Do you think I always wear jewelry for appearances? Most serve a purpose." I twist one of the rings, revealing a hidden compartment. "I even have a tiny amount of poison in one. Hell, my bracelet is a garrote."

Understanding dawns on his face as I tap the screen, activating the tracking on the twins' rings. Two blinking dots appear, moving rapidly away from our location.

"They're heading east," I say, already moving toward the door. "Toward the industrial district."

Hudson grabs my arm. "Wait. We need backup."

I wrench free of his grip. "We don't have time. Whoever took them isn't going to wait while we round up people we can trust—which, by the way, seems to be a shrinking list." I head for the exit, not bothering to look back. "You can come with me or not, but I'm going after them."

I hear his muttered curse, then his footsteps following me. Good. I could use the backup, though I'd never admit it.

We slip out through a service entrance, avoiding the chaos of the main floor. The night air hits my face, cool against my flushed skin. Hudson's SUV is parked in the reserved section at the back of the club. I climb into the passenger seat without a word, eyes fixed on my phone as the dots continue to move across the city map.

Hudson slides behind the wheel, starting the engine with a low growl that matches his expression. "Where are they headed?"

"Keep going east," I direct, watching as the dots finally slow. "They've stopped. Some kind of warehouse on the waterfront."

Hudson drives like a man possessed, taking corners at speeds that would terrify anyone with a normal sense of self-preservation. I grip the door handle, not out of fear but impatience—even this breakneck pace feels too slow when the twins are in danger.

"Slow down," I say as we approach the warehouse district. "We need to be smart about this."

He eases off the accelerator, navigating the maze of abandoned buildings and storage facilities until we're a block away from the tracking signal. We park in the shadow of a derelict factory, weapons ready as we exit the vehicle.

"Four guards that I can see," Hudson murmurs, peering around the corner at our target. "Two at the main entrance, two patrolling the perimeter."

I nod, already calculating angles and approaches. "Take the perimeter guards. I'll handle the door."

We move in perfect sync, years of working together making words unnecessary. Hudson disappears into the shadows to circle around while I advance on the main entrance. The guards are masked but sloppy—too confident, too relaxed. Their first mistake.

I approach from their blind spot, knife in hand. The first guard doesn't even have time to turn before my blade slices across his throat, cutting off any sound he might have made. The second reaches for his weapon, but I'm faster, driving my knife up under his ribs and into his heart. He crumples without a sound.

Hudson reappears moments later, blood on his knuckles but otherwise untouched. "Clear," he says simply.

We enter the warehouse cautiously, staying low and using the stacks of crates for cover. The space is cavernous, most of it shrouded in darkness, but a pool of light at the center reveals a scene that makes my blood freeze in my veins.

Rev and Kai are bound to metal chairs, their faces bloody and bruised. Rev's right eye is swollen shut, blood trickling from a cut above his brow. Kai's lip is split, his normally perfect hair matted with crimson. They're conscious but dazed, heads lolling as they struggle to focus.

And pacing in front of them, a gun held casually in one hand, is Camden.

"—years of loyal service," he's saying, his voice echoing in the cavernous space. "Years of following orders, of doing your dirty work, and for what? To be treated like a fucking errand boy?"

He stops pacing to lean in close to Rev's face. "You never even saw me, did you? Never gave me a chance to prove what I could really do."

I signal to Hudson, pointing to a path that will circle around behind Camden. He nods, slipping away while I work my way closer, using the shadows and stacked crates for cover.

"I watched him play lapdog to a little girl," Camden continues, gesturing with the gun toward Kai. "Hudson—a fucking war hero—reduced to babysitting some skinny bitch with daddy issues because you two said so."

I clench my jaw so hard my teeth ache, but I force myself to stay focused, to keep moving silently toward my target.

"We could have ruled this city like kings," Camden rants, his voice rising with fervor. "Created real chaos, real power. Instead, you imposed order. Rules. Boundaries." He spits the last word like it's poison. "You tamed what should have been wild."

I'm close enough now to see the twins' eyes, to catch the moment they spot me moving in the shadows. Neither gives any sign, their expressions remaining carefully blank despite the recognition I see flicker across their faces.

"You have no idea what real power looks like," Camden continues, oblivious to my approach. "What it means to truly control a city. You're just playing at being devils, while I—"

"Oh my God, just shut up already," I say, driving my knife between his shoulder blades.

Camden howls, whirling with surprising speed despite the blade buried in his back. His gun comes up, but Hudson emerges from the shadows, tackling him to the ground.

"You treacherous bastard," Hudson snarls, his fist connecting with Camden's jaw with a sickening crunch. "I trusted you!"

I leave them grappling on the floor and rush to the twins, pulling another knife from my boot to cut their bindings.

"Hey, gorgeous," Kai mumbles, his voice thick with pain. "Took you long enough."

"Save your breath," I reply, sawing through the zip ties around his wrists. "Can you stand?"

He nods weakly as the restraints fall away. I move to Rev, whose eyes track me with slightly more clarity.

"You okay?" I ask, freeing his hands.

"Been better," he admits, wincing as he flexes his fingers to restore circulation. "Watch your back."

I turn just in time to see Camden throw Hudson off, scrambling for the gun that skittered across the floor during their struggle. Hudson lunges after him, but Camden reaches it first, swinging around with the weapon raised.

Time slows as I see his finger tighten on the trigger, the barrel aimed directly at my chest. I'm too close to dodge, too exposed to take cover. In that frozen moment, I have the absurd thought that at least I'll die with the twins free.

Then Hudson is there, throwing himself between me and the gun as Camden fires.

The sound is deafening in the enclosed space. Hudson jerks with the impact, stumbling back a step but somehow staying on his feet. For a heartbeat, I think maybe the bullet missed—but then I see the dark stain spreading across his shirt, and my world narrows to that single point of crimson.

"No!" The scream tears from my throat as Hudson drops to one knee, pressing a hand to his abdomen.

The twins move with synchronized precision despite their injuries. Kai lunges for Camden while Rev grabs the gun, twisting it from his grip with brutal efficiency. Camden fights back, but he's outnumbered and outmatched, even against injured opponents.

I rush to Hudson, catching him as he slumps further. My hands press against the wound, blood seeping between my fingers, hot and slick. "Stay with me," I order, my voice breaking. "Don't you dare die on me, old man."

He coughs, a thin line of blood appearing at the corner of his mouth. "Not planning on it," he manages, his eyes meeting mine with surprising clarity. "Just a flesh wound."

"Shut up," I snap, tears blurring my vision as I apply more pressure to the wound. "Just shut up and focus on breathing."

Behind me, I hear the sounds of the fight winding down—a grunt of pain, a thud of bodies hitting concrete, then silence. Footsteps approach, and Rev kneels beside me, his face grim as he assesses Hudson's injury.

"How bad?" he asks, already pulling off his shirt to create a makeshift pressure bandage.

"Bad enough," I reply, trying to keep my voice steady. "But he'll live if we get him help soon."

Rev nods, taking over the pressure on the wound while I pull out my phone to call for medical assistance. As I dial, Kai drags Camden over, the traitor's face bloody and swollen but still conscious.

"You want to finish him?" Kai asks, his voice cold with fury.

I look at Camden, at the man who betrayed us, who shot Hudson, who thought he could take what's ours. Rage boils up inside me, hot and demanding. I hand my phone to Rev and stand, drawing another knife from my boot.

Camden's eyes widen with fear, but then something shifts in his expression. I drive my blade into his chest, twisting it with a savage jerk. His scream echoes through the warehouse as I withdraw the knife, only to plunge it into his shoulder next. Blood sprays across my face, warm and metallic.

"It doesn't matter," he laughs maniacally through the pain, blood bubbling between his teeth, body twitching in spasms. "I'm not—I'm not the leader. Silas is the true devil. You think killing me ends this?" His eyes roll wildly, unfocused. "Silas will burn everything you love. You have no idea what's coming."

Chapter 21

Rylan

I DRIVE MY BLADE into his throat, twisting it viciously. His eyes widen, a gurgling sound replacing his manic laughter as blood fountains from the wound, coating my hands, my face, my chest in crimson. I twist the knife again, severing his windpipe completely, watching the light fade from his eyes as his body goes slack in Kai's grip.

"Drop him," I order, my voice sounding distant even to my own ears. "He's garbage."

Kai releases Camden's body, letting it crumple to the concrete floor like the worthless thing it is. I stare down at the corpse, at the blood pooling beneath it, at the vacant eyes still wide with shock. It doesn't feel like enough. Nothing would be enough for what he's done.

"Ry." Rev's voice cuts through my rage-filled haze. "Hudson needs help. Now."

I turn back to where Hudson lies, his breathing shallow, face ashen beneath his tan. Rev has fashioned a pressure bandage from his shirt, but blood is already soaking through it. Too much blood.

"The medical team is five minutes out," Kai says, checking his phone. "It's Dead Devil's Night—no emergency services running, but our people are close."

I kneel beside Hudson, taking his hand in my bloody one. His skin feels cold, clammy. His eyes flutter open at my touch, focusing on me with effort.

"You need to go," Rev says, his voice leaving no room for argument. "Head back to the apartment. It's not safe here."

"I'm not leaving him," I protest, gripping Hudson's hand tighter. "I'm not leaving any of you."

"Ry," Hudson whispers, his voice barely audible. "Go. Please."

"He's right," Rev insists, his hand on my shoulder. "We don't know who else Camden was working with, who else might be coming. Kai and I will stay with Hudson. The medical team knows what to do."

I shake my head, something primal and desperate clawing at my chest. "No. I can't—"

"You have to," Kai interrupts, his expression more serious than I've ever seen it. He shrugs out of his leather jacket and drapes it over my shoulders, the familiar weight and scent of him momentarily grounding me. His hands move to the pockets, and I feel the solid weight of metal as he slips a gun inside. "Take this. Anyone gets in your way, you shoot first, ask questions never."

"Take Hudson's car," Rev adds, pressing the keys into my palm. "Go straight to the apartment. No stops, no detours. Don't go through the Lair. Use the parking garage entrance."

"They'll be watching the main entrances," Kai explains, his voice tight with urgency. "The garage is secure, and you can take the private elevator straight up."

I look between them, then down at Hudson. His eyes have closed again, his breathing growing more labored. The rational part of me knows they're right—splitting up is tactically sound, and someone needs to secure our home base. But leaving them feels like tearing off a limb.

"Five minutes," I say finally, my voice hard with determination. "If the medical team isn't here in five minutes, I'm coming back with reinforcements."

Rev nods, relief flickering across his battered face. "They'll be here. Now go."

I lean down, pressing my lips to Hudson's forehead. "Don't you dare die," I murmur against his skin. "I haven't finished making you pay for choking me out."

Then I kiss Rev, hard and desperate, before turning to Kai and doing the same. "Keep him alive," I order. "Keep each other alive."

"Always do," Kai says with a ghost of his usual smirk.

Then I stand, forcing myself to turn away from the three men who have become my whole world. My family. My everything.

"I love you," I say, not looking back as I walk away, knowing if I see their faces I won't be able to leave. "All of you."

I hear Kai's voice behind me, soft but carrying in the cavernous space: "Go, Ry. We'll be right behind you."

The drive back to the Lair is a blur of neon lights and deserted streets. Dead Devil's Night has driven most sensible people indoors, leaving the city to predators and prey. Usually, I'd be reveling in the controlled chaos of our creation. Tonight, I just feel hollow.

Camden's words echo in my head as I navigate the empty streets. Silas is the true devil. You have no idea what's coming.

It's impossible. There's no way he could have survived.

And yet...

My hands tighten on the steering wheel, Hudson's blood still drying under my fingernails. What if we were wrong? What if somehow, Silas survived? The thought sends ice through my veins.

I force the thoughts away, focusing on the road ahead. It doesn't matter. Either way, they've made a fatal mistake. They've hurt what's mine. They've threatened my family.

Hudson is fighting for his life because of me. Because I didn't see the danger in time, didn't protect what's mine. The thought of losing him sends a spike of pain through my chest so intense I nearly swerve off the road.

When did he become so essential? When did this gruff, infuriating man work his way past my defenses to stand alongside the twins in my heart?

I don't have an answer, but I know with bone-deep certainty that I can't lose him. Not now. Not when I've just realized how much he matters.

By the time I reach the Lair, rage has crystallized into something cold and deadly inside me.

And I will burn the world to ash before I let anyone take them from me.

I pull into the underground parking garage beneath the Lair, the security gate recognizing the car's transponder and lifting automatically. The garage is eerily quiet as I park close to the private elevator that will take me directly to the apartment.

As I step out of the car, a wave of exhaustion hits me so hard I have to lean against the hood for support. The adrenaline that's been keeping me going is finally wearing off, leaving me shaky and light-headed.

I force myself to stand upright, to walk to the elevator with my head high even though there's no one to see my moment of weakness. The twins would be here soon with Hudson. Our medical team is the best money can buy—they've patched us up from worse. He'll be fine. They'll all be fine.

The elevator ascends silently as I lean against the mirrored wall, avoiding my reflection. I don't need to see the blood, the exhaustion, the fear I know is written across my face.

The doors slide open with a soft ping, revealing the familiar darkness of our home. I step into the apartment, not bothering with the lights. I know this space like I know my own body—could navigate it blindfolded if necessary.

My mind churns with plans and contingencies as I move through the darkened living area. We need to secure all properties, verify the loyalty of every member of our organization. If Camden betrayed us, others might have too. We need to find out how deep the corruption goes, who else might be working against us.

I'm halfway across the living room when a voice speaks from the darkness.

"Rough night?"

Every muscle in my body locks into place. The air vanishes from my lungs as though someone has punched me in the chest. That voice—impossible, familiar—reaches into my core and twists.

Time stops. The ground seems to vanish beneath my feet, leaving me floating in a void where nothing makes sense. I must be hallucinating from stress and exhaustion. He can't be here. He can't be alive.

My eyes strain against the darkness, finally making out a silhouette standing near the floor-to-ceiling windows that look out over the city. A tall, solid frame backlit by the ambient glow of the city lights.

"What's the matter?" the voice continues, a smile evident in its tone. "You look like you've seen a ghost."

I can't breathe. Can't move. Can't think past the roaring in my ears and the single, impossible thought circling my brain: He's here. He's alive.

My body feels disconnected, moving through molasses as the figure takes another step forward, still mostly shrouded in shadow.

"Did you miss me?"

The figure steps fully into the glow of the city lights stream-ing through the windows, and my breath catches in my throat. Oliver—alive, unharmed, pristine in a perfectly tailored suit—stands before me. Not floating face-down in the harbor, not riddled with bullets, but here in my apartment, looking at me with those familiar eyes that now hold something I never noticed before: cold calculation.

"Oliver?" I whisper, my voice betraying me with its tremor.

He smiles, that same boyish, eager smile that had made me trust him, and lifts a crystal tumbler filled with amber liquid to his lips. I recognize the glass—part of a set we keep for our most expensive bourbon. He takes a long, appreciative sip, savoring it as though we're at a casual social gathering rather than standing in the aftermath of betrayal and bloodshed.

"This is excellent," he comments, swirling the bourbon in his glass. "Your taste is impeccable, as always."

"You're dead," I manage. "I saw you get shot. You fell into the water."

He laughs, the sound nothing like the nervous chuckle I'd grown accustomed to. This laugh is confident, controlled—the laugh of someone who's exactly where they planned to be.

"A necessary performance," he says with a dismissive wave. "And quite convincing, apparently. The look on your face when I went into the water..." He makes a chef's kiss gesture with his free hand. "Perfection."

My mind races, trying to process this new reality. If Oliver is alive, if he staged his own death, then everything—absolutely everything—comes into question.

"Why?" I ask, buying time as I assess my options. I'm exhausted, covered in blood, emotionally drained. Not ideal conditions for a fight.

"Why?" he repeats, taking another leisurely sip of bourbon. "Because this is what I've been waiting for, Rylan. This night. This moment. Taking my rightful place."

"Your rightful place?" I echo, edging slightly to my left, positioning myself for a better angle.

"At the top," he says simply, gesturing to the apartment around us. "Where I belong."

"And where do I belong in this scenario?"

His eyes darken as they trail over me, lingering on the blood splattered across my skin. "With me, of course. Now that the twins are... disposed of... you belong to me."

Ice slides down my spine.

"Camden was quite enthusiastic about handling that particular task." He smiles, a predator's smile that transforms his face into something I barely recognize. "By now, they should be cooling on a warehouse floor. Hudson too, I imagine, judging by that blood and how he isn't hovering over you like a ghoul."

Rage wars inside me, but I keep my expression neutral. If he thinks they are dead, I have an advantage. Let him underestimate what he's dealing with.

"You've been playing us this whole time," I say, putting the pieces together. "The sabotage at the club, the fires, the overdoses—that was you?"

He inclines his head in acknowledgment. "Not personally, of course. I have people for that. Or, Silas does."

Something about his demeanor, his confidence—it's all wrong. This isn't the nervous dancer seeking approval. This is someone else entirely.

"Why did you use the name Silas?" I ask, it's now starting to click together in ways I don't want to believe.

His smile widens into something wicked as he raises the glass in a mock toast. "Well, that's because it's my real name," he says with a casual shrug. "Silas Oliver Holt."

Chapter 22

Rylan

The room seems to tilt beneath my feet. "That's impossible."

"Is it? Hudson can look all he likes at Oliver Hart and he'll only find what I wanted him to. But had he looked at Silas Oliver Holt, he would have found a completely different result." He laughs, the sound chilling. "You can't really be angry at Hudson for that. My relationship with my father was very well hidden."

My hands slip into the jacket, trying to come across as casual and non-threatening, I need more information. "Silas Holt is dead."

"No," he corrects, "my father is dead. Murdered by your precious twins." His expression hardens, something ugly flashing in his eyes. "I at least wanted to take after him, unlike the twins. I had started learning from him, you know, before they ruined it and killed him."

None of my research over two years ago mentioned that Silas had another son. But then there wasn't much to link the twins to him either.

"If you're who you say you are," I challenge, "why the elaborate charade? Why not just kill us all?"

"Where's the satisfaction in that?" He moves closer, and I have to force myself not to retreat. "I wanted you to know me. To trust me. To like me." His smile turns cruel. "And you did, didn't you? Poor, eager Oliver, so desperate to please. So useful."

I think of all the information he fed us that led us exactly where he wanted us to go. The sick feeling in my stomach intensifies.

"I've spent years planning this," he continues, his voice taking on a fervent quality that reminds me unnervingly of Silas himself. "Learning everything about you three. About how you stole what should have been my inheritance. My father was building an empire, and you—" he points at me accusingly, "—you helped them destroy it."

He's delusional. Or he only knows what information Silas fed him, because the empire was never Silas'... it was David's. But I doubt that matters.

Because I see it now—the family resemblance that was hidden beneath Oliver's carefully cultivated softness. The same bone structure, the same cold intensity in the eyes. How did I miss it?

"Your father was a monster, he deserved worse than the death we gave him," I say, my voice steady despite the storm raging inside me.

Oliver takes another step forward. His jaw twitches, a muscle pulsing beneath the skin as he attempts to school his features into something controlled. But his eyes betray him—cold fury burns there, turning them to shards of ice. "It doesn't matter now. The twins are dead. Hudson is dead. And you..." His eyes rake over me possessively. "You belong to me now."

I laugh, and even I can tell it sounds a little unhinged. The sound echoes through our apartment, bouncing off the walls like something feral and wounded.

"You stupid, stupid fool," I say, shaking my head as if I'm disappointed in a child. "You've got it all backward. I never belonged to the twins." I take a step toward him, watching his eyes narrow in confusion. "The twins belong to me. Always have. And you?" I smile, feeling my lips stretch too wide. "You're nothing but a pale imitation of a man who was already pathetic to begin with."

His face contorts with rage, fingers tightening around the crystal tumbler. "You bitch. After I'm done—"

The soft ping of the elevator behind him interrupts his tirade. His head whips toward the sound, body tensing as he realizes he might not be as in control as he thought.

In the mirrored glass behind him, I catch the reflection of three figures stepping out of the lift—Rev and Kai, supporting Hudson between them. Their faces register identical expressions of shock as they take in the scene.

I pull the gun from my pocket and fire once, the bullet catching him in the shoulder before I adjust my aim and shoot the glass behind him. The massive pane shatters into a million glittering pieces, the sound like a cascade of diamonds hitting marble.

Before he can recover from the shock of the bullet, I launch myself forward, driving my boot into his chest with every ounce of strength I have left. The impact sends him stumbling backward through the shattered wall, his eyes wide with disbelief as he realizes what's happening.

For one suspended moment, he hangs in the empty air, framed by the jagged edges of the broken glass, the lights of the city twinkling far below. Then gravity claims him, and he's gone—plummeting to the unforgiving concrete below.

I don't wait to hear the impact. Instead, I whirl toward the men behind me. "You're alive," I breathe, the gun dropping to the floor as relief washes through me like a tidal wave. "You're all alive."

"Told you we'd be right behind you," Kai says, his usual smirk struggling to form on his split lip.

The three of them look like hell. Rev's right eye is swollen nearly shut, purple bruising spreading across his cheekbone. Kai's split lip has started bleeding again, and there's a gash at his temple that's been hastily bandaged. But it's Hudson who makes my heart stutter in my chest. He's conscious, but barely, his face ashen beneath his tan. A fresh bandage is visible beneath his torn, blood-soaked shirt.

"You need a hospital," I say, rushing to Hudson's side as he sways dangerously between the twins.

"No hospitals," he growls, his voice weak but stubborn as ever. "Too dangerous."

"Our medical team patched him up at the warehouse," Rev explains, adjusting his grip to better support Hudson's weight. "We would have been here sooner, but this stubborn bastard insisted on coming with us rather than going to the safehouse."

"I'm fine," Hudson grunts. "Just a through-and-through. Missed anything vital."

"Refused anything but basic field dressing too," Kai adds, shooting Hudson a look of exasperated admiration. "No painkillers stronger than over-the-counter shit."

"I need to stay alert," Hudson argues, wincing as they help him to the couch. "Can't afford to be drugged up with everything that's happening."

"So you'd rather bleed out while fully conscious?" I snap, the fear I've been suppressing bubbling up as anger instead. "That's your brilliant plan?"

Hudson's eyes find mine, startlingly clear despite his condition. "Better than missing something important because I'm high as a kite."

I kneel beside him as Rev and Kai carefully lower him onto the couch. His breathing is shallow, each inhale clearly causing him pain.

"He also refused the IV," Rev says, his tone making it clear what he thinks of that decision. "Wouldn't let them put in the line."

"What?" I look up at Hudson incredulously. "You need fluids. You've lost too much blood."

"No needles," Hudson mutters, closing his eyes briefly as a wave of pain washes over him.

That's when it clicks, and despite everything—the trauma of the night, the betrayal, the violence—I feel my lips twitch with the beginning of a smile.

"Oh my God," I say, staring at him in disbelief. "You're afraid of needles?"

Hudson's eyes snap open, narrowing at me. "I'm not afraid of anything."

Kai snorts, wincing as the movement pulls at his split lip. "Tell that to the nurse whose hand you nearly broke when she tried to start the IV."

"I didn't—" Hudson starts to protest, then grimaces as the movement pulls at his wound.

"My big, bad security expert," I tease, relief making me giddy as I brush sweat-dampened hair from his forehead. "Fearless in the face of bullets and knives, but brought to his knees by a tiny needle." I shake my head in mock disbelief. "Your cock is pierced, for fuck's sake."

His eyes widen slightly, darting to the twins, who both smirk despite their injuries.

"That was different. I took a bullet for you," he reminds me, but there's no heat in his words. "A little respect would be nice."

"Oh, I respect you," I assure him, my voice softening as I take his hand in mine. "I respect the hell out of you, old man. But I'm still going to give you shit about this forever."

A ghost of a smile touches his lips before pain wipes it away. "Looking forward to it."

I look at the three of them—bruised, bloody, but alive. My family. My heart. The relief is so overwhelming I could drown in it.

Rev looks toward the now empty space in the glass wall and says, "Ummm so, what did we miss? Was I hallucinating or did I see you throw a not so dead Oliver out the window?"

"Technically I kicked him out, pun intended... Oliver was Silas's son," I tell them, the words tumbling out in a rush. "He orchestrated everything—the sabotage, Camden's betrayal, all of it. He's been playing us from the beginning."

"Not us," Hudson corrects, his voice stronger now. "Me. I should have seen it. Should have dug deeper."

I shake my head, sinking onto the couch beside him. "None of us saw it. He was good."

"Not good enough," Kai says with grim satisfaction. "Not anymore."

Rev shifts his weight, wincing slightly as he puts pressure on what must be an injured leg. "We need to sweep all the properties," he says, running a hand through his blood-matted hair. "Check every single employee, anyone who might have been working with Camden or Oliver—Silas—whatever the fuck his name was."

"Tomorrow," I say, suddenly overcome with bone-deep exhaustion and a fierce need to reclaim what's ours. "We can do all that tomorrow." I push myself up from the couch, my muscles protesting every movement. "It's still Dead Devil's Night, and I should go back to the Playground."

I walk across the room to retrieve the SUV keys I dropped during my confrontation with Oliver.

Kai raises an eyebrow, his split lip twisting into something between a grimace and a smirk as he takes in my appearance. "You're still covered in blood, gorgeous."

I look down at myself, at the crimson stains drying on my skin, at Camden's blood splattered across my chest and face. I shrug, a cold smile spreading across my face. "What better time to make a statement than covered in the blood of our enemies?"

Chapter 23

Rylan

THE DRIVE BACK TO the Playground is a blur of neon signs and empty streets. My city looks different tonight—not just because of Dead Devil's Night, but because for the first time in years, I'm seeing it with absolute clarity.

The SUV hums beneath us, Rev driving while I sit in the back with Hudson's head in my lap. His breathing is labored but steady, his eyes occasionally fluttering open to meet mine before pain forces them closed again. Kai rides shotgun, constantly checking his phone as reports filter in from our people across the city.

"Status update on Oliver?" I ask, gently stroking Hudson's hair.

"Definitely dead this time," Kai confirms, not looking up from his phone. "Our clean-up crew confirms he's a very messy stain on the pavement. They're handling it."

"Good." The word comes out colder than I intended, but I can't bring myself to care. Oliver—Silas—whatever he called himself, deserved worse than the quick death I gave him.

"And Camden's body?" I continue, needing to tie up all loose ends.

"Disposed of," Rev answers, his eyes meeting mine in the rearview mirror. "No trace left."

I nod, satisfied. "Any other problems?"

"Not tonight," Kai says with a grim smile. "Word's spreading fast about what happened. Nobody's stupid enough to make a move now."

As we approach the Playground, I can see the club is still in full swing despite the earlier chaos. Lights pulse in the darkness, and the bass from the music vibrates through the car windows as we pull up to the VIP entrance.

"Are you sure about this?" Rev asks, turning to look at me. "We could just go back home, deal with it tomorrow."

I shake my head, determination hardening in my chest. "No more shadows. No more hiding. It's time they knew exactly who they're dealing with."

Hudson stirs in my lap, his eyes opening with effort. "I'm coming in too," he says, his voice rough with pain.

"You can barely stand," I argue, though I know it's futile.

He meets my gaze, unwavering despite his pallor. "I'll stand next to you or die trying."

I should protest more, but the truth is, I want them all with me for this. My men. My family. My strength.

The moment we enter the club, Stella's face is a masterpiece of horror. Her eyes widen to almost comical proportions as she takes in my blood-splattered appearance, her gaze darting between me and the three battered men flanking me like avenging angels.

"What the actual fuck?" she hisses, rushing toward us as we enter through the back entrance. "I've been trying to reach you for hours! The whole place went dark, people were panicking, and then—" She stops short, finally registering the full extent of our injuries. "Is that... is all that blood yours?"

"Not mine," I reply, the ghost of a smile playing on my lips. "Not theirs either. At least, not most of it."

Her eyes land on Hudson, who's standing through sheer force of will, his face ashen. No pain medication, no rest—just a fresh field dressing and that insufferable stubbornness that makes me want to simultaneously slap him and kiss him.

"Jesus Christ, he needs a doctor," Stella whispers.

"Tell him that," I say dryly. "I've tried."

"I'm fine," Hudson grits out, the words becoming his mantra for the night. His hand presses against his side.

Stella looks like she wants to argue, but something in my expression must warn her off. Instead, she turns back to me, switching to business mode with the adaptability that makes her invaluable.

"The club is still packed," she reports. "Most people thought the earlier glitch was part of the show, especially when that spotlight came on for Malik's performance. The important people are all still here—mayor, police commissioner, district attorney, all the key players."

"Who's running the lights and sound right now?"

She blinks, thrown by the abrupt change of subject. "Marco. He stepped in after the blackout when Dylan didn't come back."

"Dylan was on Oliver's payroll," Kai supplies, his split lip curling into a snarl. "He'll be dealt with."

Stella's eyes widen slightly, but she recovers quickly. "Good fucking riddance," she mutters. "Never liked him anyway. Always leering at the dancers."

"He won't be a problem anymore," I assure her. "I need to make a statement."

Stella nods, already understanding what I need. "I'll have them kill the music and put a spotlight on the mezzanine. Five minutes enough prep time?"

"Perfect," I confirm. I turn to my men, my gaze lingering on Hudson. "Last chance to wait this out downstairs."

He straightens despite the pain it clearly causes him, his jaw set in stubborn determination. "Not a chance in hell."

The twins flank him without being asked, ready to catch him if his strength fails. The sight of their automatic coordination, their unspoken understanding, makes something warm unfurl in my chest despite the night's horrors.

"Let's go," I say, leading the way to the mezzanine that over-looks the main floor.

I feel a strange calm settling over me. For two years, we've ruled from the shadows, letting rumor and fear do our work for us. The mystery was part of our power—the unseen hand that controlled the city's underworld. But tonight has changed everything. Tonight, the shadows were used against us.

It's time for a new approach.

We reach the mezzanine, and I position myself at the railing that overlooks the main floor. From here, I can see the entire club—the dance floor packed with bodies moving to the music, the VIP booths where the city's elite pretend they're not rubbing shoulders with criminals, the performance spaces where dancers twist and turn in hypnotic patterns.

I nod to Stella, who's watching from below. She speaks into her headset, and seconds later, the music cuts out abruptly. Confused murmurs ripple through the crowd as the lights dim, leaving only a single spotlight that finds me on the mezzanine.

The reaction is immediate and dramatic. Gasps echo through the suddenly silent club as people take in my appearance—the blood still staining my skin despite my hasty cleanup, the cold fury in my eyes, the three battered men arrayed behind me like harbingers of death.

I let the silence stretch, let them look their fill. Let them see what happens when someone crosses us.

"Good evening," I say, my voice carrying through the sudden silence. "I apologize for the interruption, but I have an announcement to make."

Below me, I can see officials from the mayor's office, police captains, district attorneys—all the power players who came to curry favor with the mysterious owners of the newest hot spot in the city. Their faces register shock, confusion, fear as they realize who stands before them.

Perfect.

"For two years I let the city whisper about the ghost in its veins—the phantom who ruled from the dark. You thought that meant I was hiding. You were wrong. The dark was never my cage—it was my weapon."

The crowd stills completely, hundreds of eyes fixed on me as I continue.

"You wanted a name. A face. A devil you could see? Here I am."

I let my gaze sweep over them, lingering on the officials who've profited from our rule while pretending not to know who really runs this city.

"If you touch me, or mine, you'll learn why the graves are already full of fools who tried. You'll join the other dead devils who thought they could take what's ours and walk away breathing."

Behind me, I feel rather than see Hudson sway slightly. Without missing a beat, Rev and Kai shift closer, supporting him while maintaining the illusion of strength. My heart swells with fierce pride and love.

"We didn't build this place for ourselves alone. We rebuilt it so people could walk home without looking over their shoulder, so kids could run these streets without hearing footsteps they feared. I took the night so the city could sleep. I bled so others wouldn't have to."

The silence is absolute now, the air charged with tension and something else—respect, perhaps. Or fear. Or both. I don't care which, as long as they listen. As long as they understand.

"So remember this moment before you cross us—the shadow has a face, and she's smiling."

I bare my teeth in what only the most generous observer would call a smile, letting them see the predator I've always been.

"Welcome to my playground. Play nice or you will become a dead devil too."

For a heartbeat after I finish, the silence holds—a perfect, crystalline moment suspended in time. Then, from somewhere in the back of the crowd, a single person begins to clap. The sound is joined by another, then another, until applause thunders through the club, punctuated by whoops and cheers.

I hadn't expected applause. Screams, maybe. A stampede for the exits. Not this strange, almost reverent recognition.

I turn slightly, catching Hudson's eye. Despite his pain, there's pride shining in his gaze, a fierce approval that warms me from the inside out. Rev and Kai wear matching expressions—part admiration, part possessive heat that promises retribution of a different sort once we're alone.

Stella takes the cue without being told, getting the music started again as the spotlight fades. The spell breaks as the crowd returns to their drinking and dancing, though the energy has shifted. There's an edge to the revelry now, a heightened awareness that they're dancing in the devil's domain.

I'm left bathed in the ambient glow of the club lights. I should feel triumphant. I should want to descend to the main floor and lose myself in the rhythm, feel the bass vibrating through my bones until I forget everything but the music. That's what I would normally do on Dead Devil's Night—dance until dawn, celebrating our power, our victory, our survival.

But not tonight.

Tonight, all I can think about is getting home. Getting clean. Crawling into bed with my men and sleeping for a week. My body aches with exhaustion, every muscle screaming for rest. The dried blood on my skin feels tacky and uncomfortable, a constant reminder of everything we've been through.

"Let's go home," I say, turning to face my battered family.

Hudson sways slightly, his jaw clenched against the pain. "I'm fine," he insists before any of us can comment.

"Sure you are," I say dryly. "And I'm the Queen of England."

"No, you're not," Kai interjects, his eyes glittering dangerously in the low light as he slides a steadying arm around Hudson's waist. "But you are the queen of the dead city. And we're your loyal subjects."

"I can walk," Hudson protests, though his complexion has gone from ashen to nearly translucent.

"Shut up," I tell him, with no real heat behind the words. "I love you, you stubborn asshole, but you've proven your point. You're the toughest bastard in the room. Now let us take care of you before you actually die and ruin my night completely."

A ghost of a smile touches his lips before pain wipes it away. "Wouldn't want to inconvenience you."

"Damn right," I mutter. "Old man."

Epilogue

Rylan

One Year Later

I SINK DOWN SLOWLY onto Hudson's cock, my body stretching to accommodate him as a moan escapes my lips. The sound is echoed by Hudson's deep groan as he fills me completely. His eyes lock with mine, dark with desire as he reaches up and fists a handful of my freshly dyed hair, pulling me down until our mouths meet.

His kiss is hungry, demanding, swallowing more of my moans as I begin to rock in his lap. The metal barbells of his piercings rub against my inner walls in the most delicious way, hitting spots that make my thighs tremble. I've developed quite the appreciation for those piercings over the past year.

Warm fingers trail up my spine, tracing each vertebra with deliberate pressure before joining Hudson's grip in my hair. I know what's coming even before Kai presses his slick cock against my ass, already prepped and ready for him. My breath catches as he pushes inside me slowly, the familiar burn of the stretch making my back arch.

"Fuck, gorgeous," Kai murmurs against my ear, his chest pressed to my back as he seats himself fully inside me. "You feel so perfect."

I'm trapped between them, filled completely, my body stretched to its limits in the most exquisite way. Hudson's hand tightens in my hair, tugging just hard enough to make my scalp tingle. They've developed such an attachment to my hair this year—especially since my latest salon visit.

When I'd returned from the newly opened salon a few doors down from the Lair this morning, Kai had nearly doubled over with laughter before grabbing me and devouring my mouth. "Always wanted to taste the rainbow," he'd growled against my lips, fingers combing through the vibrant streaks of red, blue, purple, green and yellow that now cascade down my back.

They start to move in tandem, a rhythm perfected over months of practice. Hudson thrusts up as Kai pulls back, never leaving me empty, never giving me a moment to catch my breath. The dual sensation is overwhelming, pleasure building at the base of my spine as they take me higher.

A new hand threads through my hair, strong fingers tangling in the rainbow strands. I break away from Hudson's kiss as the hand gently but firmly guides my face to the side. Rev kneels beside us on the massive bed, his cock hard and waiting mere inches from my lips.

I dart my tongue out, tasting the salt of his skin before taking him into my mouth. His groan of satisfaction vibrates through me as his hand tightens in my hair, guiding my movements as Hudson and Kai continue their relentless pace.

This is my world now—surrounded by these three men, claimed by them as thoroughly as I've claimed them. The past year has transformed us all, forged us into something stronger, something unbreakable.

After my speech at the Playground last Dead Devil's Night, the city's power structure shifted dramatically. Officials and criminals alike scrambled to cement discreet alliances with us, eager to secure their places in the new order. The refurbishment of the city has been flourishing under our watchful eye. Crime hasn't disappeared—I'm not naive enough to think it ever could—but it's organized now, controlled, channeled into avenues that benefit rather than harm.

Certain crimes have vanished entirely. No one dares commit rape or domestic abuse in my city anymore. Not when everyone knows the queen of the dead city might slink out of the shadows to slit their throats. I've made examples of those who tested this boundary, and the message has been received loud and clear.

I'm pulled from these thoughts as Rev's hand tightens in my hair, his cock hitting the back of my throat as his breathing grows ragged. Hudson and Kai increase their pace, driving into me with an intensity that borders on desperation. My body is a conduit for their pleasure as much as my own, every nerve ending alive with sensation as I'm filled from all sides.

"Our queen," Hudson murmurs, his voice rough with exertion as he drives up into me. The bullet wound in his side healed months ago, leaving behind a star-shaped scar that I trace with my tongue when he sleeps. "Our beautiful, deadly fucking queen."

I moan around Rev's cock, the vibration making him curse as his hips stutter. The sound of skin against skin fills our bedroom, punctuated by grunts and gasps as we chase our release together.

Kai's teeth find the sensitive spot where my neck meets my shoulder, biting down just hard enough to send a jolt of electricity straight to my core. It's the final push I need, my orgasm crashing over me in waves that make my vision blur at the edges. I convulse around them, pulling them deeper as my body clenches and releases.

Rev is the first to follow, his hand tightening almost painfully in my hair as he spills down my throat with a hoarse shout. I swallow everything he gives me, my eyes watering as I struggle to breathe through the intensity of my own climax.

Hudson and Kai fall over the edge together, their movements becoming erratic as they chase their release. I feel them pulse inside me, filling me from both ends as their groans harmonize in a symphony of satisfaction.

For a long moment, we stay locked together, our bodies slick with sweat, chests heaving as we struggle to catch our breath. Then, slowly, they disentangle themselves from me, careful not to cause discomfort as they withdraw.

I collapse onto Hudson's chest, his heartbeat strong and steady beneath my ear. Rev stretches out beside us, his hand still playing with strands of my multi-colored hair. Kai disappears briefly, returning with a warm, damp cloth to clean me up gently before tossing the cloth in the general direction of the bathroom.

"I still can't believe you actually did it," Kai says, gesturing to my hair as he settles on my other side. "When you said you were thinking about going rainbow, I thought you were joking."

I smile lazily, too sated to move. "Thought it was appropriate after all these years. Dead Devil's Night is tomorrow, after all. Gotta look my best for our anniversary."

"I love the hair," Hudson murmurs after a moment, twirling a strand of purple and blue around his finger. "Though I'm not sure the mayor knew where to look during our meeting this morning."

I laugh, remembering the official's poorly concealed shock when I walked into the boardroom with my rainbow-colored locks. "That was half the point. Keep them off-balance."

"It's a good strategy," Rev agrees, his thumb tracing lazy circles on my thigh. "They never know what version of you they're getting—the businesswoman or the devil."

"They're the same person," Kai points out, pressing a kiss to my shoulder. "That's what makes her so goddamn terrifying."

I smile at that, a warm glow of satisfaction spreading through me. It's taken time to find this balance—between the ruthlessness needed to maintain our control and the compassion that drives us to make the city better. Between the public face of our legitimate empire and the shadows where we still operate when necessary.

"The new hospital wing opens next week," I remind them, thoughts drifting to our latest project. The children's medical center, funded entirely by our businesses, will serve the poorest neighborhoods in the city. My hand unconsciously drifts to one of the scar below my navel, the permanent reminder that I'll never carry a child of my own. Maybe that's why this project matters so much.

"David would be proud," Rev says quietly, his eyes meeting mine with understanding.

The mention of the man who saved me four years ago still brings a pang of grief, but it's softer now, tempered by time and the knowledge that we've built something he would have approved of. Something lasting.

"He would," I agree, reaching up to trace the scar on Hudson's abdomen—a permanent reminder of how close I came to losing him. "He would have even approved of my methods, he did teach me most of them afterall."

Kai snorts. "Your methods are what keep this city in line. Fear works."

"Fear and hope," Rev corrects, his gaze thoughtful. "That's the balance we've found. They fear what happens if they cross us, but they hope for what we can help them build."

I consider this, thinking of the changes we've implemented over the past year. The social programs funded through our clubs. The rehabilitation centers for addicts. The shelters for those escaping abuse. All operating alongside our more ruthless activities and criminal enterprises that will never truly disappear.

"It works," I say finally. "This city is ours—not just to rule, but to protect."

Hudson's arm tightens around me, his lips pressing against my temple. "And no one's going to take it from us."

"They can try," Kai snickers with a dangerous smile. "We could use the entertainment."

I laugh, the sound free and genuine in a way it wasn't a year ago. We've earned this peace, this moment of contentment amidst the chaos we still sometimes create.

The city stretches out below our penthouse, visible through the floor-to-ceiling windows we replaced after I kicked Oliver through one a year ago. Lights twinkle like earthbound stars, a testament to the order we've created from chaos. My city. Our city.

I think sometimes about the girl I was before all this—before that fateful night with the twins, before Hudson, before I claimed my crown. She would hardly recognize me now, this queen who rules this dark city. But I think she'd approve of what I've become, of the family I've built, of the peace I've carved out with blood and sheer force of will.

"What are you thinking about?" Hudson asks, his fingers tracing my spine.

"The past," I admit. "The future. How far we've come."

"Regrets?" Kai asks, though his tone suggests he already knows the answer.

I shake my head, rainbow strands falling across my face until Rev gently tucks them behind my ear. "Not a single one."

And it's true. Every scar, every fight, every drop of blood spilled—it was all worth it to end up here, surrounded by the men who are my heart, my soul, my everything. Soon enough we'll face the city again, remind them why they fear us, why they need us. But in this moment, we're just us—Rylan, Hudson, Rev, and Kai—tangled together in the aftermath of pleasure, secure in the knowledge that what we've built will endure.

The dead devils of our past remain where they belong—in their graves. And we, the living devils, rule on.

I stretch languidly between them, already feeling desire stirring again. "So, before we head out to go dancing... as is tradition now," I purr, trailing my fingers down Hudson's chest toward his already hardening cock, "who's ready for round two?"

Their answering grins are all the response I need.

It's good to be the queen.

The End

Stalk Me

Please feel free to stalk me.
Like metaphorically, not literally of course!

Also By

DARLING WORLD

hunt me darling
hide me darling
seek me darling

DEAD CITY WORLD

Dead Devil's Night
Dead Devil's Playground

WHISPERS OF WICKED FAE

The Wild Hunt

SHATTERED WORLD

Shattered Safety Duet:
Untouchable & Unbreakable
Shattered Memories Duet:
Unforgettable & Unstoppable

STANDALONES

Home Sweet Home
Pose For Me
Push My Buttons
The Darkest Gift